THE FOLDED LAND

A RELICS NOVEL

ALSO AVAILABLE FROM TIM LEBBON AND TITAN BOOKS

Coldbrook
The Silence

THE RELICS TRILOGY
Relics
The Folded Land
The Edge (forthcoming)

Alien: Out of the Shadows

THE RAGE WAR
Predator: Incursion
Alien: Invasion
Alien vs. Predator: Armageddon

The Cabin in the Woods
Kong: Skull Island

THE FOLDED LAND

A RELICS NOVEL

TIM LEBBON

TITAN BOOKS

THE FOLDED LAND
Mass-market edition ISBN: 9781785656095
Electronic edition ISBN: 9781785650345

Published by Titan Books
A division of Titan Publishing Group Ltd
144 Southwark St, London SE1 0UP

First mass-market edition: February 2019
2 4 6 8 10 9 7 5 3 1

A CIP catalogue record for this title is available from the
British Library.

Printed and bound in the United States.

Did you enjoy this book?
We love to hear from our readers. Please email us at
readerfeedback@titanemail.com or write to us at
Reader Feedback at the above address.

To receive advance information, news, competitions, and
exclusive offers online, please sign up for the
Titan newsletter on our website
www.titanbooks.com

This one is for my yearly walking buddy,
the magnificent Guy Adams

1

There were three men running toward him. He stood his ground as they dashed past, and ignored their panicked, shouted warnings, swapping a glance with one of them. There was sheer horror in the man's eyes.

Gregor smiled. He'd come to the right place.

He walked on toward the source of their terror. It was a direction he was used to taking. When there was fear amongst people, that was where he often found what he was searching for. Sometimes those frightened people thought of him as a kind of savior, that he had come to rescue them from things with teeth and claws, and faces unlike their own. He did nothing to disabuse them of the notion.

They ran, he arrived, and the monsters went away.

Gregor had been watching the illegal logging camp for seventeen days, hiding out in the jungle, circling by day and hunkering down at night. He grabbed ten minutes of sleep here and there, but most of the time forced himself to remain awake. He'd been watching for signs, and didn't want to miss anything.

The settlement was large. During the day it often took him ten hours to complete a full circuit of the rough camp and the logging operations that spread out from its heart. Down ravines, up steep hills, always alert for movement and careful not to be seen, he enjoyed the physical challenge. He liked pushing himself. The pain was cathartic. Nothing good came to those who did not strive.

The Amazon jungle was sweltering. Even the regular afternoon downpour was warm, but at least the water swilled a little of the stale sweat and dirt from his clothes, and he caught some in his hat to drink. He ate acai and figs from hanging branches, and sometimes he plucked grubs and spiders from damp, dark places in the bark of giant trees. The loggers would be destroying their habitats soon enough. At least he was putting their succulent, crunchy bodies to good use.

With his time here almost over, he felt a flush of satisfaction. It had been wise to wait and watch. The landscape felt right, the surroundings and location perfect, his information had been correct. He'd known that given time the loggers would uncover what he sought.

In the distance he heard mewling in the naked sunlight.

Gregor broke into a jog. In any normal jungle, moving at such speed would have been impossible, but this place was dying. He vaulted felled trees, climbed onto pale fleshy stumps, leapt off and kicked through thigh-high piles of chopped branches and lank vines. Skirting around a massive stack of stripped trunks, he almost ran into two more men who were running away. One of them skidded to a stop and grabbed Gregor's arms, opening his mouth to shout a warning, snot running from his nose, sweat washing dirt and sawdust into his wide, terrified eyes.

The man saw something in Gregor's expression that gave him pause, and the warning remained unvoiced. Pushing away, Gregor ran on, turning his head slightly from side to side, sniffing the air.

A machine idled nearby, sitting at the end of a trail of deep ruts in the jungle floor. Its caterpillar tracks had churned harsh wounds into the ground. Its heavy clasping claws held a tree horizontally, ready to drag it through a macerator that would chew off limbs, bark, and thick side branches, processing it for future use. It was a mechanical version of Gregor himself, albeit larger and far clumsier.

Gregor grinned at this comparison. It pleased him, and he laughed as he ran past.

A flock of birds took flight, startled by the sound.

He stopped at the edge of a large hole. It had once been home to the roots of a massive tree, now tumbled ready to be chopped. The upended root ball formed a tall wall to his left, and crawling blind things still scampered for shelter.

In the hole, the pale thing also tried to crawl back into dank shadows. Tropical sunlight hit its slick skin. Steam rose from its body. It looked up at Gregor. Perhaps it smiled, or grimaced, and the faint whisper might have been an attempted growl to see him away.

Gregor jumped into the hole and landed several feet away from the naked beast. It was the size of a small child, thin and weak-looking, despite its long limbs that seemed to flex and curl around it. It pulsed and moved as if unused to such exposure.

"You're not afraid of me," the creature said, the

words sounding unfamiliar in its mouth. It must have been a long time since it had felt the need to speak.

"Should I be?" Gregor asked. He pulled a long curved knife from a sheath on his belt. It was razor sharp on its outer edge, the inner blade serrated for sawing through bone. Though well-used, it was still keen and clean. Gregor knew how to look after the tools of his trade.

The creature hissed, but the sound turned into a low, pained sigh.

"Poor leshy," Gregor said, kneeling in the mud. "How long have you lain here?"

"Too long to remember," the leshy said, eyeing the blade. It was a tree spirit of this jungle, and it had used the living weight of this giant kapok tree to hide itself away. It might have been there for five hundred years.

Gregor reached out, not with the knife but with his free hand. He touched the creature's slick brow and whispered words of comfort. Its heavy eyes drifted shut and it purred, twisting itself against his hand.

"Please don't hurt me," it said, and although its language was one that no human should know, Gregor understood.

"Tell me where you came from," Gregor said.

"I've been here for..."

"Not here. Before here."

The leshy opened its eyes again, onto a whole new world. Gregor saw a shred of understanding there now. He would have to be careful. This creature was weak, pitiful, but appearances could be deceptive.

"North," the leshy said. "There were too many of us there. I came here to be on my own."

"So sad," Gregor said.

"Have you come to save me?"

"Yes," Gregor said. "Yes, I have."

The leshy blinked and its limbs curled in on themselves.

Gregor lashed out with his knife and sliced the creature's throat. Its eyes snapped wide. He saw its surprise, but behind the surprise there was something else. Perhaps it was relief.

He cut again, reversing the knife and pressing down, sawing until the leshy's head parted from its body. Above and around him a heavy sigh passed through the canopies of those trees that were still standing, but Gregor did not let such a thing distract him from his task.

He dug in deep and cut out the dying creature's heart. As he held it up, sunlight touching where it never should caused the dripping organ to shrivel and cauterize.

A nearby tree began to shed its heavy leaves. Further away, several other trees collapsed with a grief-stricken roar.

"You're saved," Gregor said. He pocketed the heart, climbed from the hole, and started walking north.

Half an hour later he came across two of the men he'd seen fleeing. They were huddled in the cab of a truck, doors and windows closed despite the humidity and heat of the midday sun. They were smoking, their frightened faces hazy behind a miasma of fumes.

As Gregor passed by, one of them wound down his window, just a few inches.

"It's gone?" he asked.

"Gone." Gregor did not stop walking.

"What was it?" the man called after him.

"Amazing," Gregor said, and he walked on, looking forward to leaving that awful fucking place.

2

When storms blew and raged, Sammi remembered her mother.

Mom had always enjoyed storms, and used to sit watching thunder and lightning from Sammi's bedroom window seat, holding her daughter's hand and telling her there was no reason to be afraid. Sammi once read about a football team being struck by lightning in Brazil. Six of them had died.

"You've got more chance of being eaten by a crocodile," her mother would say.

"Here in Massachusetts?"

"Precisely."

In truth, Sammi had never been afraid of lightning. The power and strength of those superheated bolts fascinated her. Hurrying along the street toward their riverside holiday home, Sammi kept away from the gutters. The storm drains weren't that large here, but they were still big enough for a snapping snout to poke through.

It was a ridiculous thought, she knew, but it reminded her of her mom. That was another thing she'd said.

"You've got a vivid imagination, Sammi. It's richer

than most. Sometimes it might make you afraid, but that's a small price to pay for knowing the world." At the time Sammi had been too young to ask exactly what she meant, and later there were other things to talk about, but now she often wished she had. She'd never mentioned it to her dad. It was a private memory.

She was beginning to wish she'd come on the bike, as her dad had suggested. He'd already had a couple of beers, so couldn't drive, and when Sammi had developed a sudden craving for Dunkin' Donuts, and his face lit up at the idea of one of their coffees, the skies had just been overcast. If she'd taken the bike, she would have had trouble carrying the bag in one hand and steering with the other. And it was only a mile's walk.

Then the skies opened, rain hammered down, and sizzling arcs of lightning clashed in the clouds above her. She huddled the paper bag to her chest to prevent it from getting soaked and falling apart. It contained four donuts and two steaming hot coffees in a cardboard holder. She wasn't dressed for the weather, and she passed a few other people who'd been caught out by the sudden downpour, wearing shorts and tee shirts and dashing here and there. She swapped amused glances with some of them. One teenaged boy about her age smiled shyly. An older woman frowned, appearing confused at the storm.

It had come from nowhere.

Sammi didn't mind. She wasn't afraid of thunder and lightning, because her mother had told her not to be. Trying to know the world honored her memory. So did not being scared of the storm.

Besides, the rain was warm on her skin, the smell of a summer downpour sweet, and she still had six more glorious days on Cape Cod.

"Hey, Sammi, hope the donuts are worth it!" Mrs. S. called from her front porch. Sammi smiled and waved back, still trying to shelter the bag with her body. Mrs. S. was a huge, round woman who seemed to spend morning, noon, and night sitting on her porch, watching the world go by and swigging soda from a glass the size of a fishbowl.

Sammi had never known her as anything other than Mrs. S., and Dad claimed not to know her real name. They only came to the Cape Cod house two or three times each year, and their interactions with their large neighbor rarely went beyond a wave and a comment about the weather. That Mrs. S. knew their names didn't faze them. She was a permanent resident, and the sort of person Sammi's mother had called a sponge, sitting out there and soaking up information whether offered openly or not.

Sammi felt like a sponge. She was soaked through, and would have to change before dinner. At the entrance to the winding road that led down to the inlet's edge, she felt the bag beginning to split. She hugged it close, both hands folded beneath it to hold in the contents.

Another great crack of thunder smashed across the sky, lightning flashing immediately overhead, so powerful that she felt it thud against her chest. Sammi paused, looking up and around. Rivulets of water ran across the lane and the normally dusty surface was dark and soaked, muddy puddles growing here and there. The river would be flowing faster in the morning, and heavy with sediment. Pity. She'd been hoping for an early morning swim.

It didn't matter, really, because she and her dad would take a day trip, instead. The trouble was, everywhere they went across the Cape reminded them of her mother.

The house was owned by her mother's side of the family. A couple of times they'd all come here together, crowding into bedrooms and enjoying a big family get-together.

Then her Aunt Angela went to Britain, and...

Sammi had never believed any of the stories about Angela and her boyfriend. Neither did her dad. Sometimes the news reminded them, but she and Dad no longer talked about the couple.

"Too painful," he said. *Too many lies*, Sammi thought. There was a pause button pressed in her life, one branch blocked, and something inside told her that one day, it would be unpaused, and the truth would play out.

Despite that, the house was bursting at the seams with fond memories, the scene of many of her first real recollections. They'd taken regular vacations there every year since she had been born fourteen years before, and she could scroll through the times in that house like a flip-book of images showing her growing up. Barbecues in the garden, playing softball on the lawn, jumping from the dock into the inlet, paddling the inflatable kayak that had somehow lasted nine summers and the abuse of family members and friends. Watching TV in the warm, humid evenings, sitting in her favorite wicker chair while her parents shared the sofa and a bottle of wine, or sat out on the patio, the warm murmur of their voices a comfort behind cartoon chaos or Disney frolics.

Sitting in the window seat with her mother, watching lightning dance across the ocean horizon to the south.

Her mother had died six months earlier, in a car accident. This was their first time here without her, and the house seemed larger than before, harder to fill. She knew that her dad was still struggling. He'd aged years over the past few months, and he was quieter now, more prone to long periods of silence staring at nothing.

Sammi knew what he was looking at.

Splashing through puddles, she was no longer concerned about how wet her tennis shoes became, and giggled at the memories of doing this as a child. There must have been a last time she'd ever jumped into a puddle and thought it fun. The next time she'd walked around them, not wanting to get her new jeans wet, or conscious that her parents would roll their eyes, more concerned with the laundry they'd have to do than the enjoyment she was having. She supposed these last times doing childish things were a part of growing up, and it was sad that they happened and drifted by unnoticed. If she noticed when they came, she would relish every one.

She passed a couple of houses on her left and right, each in its own generous yard with an entrance lane, fencing, and trees and hedges planted to identify the garden boundaries. These were also holiday homes, and she'd never got to know the people staying there.

Lightning flashed again. Thunder cracked. She wondered where it struck, and whether another tree had just died.

As she neared the driveway to the house she saw her father huddled under an umbrella and waiting for her on the porch. He waved and moved out toward her, smiling broadly. She smiled back. There was something about an unexpected, unforecast storm like this that was exciting, and she was pleased to see he shared her pleasure.

She passed their parked car, and when they were within hailing distance she heard him shout. "You better not have spilled my—"

Something changed. The moment froze. For an instant quicker than a blink Sammi was aware of her surroundings with a stark, utter clarity. Her father partway across the garden toward her, one foot raised, mouth open mid-sentence. The house behind him, lights casting shadows across several windows, paint flaking from wooden siding, rose trellis heavy with summer blooms. Rain hanging in the air like glass shards, catching light from the house and reflections from elsewhere. *If I look closely enough I'll see myself in every raindrop*, she thought.

A sharp, loud crack split the world. A bright flash, bright as the sun, blinded her. Something struck her so hard that she felt shifted aside.

All became darkness.

"I feel fine, Dad. Really. A bit fuzzy in the head, like I'm drunk."

"And what would you know about being drunk, young lady?"

Sammi grinned and looked aside. She knew when she could play her dad and when she couldn't, and this was one of those times she could. *"You might have died,"* he'd said when they were in the ambulance, and the terror in his eyes had made her cry. The terror, and the deep loss that resided there, despite the fact that she was still breathing.

"Last Christmas," Sammi said. "Remember when Chris and Lennie came over for the evening? I was in my room with Jenn."

Her dad frowned, half-smiling. No, he couldn't remember, she realized, and she felt a pang of guilt, because sometimes he told her he could hardly recall any good times with her mother at all. It was something to do with the way he was processing the grief. Every memory was in there, he said, but the shock of her death had put a buffer around them. Like bubble-wrap.

Making him try to remember felt cruel.

"I snuck downstairs," Sammi said. "Mom was laughing, Lennie was all embarrassed, 'cos you and Chris were talking over each other about some holiday you'd been on when the hotel staff caught you all skinny-dipping in the pool past midnight."

"Shhh!" he said, looking around the emergency room as if afraid someone would hear. She saw how pleased he actually was, because now he was remembering that evening, and that was a good thing.

"Yeah, Sally was laughing," he said, nodding slowly.

"Well… I poured Jenn and me a glass of punch in

the kitchen and crept back upstairs with them."

"You little sneak! You stole two glasses of punch?"

"No, Dad," Sammi said. She paused for effect. "I stole six." She started laughing, then trailed off when it hurt her head.

"So is this the famous young lady who got struck by lightning?" A doctor entered the treatment cubicle. He might have been the tallest man she'd ever seen, with dreadlocks down to the small of his back and hands the size of footballs. His voice, high and soft, didn't match his appearance, and though he looked stressed, his eyes smiled.

"That's me!" she said. "Do I have superpowers now?"

The doctor picked up her charts, flipped through a few pages, and raised his eyebrows.

"Well, it says here you can travel through time and move things with your mind."

She shrugged, trying for nonchalant.

"Mind if I look you over?" he asked. "It's not every day I treat a time traveler."

"How do you know?" Sammi asked.

"Touché." The doctor shone a little flashlight into her eyes, took her pulse and blood pressure, listened to her heart. Her dad watched quietly, letting the man do his job, but Sammi could see he was itching to ask a million questions.

"Yep, you're fine," the doctor said at last. "Very slight burns on your right shoulder, no worse than a sunburn. A few singed hairs on your neck."

"I do *not* have a hairy neck!"

"Not anymore you don't."

"And my new tats, of course."

"Yeah, they're quite something." Sammi turned her arm slowly as the three of them stared at the patterns on her left shoulder and down her arm, around her bicep and tricep and finishing just below her elbow. They were a light brown and golden color. Her dad had said they looked like a satellite photo of a river delta. She thought they resembled the delicate fronds of a big leaf with sunlight shining through it.

"They look like sheet lightning in the clouds," the doctor said, and the similarity struck Sammi so hard that she wondered why she hadn't seen it before.

Of course they do! she thought. *It's the bolt that hit me, echoing on my skin.*

"Will they stay?" she asked. It was sort of cool, but she was also worried that the freak accident might have scarred her for life.

"They'll fade over time," he said. "Few days, maybe a week or two. You should probably take pictures."

"Way ahead of you," Sammi said.

"They're burst capillaries," the doctor continued. "At least, that's what all the research says. Microscopic damage to lots of really tiny veins."

"That sounds bad," her dad said.

"No worse than bruising," the doctor said. "Just in much nicer patterns."

"So she's really okay?"

"Right as rain."

"But she was struck by lightning!"

The doctor's face broke into a smile at last. "And that's very cool. She's got a great story to tell her friends."

"But…" Her dad shook his head. "The electricity. Her heart."

"This isn't something I've ever seen before," the doctor admitted, sitting on the edge of the bed. "So I did a quick bit of research. Usually, people who get electric shocks from a wire or socket become injured or even die because it's a sustained dose. A second, two seconds or more, long enough to damage cells and induce organ failure. With a lightning strike, it's over in a millionth of a second. The charge usually travels across the surface of the body, not through, especially in this case when she was soaked to the skin. There's a case of a guy in Florida being struck while playing volleyball, getting up afterward, finishing his game."

Sammi concentrated on a pen in the doctor's top pocket. She focused, trying to make it lift out and drop to the floor. It didn't work. She was disappointed.

Silly sausage, a voice said. She blinked, startled. It had sounded just like her mother, whispering to her from the past.

"But Sammi passed out," her father said.

"It's like being punched," the doctor said. "Hard. By a grizzly. That's where the fuzzy head comes from. Trust me, the scans all came out clear. No bleeds, no internal scarring. Heart trace is fine."

"So I'm free to go?"

"Free to go." The doctor held out his big hand for a high-five. She didn't leave him hanging.

"Thanks," her dad said. "Thanks so much." His voice broke a little, and so did Sammi's heart. For a while he'd been afraid that he had lost her, too.

"Don't mention it," the doctor said. He turned and left the cubicle, heading to someone more needy.

"So," Sammi said. "Now that I'm a superhero, can we get take-out on the way home?"

"It's eleven in the morning."

"Don't care. I'm starving. Besides, I can time travel, so I'll make it dinner time."

He grinned. "Chinese?"

"Chinese."

They left the hospital together, and he held her hand. He hadn't done that for some time. She was too old, really. She squeezed back.

Pulling up outside the house, Sammi felt strange. Last time she'd been here she hadn't come home properly— the lightning bolt had seen to that. She scanned the graveled parking area and lawn, looking for scorch marks. There was nothing. He must have picked up the spilled coffee, too, and she mourned the lost donuts.

"You okay, honey?" her dad asked.

"Yeah, Dad, I'm good. Kind of tired."

"Still hungry?"

She nodded. It felt strange. Like coming home to a place so safe and familiar, and returning somewhere after a long time away. The familiarity held a deep nostalgia that someone her age should hardly recognize. *"You've got an old head on your shoulders,"* her mom used to say, and Sammi sometimes imagined herself with gray hair and strange, knowing eyes.

"I'm just going out on the dock for a little bit," she said. "It's a nice day, and some sun will make me feel better."

"You're sure?" That look of uncertainty. He asked her questions like that a lot nowadays. *You're sure? Do you really think so? Are you certain you want to do that?* It had something to do with grief and the uncertainties he felt about her mother dying. In some ways he was being overprotective, making sure that every action Sammi took was a safe one. It was as if he couldn't bear to have her to grieve on her own. They often spent time together, walking or sitting on the sofa and talking about Mom, looking through photos or old videos, crying and laughing and struggling to move on in their own individual ways.

But sometimes it became cloying.

Sometimes, Sammi just wanted to be on her own.

"I'm sure," she said, smiling. "It's one of *those* moments." They both had moments that they talked about. Unremarkable memories of her mother, his wife, sitting somewhere and telling a joke, planting a rose bush, pointing at a flock of birds sheeting back and forth across the estuary. They might be years old, random recollections of lost times that meant so much. Every one of them was special.

"Right," he said, smiling, nodding. "They're important. Every moment is important." He paused, and then added, "I'll put the food in the oven to keep it warm."

"I won't be that long, Dad," she said. "Ten minutes."

"Okay. Still want to go kayaking this afternoon?"

"Absolutely! I'll race you."

"You'll lose." He always said that, and until lately he'd been right. Last summer, though, Sammi started beating him in their races. She remembered her mother laughing as they'd both splashed and sweated their way past the spot where she sat in a boat, Sammi edging ahead by half a length and lifting her paddle skyward in triumph. She'd been so pleased that she hadn't stopped mentioning it for the rest of the day. That long-ago, hot and perfect day.

While her father carried their early take-out to the house, Sammi crossed the lawn toward the dock. Though the sky was a searing blue and the midday sun beat down, the lawn was still damp from the previous day's surprise downpour. Water soaked through her shoes and into her socks. It was a nice feeling, cool and calming. She stepped onto the dock and kicked off her shoes, pulled off the socks, and enjoyed the feeling of warm wood on the soles of her feet.

She walked to the end of the dock and felt as if she should continue onward. As if there was somewhere else to go. As if there was more to see. This was her favorite place in the whole wide world, but something inside seemed to be urging her elsewhere. Across the wide inlet she could see a dozen houses sitting close to the water, boats docked beside some, flags flying from poles, a few people just visible in gardens, heat haze making ghosts out of them. Several boats chugged up and down the river. A group of kayakers paddled past. She felt an unaccountable need to keep walking, because this wasn't where she needed to be.

Sammi's heart hammered in her chest, and as she turned to go back to the house a splinter slid into her skin just beneath her big toe.

Ow!

Silly sausage! a voice said just over her shoulder, and she spun around. Her mother's pet name for her, spoken in a voice so like her mother's and yet with a weird lilt, like the distorted echo of someone impersonating her almost perfectly.

"Mom?" Sammi asked.

A shadow passed across the sun and she looked up. Clouds were forming, wispy, darkening. Her skin prickled all across her body. The hairs on her arm stood on end. She looked back toward the house. Her father stood outside the open patio door, smiling and waving her over so that they could share lunch. He and the house were a million miles away.

A sharp, loud crack split the world.

3

Sammi knew that she wasn't dreaming, but every step felt light, every moment loaded with remarkable potential. Each time she blinked she expected the world to have changed, and in a way it did. One moment to the next presented a whole new existence, although each world contained constants—her father's love, her own grief, her mother's unending, unbearable absence.

Everyone sees the world in a different way, a voice whispered in her ear, and it was something her mother used to say, uttered in her voice. *So when you look at it like that, we each live in our own world*. She felt no threat from the strange presence. In fact, it was comforting. Sammi glanced around, blinking rapidly as if to renew, renew. The shimmer remained in the air, a heat haze that enclosed her all around and guided her onward.

She was tugged in two directions. From behind, the love and need of her father. She knew how worried he would be, how confused, and instinct sought to turn her around and take her right back to the riverside house. From ahead, something *else* drew her on. She couldn't be quite sure what it was yet, but the presence accompanying her promised that it was wonderful.

Sammi had always been a curious girl.

We'll ride the breeze and take a look. Her mother's voice again. She'd used that saying whenever they embarked upon a family journey somewhere they'd never been before. She'd said it the first time they'd driven down to New York, and along the way Sammi had been wondering where they would park their car and mount the wind that would take them into the city. By the time the great skyscrapers had come into view, however, she'd forgotten about riding the breeze.

"I'll be back soon," she whispered to the warm summer day. It was lunchtime, and the roads were busy with workers going out for food, tourists choosing their restaurant for the day, and other vehicles going on a hundred errands she would never know. "Be back soon, Dad. Keep the food warm."

Just another girl walking along the side of the road, she stepped onto the grass verge whenever a vehicle came past, and every time she locked eyes with the driver, wondering whether they could see the shape that accompanied her and what they might think of it.

Although she knew what her father must be going through, the shape told her that it would be all right.

He'll be fine, it said, no longer in her mother's voice. Its own voice was just as calm, though a little colder, and not imbued with the love her mother always had for her. *He'll barely know you're gone, and you'll be back before you know it.* Something about the voice, its words, sounded fake.

Fakery didn't matter in a dream.

"Is this real?" she asked.

As real as it needs to be.

She felt the soft warm breeze on her face, smelled exhaust fumes and the sea, heard the shouts of children playing in a school to her left and the busy mutterings of adults shopping at a line of stores across the road to her right. Dunkin' Donuts was over there. The one she'd visited before she'd been struck by lightning.

Her left shoulder, back, chest, and arm tingled as if from sunburn, yet it was a strangely pleasant discomfort. She pulled up her sleeve and looked down, and the pale frond-like pattern from yesterday was darker, deeper, more textured and elaborate. She gasped at the exquisite detailing, pausing by the side of the road and turning her arm slowly left and right. It was as if she were flying above a jagged landscape, looking down upon ridges and valleys, woodlands and plains. In places her pale skin was darkened several shades, in others burnt to a vivid pink. She blinked and if anything the vision became deeper, more defined.

Between ridges on her skin she saw the glinting curve of a river.

A familiar freckle became a clearing in a darker woodland.

A swath of fine hair close to her elbow, darkened into nubs by intense heat, was a landscape of tumbled boulders.

A car horn blared, startling her back from the strange distance that had grown between her and the world. She stumbled onto the verge. Fingers dug into her right arm and helped her, and when she looked that way a shape manifested from the heat and sunlight. She felt its shadow cool on her bare arm before it became fully solid, and though she knew she should be afraid, she wasn't.

Because none of this is real, she thought, and at last the idea settled that she was still lying out there on the dock. She'd been struck by lightning a second time, and her dad was leaning over her, phone in hand while he talked to paramedics. Making sure her airways were open, tipping her onto her side and into the recovery position.

She thought about this for a moment, but then the shape was almost whole.

It'll be Mom, she thought. *I'm lying here, maybe even dying, and Mom has come to me to make sure I'm not afraid.*

Yet the shape was not her mother. Taller, slimmer, Sammi wasn't sure what sex it was, if any. With a cool finger it traced some of the veinous marks across her bicep, and looked as amazed at the patterns as she was. Then it leaned forward, like a sapling in the breeze, and she felt cool breath against her ear.

Your mother sent me, it said. When it started along the side of the road, Sammi could only follow.

The man lay in the gravel and watched as his girl was taken away.

He could barely move. His limbs shook, rattling stones together like old bones, and he clawed his right hand in an effort to dig in and drag himself forward, but there was no strength. His left arm was bent beneath him, trapped by his own dead weight. He tried pushing with his toes but felt nothing past his waist. That didn't matter. All that mattered was Sammi and the shape beside her, holding her arm and guiding her away from him.

He doubted his vision, his senses. Heard only a low, rumbling hiss, like water under pressure, spurting through a crack. He could taste metal on the air. He felt hot, as if his skin was naked to the blazing sunlight, stretched and burnt.

The shape he saw with Sammi was impossible.

It held human form, a blur in the air to her left, leaning forward to whisper into her ear. The figure drifted just above the ground, and through it and beyond he could see the wooden dock, the shimmering water, and across the inlet a large, pale blue house with a flag hanging limp in the motionless air.

The lawn was singed in a pattern that originated where Sammi stood. The grass had been bleached brown in uneven lines radiating out from her feet like frozen ripples. Here and there it appeared to steam or smoke, but when he blinked the effect shifted, and he wondered whether it was his damaged eyes causing it.

The sky blazed blue. No clouds, no rain, no hint of thunder and lightning.

That's what I saw, he thought. *That's what I felt*. He tried to move, struggled, but his muscles did not obey his commands. His heart felt hot and molten in his chest. His whole world was a paused breath.

And when he tried to breathe, nothing happened.

He gasped and tried to shout his daughter's name. Darkness closed in. His heart, heavy and hot, became a blazing rock. Sparks of agony passed through his body, from the tips of his limbs into his core, as if the lightning was still there hammering at him, punching in again and again until its malevolent work was done. A millionth of a second, the doctor had said, and the father understood now that he was trapped in that moment, his last moment.

He understood also that this was no accident or coincidence.

He struggled and fought, as he had every day since his wife had been taken from them. He fought for his daughter. Sometimes, though, the will to fight is not enough.

Senses fading, death stalked in and pulled him down to its eternal bosom. With only his hearing left, he expected at any moment to hear the calming whisper of his dear departed wife.

He heard nothing, and then there was nothing.

No more moments at all.

4

Angela Gough knew that the best way to reveal herself was to acknowledge that she was hiding.

The man looking at her in the coffee shop was probably just some guy, bored or distracted, catching her eye and gazing for just a little too long. She had that effect on people sometimes. Perhaps it was to do with all the things she had done, and all the things she had seen, reflected somehow in her eyes.

She looked back down at the phone in her hand. For the thousandth time in three months she switched it to selfie mode and gazed at her image, wondering what people saw. It surprised her every time. Her dark, shoulder-length hair was now dyed silver and trimmed shorter. Her blue eyes were darkened with tinted contact lenses. The heavy framed glasses she wore contained plain glass. Everything about her appearance had changed.

A lot about *her* had changed.

If he recognized her, it was because he already knew who she was, and had followed her here.

She tapped the phone back into photo mode, snuggled down in the seat, leaned across to pick up her coffee. Then she settled again with the phone angled toward him. With another tap she zoomed in.

Coffee Man was no longer looking at her. In fact, he was pointedly *not* looking at her, holding his mug up with both hands and glancing everywhere around the bustling café, apart from in her direction. He wore a Bluetooth earplug and a small microphone clipped to the inside of his polo shirt collar. That meant nothing. Plenty of people spent their lives permanently connected.

"Paranoid," she whispered. She talked to herself a lot now. Sometimes it held the demons at bay. Other times it was an attempt to make herself feel less lonely, although it usually succeeded in doing the opposite. "Just some guy."

She took a picture anyway.

The café was a small independent place she'd only been to once before. She'd stopped in Albany for a while on her way through to somewhere else, *anywhere* else. She never made a habit of becoming a regular. She tried not to develop any habits at all, but she'd liked this place when she'd visited a couple of days ago, enjoyed its busy atmosphere and the sense of calm welcome extended by the staff and customers.

Almost without thinking she flicked through to her photograph album, and there was a picture of Vince. She knew it was foolish, keeping this snapshot on her phone, but it was the one she'd been unable to delete. He was sitting in their small back garden in London, beer bottle in one hand, the other held up to shield the sun from his eyes, and he was grinning the smile she loved. From the first time she'd seen the photo, she'd known that he was shielding the sun so that he could see her more clearly. He'd told her so. She had been lucky to take the shot at just the right moment, before he realized what she was doing. It was an honest reflection of their love.

Someone laughed. Music blared. The hubbub of voices merged into a single mass, and she wasn't able to make out anything that was being said. It was a nicely appointed café, walls lined with posters about regional Albany events and artwork from local artists. The counter was heavy with homemade cakes and pastries, and she could tell that many of the clientele were regulars. The way the barista smiled at them was different from the smile he'd offered Angela when she'd arrived, still open and friendly, but also businesslike.

Angela was getting very good at telling stories from expressions.

Like the guy not looking, displaying his interest in her like a brand.

Finishing her coffee, she glanced around the rest of the room as she tilted the cup back against her lips. If he was a cop, he'd have at least one other companion, with probably more waiting outside. No one was going to risk arresting a mass murderer on their own.

She couldn't see anyone obvious, but that didn't mean they weren't there.

The bathrooms were at the rear of the café, and although there also was a private staff doorway, there was no telling if that led toward a back entrance. Even if it did, there was no way to guarantee it would be open. It wasn't worth taking the chance. Angela did her best to live life without risks. She'd have to leave via the front door, and prepare to engineer a distraction if the guy stood to follow her out.

For weeks, Angela had expected to be caught. After the horrors in London—the revelation of Vince's secret life, her involvement with Fat Frederick Meloy, the murders, and Kin and humans meeting in a bloody, terrible clash—she and Vince had fled to the USA on separate flights. She was met at the airport by police. Vince got through.

She'd believed that was it for her, and from that moment on she'd stuck to their story, and maintained that Vince was dead.

Then he and the Kin had rescued her from the police precinct, and the world of the Kin had opened up for her. Turned out those fantastical creatures existed not only in London, as she'd grown to believe.

The Kin were everywhere.

Coffee Man, sitting in the café and watching her by not watching, was not Kin. There was no wonder in his eyes. No fear.

She stood, picked up her backpack, pocketed her phone, and made her way toward the front door. The barista caught her eye and nodded, and she smiled back. In the wide mirror behind the counter she saw the man muttering something as he stood.

That was it, then. He was here for her, and he was talking to a partner she had yet to see.

Angela's heart sped up but her senses remained sharp. She had been mentally preparing for an occasion such as this, and knew that it would come at some point. Her drifting might have been aimless, but her existence was not. She lived life with a keen focus. She wished it didn't have to be so, but she had to believe that danger stalked her every minute of the day.

As she pushed the glass door open, her attention was ahead of her. She knew the threat behind was a good fifteen seconds away, having to negotiate his way around tables, chairs, and other customers. By the time he reached the door she needed to be gone. To do that, she had to know where his partner was.

The sidewalk outside was home to half a dozen tables, all of them occupied by couples or groups eating and drinking. She scanned them and saw no one who appeared to be on their own. No one who was looking at her, or at the doorway behind her. That was no comfort. She was in flight mode now, and she'd been here before, ready and willing to run at a moment's notice. She had been forced to run twice since being sprung from police custody by Vince and the Kin. The first time had been just a few hours later, when she and Vince had escaped pursuit thanks to the intervention of a small, skinny man who'd punctured a police car's tires.

The second time she had been on her own. She'd run so quickly, escaped so efficiently through the streets of Boston's docklands, that she'd never even been certain she was being followed.

Turning left now, she headed along the sidewalk. After counting to five, she spun on her heel and strode back past the tables.

Coffee Man was standing just outside the café, the door swinging shut behind him, still muttering into his hands-free. As she fixed him with her gaze and marched toward him, his eyes went wide with surprise.

He froze to the spot.

She had maybe two seconds.

"You touch me again and I'll call the cops, you

fucking prick!" She pointed at him from just a few feet away, then turned and rushed along the sidewalk, not quite running. From behind she heard the scrape of several chairs on concrete, a table knocked, cups rolling and spilling.

"Hey, pal, where d'you think you're going?"

Angela chanced a quick glance back. A woman and two men stood in front of her pursuer, blocking his route along the sidewalk. One of the men looked her way, concerned. She nodded her thanks and gave him a grateful wave. She tried to look afraid. It wasn't hard.

If he was a cop he'd be after her within a few seconds. If he wasn't, it might take him a little longer to forge a path through the people. She hated playing the victim, but that precious head start might make all the difference.

Angela glanced around as she went, frowning, wondering where the hell his partner was. She also wondered whether she might truly be paranoid, and if the poor guy had just been someone taking a mid-morning coffee, catching her eye, maybe looking away in embarrassment at being caught.

As she turned a corner, however, and prepared to start running, the truth hit home. Not only was the man coming for her, but his partner was here as well.

And they were going to kill her.

"Claudette," Angela muttered, and a flush of memories assaulted her.

Claudette and Harry, Mary Rock's goons, haranguing her in the coffee shop in London and demanding to know where Vince had gone, because he'd killed her brother and she wanted revenge. Claudette ushering her into the car outside her maisonette, while Angela was certain that Vince was dead on the road behind her.

It hadn't been him, but Claudette hadn't cared. She wasn't the sort of woman to care, but she *was* the sort to inflict pain. Later, at Mary Rock's house, she'd stabbed Fat Frederick Meloy in the chest and fled into the night, never to be seen again.

If only.

If Angela went that way, Claudette would have her. She had no choice. Turning, she ran back the way she'd come, then cut across the T-junction away from Coffee Man, and Claudette. There was no time to slow down or even look both ways. She dodged around two cars idling at the junction, and sprinted out into the road as brakes squealed and horns blared. Out of the corner of her eye she saw a white van careening toward her.

She jigged right and jumped, sliding across the bonnet of a car a split second before the van smashed into the fender behind her. Glass smashed. The car rocked beneath her, bucking her off onto the road. She sprawled, leapt to her feet, continued running. The driver called out, angry and surprised. Claudette and Coffee Man would be saving their breath.

Reaching the opposite sidewalk and aiming for the wide-open park gates, she risked a quick glance back. Coffee Man had already crossed the street by the café and was sprinting along the sidewalk toward her. People stepped out of his way. She didn't blame them—he looked determined, strong, and dangerous. Claudette was there now, wending her way between vehicles stalled across the road following the collision. Her face was almost expressionless. Angela knew the brutality the small, slight woman possessed.

She had maybe a ten-second head start, and she'd use it well. Angela kept fit, running most days, and when she was on the move from place to place she often did much of the journey on foot. She was on the run in the truest sense of the term, and she knew the value of speed and endurance. The drivers involved in the fender bender would already be calling the police. Only as a very last resort could she put herself back in their hands.

The wide path into the park curved left and right. She went left, darting past a group of mothers with strollers and toddlers playing on the grass. She scanned the lawn ahead of her, searching for somewhere to hide, desperate for a way out. It was wide open here, an area of gently rolling landscape, paths, benches, and a small lake to her right, while on her left a bank of hedges curved around, marking the park's boundary. She could follow the hedge and hope there was another gate further on. Or she could cut straight across and skirt around the lake.

She chose the latter, and felt eyes on her as she ran. If she'd been moving slower she might have passed as a particularly energetic jogger, although her loose trousers, tee shirt, and backpack weren't the traditional runner's garb. But she didn't slow down, concentrating on form and pace, scanning the ground ahead of her for trip hazards, wondering what would happen if she fell. Would she break her ankle? Would they kill her out there in the open? Would Claudette torture her first, trying to get Vince's location?

The idea winged by that maybe she should be

looking for a cop. Certainly she'd end up being questioned again, for the gruesome deaths back in London. Deported, probably. Interrogated by Detective Inspector Volk, who was surely still searching for her, especially after her inexplicable escape from the holding cell. She'd spend life in prison, because she couldn't give up the Kin. Even if she tried, the stories she had to tell were preposterous. Insane.

Maybe they'd lock her up in an institution instead. Maybe Vince and the Kin would rescue her from there, as well.

She loped across a wide pathway, just dodging around a startled cyclist, and glanced back as she started down the gentle slope toward the lake. Coffee Man was falling back a little, but of Claudette there was no sign. Angela frowned, scanned left and right, yet the woman was nowhere to be seen.

"What the fuck?" she muttered.

The lake was just ahead of her now, and at last she could see where perhaps she might be able to escape. This side of the lake was open to lawns, with a couple of low wooden docks for the mooring of rowboats, and an artificial beach where kids played in the sand. The other side was heavy with undergrowth, and she could tell from the lay of the land that the park perimeter was just beyond. Even if there was no gateway over there, she could climb over the wall or fence. She'd done it before. Then, every second's lead she had on her pursuers gave her a better chance of getting lost in the streets.

If luck was with her, she'd jump from the wall and hail a cab.

She cut left, dashing past a couple of lovers lying in

the sun. That sparked a pang of jealousy. The last time she'd seen Vince had been more than four weeks ago. He'd been distracted, they hadn't had much time, and they'd parted with an air of loss she was convinced she felt much more than him. Back in London she'd probed into his hidden world and become ensnared, like it or not. She'd been both enraptured and horrified by the creatures revealed in the darkness of the world—Lilou the nymph, who Vince perhaps loved; Mallian the fallen angel, brutal and elemental; Ballus the mad satyr.

There were others, too. Wonderful, beautiful, terrifying, unbelievable. All the while, her love for Vince had been her driving force, and the one thing still tying her to the world she knew and could understand. It had become her foundation, to prevent her from drifting away from reality and becoming lost, afloat in the new, wider reality. It still shocked her to think about it.

She wasn't sure whether Vince was still tethered to her world. He was the same in many ways, but in some more important ways, she feared he was gone.

The woman raised her head when she heard Angela's rhythmic footfalls. She smiled. Angela looked away and concentrated on maintaining her speed, alert for threats, and more concerned as each moment passed that she'd lost sight of Claudette.

She reached the path that skirted the lake and started a clockwise circuit.

Something to her left caught her attention. A fluttering in the bushes that lined the park's perimeter, and a sound like birds cackling. When she looked directly toward the disturbance she saw nothing.

Passing a group of older teens playing frisbee, she considered stopping and confronting Coffee Man again. The youths might come to her aid, and for a while she'd be safe. Until the police arrived. But he was with Claudette, and she wore violence like a second skin. Now that Angela was running, there was no saying what she and Coffee Man would do to catch her. Or who they might hurt.

She sprinted past the teenagers and headed around the lake. There were a few people walking the path, and a couple of kids on tricycles, but the far side was quieter, with little other than a spread of grass and then the heavily planted park perimeter.

Angela aimed for that, and soon felt a tree's shadows cutting her off from the blazing sunlight. Sweating, panting, she ducked beneath the overhanging branches and risked a halt to look back.

Coffee Man was rushing around the lake toward her. Their pursuit had turned a few heads, and several of the college kids were standing with hands on their hips, frisbee now forgotten. His pace had slackened and he was visibly weakening. Good. She could outrun him, at least, and then—

"Bitch."

Angela spun around. Claudette stalked toward her from deeper in the shadows, sweat glinting on her brow, gun in hand. It was aimed at Angela's stomach. From fifteen feet away, she would hardly miss.

Angela opened her mouth, but there was nothing to say that might persuade Claudette to let her go.

"Where is he?"

"I don't know."

"Liar. Where's Vince?"

Angela shrugged.

"If you don't know, then you're useless to me, so I'll just kill you."

Angela didn't react. Her senses were heightened, everything sharp, crystal clear, slow.

"How did you find me?"

"You think you're that good at hiding?" Claudette stepped closer. There was a silencer on her gun. Angela had only ever seen them in the movies. From behind, she heard Coffee Man's heavy approaching footsteps.

"Last chance," Claudette said.

"Really, I—"

Click!

Angela gasped. Claudette turned the gun in her hand and looked down at it, surprised, annoyed. Angela took a step forward, and then the trees above them burst into life, and chaos fell around her.

Three shapes dropped down onto Claudette. At first Angela thought they were large birds, but then she saw that they were slashing, hacking, and stabbing. Claudette dropped the gun and waved her hands around her head, batting at the creatures that had attached themselves to her face, neck, and shoulder. Her startled shout turned into a gurgling scream as she fell beneath their assault. Blood splashed through the air in a graceful arc.

Angela stepped back from the violence. She'd seen its like before—and worse, much worse—but it was still a shock. More shocking still was the sudden turnaround in circumstances. From being threatened with death by this woman, now she was watching her die. Confused, unsure whether to help or turn and flee, she could only stand and watch the onslaught unfold.

A shape appeared from deeper in the undergrowth in the direction of the park wall, and Angela knew who it was simply from the way it moved, as familiar as her own shadow.

At the same time Coffee Man entered the shelter of the trees behind her, gasped at the scene that greeted him, and started backing away.

The shadow manifested as Vince. He pointed past Angela at the startled man.

"You need to go." Behind her, Coffee Man turned on his heels and ran back the way he'd come. He no longer looked tired.

Claudette was on the ground now, curled up at the foot of a tree. She shivered and bled, her wide white eyes stark against the bloody mask of her face. The three things that had dropped onto her were back on the low branches, poised ready to leap down again should the need arise. The one closest to Angela was the size of a newborn baby, but its features were that of an old man, its skin a dark grizzled gray, eyes deep-set and sparkling with an unknowable intelligence. It held out its hands, turning them slowly as it examined the gore on its clawed fingers and palms.

Claudette spluttered and gagged on her own blood.

"We need to go, too," Vince said. He was talking to Angela but looking down at Claudette. His eyes were wide, but he did not seem afraid.

"We can't just…" Angela said, unable to finish the statement.

"You want to call an ambulance?" Vince asked.

Yes, she thought.

She shook her head.

"Then come on!" He held out his hand.

Angela took a step closer to Claudette. The wounds on her neck and face were terrible, gaping, leaking blood in heavy spurts. Her shivers were lessening, her eyes glazed. Perhaps she was already dead.

Angela took Vince's outstretched hand, and despite everything it felt good.

"Where?" she asked, her voice barely a croak.

"Old gate out onto the road. Then we walk. Just taking in the sun. Okay?"

"Okay. What about...?"

"She'll be found soon enough, and she was seen chasing you, so you'll need to change your appearance again." He smiled at her. "Pity. I like the hair."

"I was thinking more about them." She nodded up at the trees.

"The gremlins? They can look after themselves."

Hand in hand, they left the dying woman behind.

5

Head down, senses alert as the bustle and chatter of ignorance washed over her, Lilou passed along the warm evening streets of London, this city that was not hers.

It was almost eight in the evening, and many of the Soho pubs were spilling their clientele onto the streets. Men in shirtsleeves and loosened ties, women in summer dresses, cigarette smoke hanging low in the still air, laughter and chatter ringing between buildings, the throngs seemed to repulse Lilou as she found the easiest route through and between the groups.

A few people saw her. Some even noticed, and one young man followed her for a while, ignoring the confused entreaties of his female companion as he left her standing alone outside a corner pub. Lilou sped up, drew herself in, concentrating on not being who she was. It took only moments for the man to slow to a halt, and she left him looking around in confusion.

Lilou could bewitch any man or woman she passed by. Her strongest instincts urged her to do so, but she was a wise nymph, and one who had seen and done so much. These past few months she had interacted with the human world more than ever before, and she'd revealed a talent for doing it well. Amongst her kind such a skill, allied with her human features, could be priceless.

Truth be told she liked being out on the streets alone. Although she had spent much of her life hiding, sometimes in plain sight, she could not deny the sense of vague superiority that overcame her when she was walking through busy London. So many people doing so many things, each of them thinking that what they accomplished was important, all of them believing they were wise in their own life, knowledgeable about the city and people around them.

None of them knew anything.

They couldn't conceive of the ancient woman who walked amongst them, and would not understand even if they knew. She was older than any of them, older than the buildings in which they lived, worked, and loved, and she carried the weight of that age with ease.

Most of the time she held back this arrogant sense of pride. It was dangerous. Most of all, it was shallow.

Lilou was comfortable being friends with humans, even though some of the Kin looked down upon them, and sometimes upon her for doing so. Lately she'd had much more cause to make human friends. Few could deny that her affinities benefited the Kin.

It was why she had ventured out.

She headed from street to street, encountering the oppressive city heat in these narrow thoroughfares. A food market drew her, its enticing smells a lure, and she bought a tray of spiced noodles. Walking and eating, she took the opportunity to glance around and make sure she wasn't being followed. It was an unconscious gesture, as much a part of her life as breathing and eating. These were dangerous times.

Excited by her mission, she hurried the rest of the way until she was standing across the road from her destination. She had not let him know she was coming—that would have been dangerous—so she knew that her arrival was likely to cause a commotion. She needed to do everything she could to ensure it remained as calm as possible.

As Lilou finished her food, she eyed the unimposing doorway. She knew what was down there. The man running the club had helped them, his sense of wonder opening up into a childlike fascination, his inbred brutality coming to the fore when he knew they were in danger. She and others like her had watched him afterward, but he'd kept his head down and done nothing to draw attention.

His part in the attack on Mary Rock's house had remained unknown. His recovery from the wounds he'd received there had been slow. Gangster, collector of relics, he now knew about those who still existed in the shadows, in hiding. That fact alone meant that they would always keep a covert watch on him.

Lilou had wanted to give him thanks, but Mallian had forbidden any more contact with Fat Frederick Meloy. Until now.

As she binned the empty food container and prepared to cross the street, the blue door to the club named The Slaughterhouse swung open. A heavyset man emerged and glanced up and down the street. He was dressed well in slacks, open-collared shirt, and a light jacket, and Lilou had seen him before. His name was Wheeler and he was a new recruit into Meloy's organization.

Lilou turned and looked into a restaurant window, pretending to scan the menu but actually watching over her shoulder in the reflection. Soon after the big man stepped aside, Fat Frederick Meloy emerged. Still not fat, he wore jeans and a plain black tee shirt, and he'd grown a light beard since the last time she'd seen him. He also looked older. The wounds he'd received at Mary Rock's house had indeed taken time to heal, but she thought perhaps it was the mental scars that drew the years down upon him.

He still carried the weight of power and confidence, though. It was an aura, a sense of restrained violence that would likely accompany him into old age, if he lived that long. It came naturally to people like him. He was a man whose personality would fill and control any space he entered.

Meloy and his companion headed along the street, chatting amiably. They stopped at a stall in the narrow road and Wheeler bought a bag of apples, then they continued on.

Lilou followed. She'd been ready to enter The Slaughterhouse, but this was better for her. She feared Meloy. She didn't think he would ever hurt her, at least not on purpose, but his was a deep fascination. An obsession. His collection was of old dead things, but now that he knew some Kin were still alive, Lilou and others feared that he might go the way of Mary Rock.

The difference was, they had Meloy in their sights. If he ever started to hunt the living Kin, they would kill him first. His death was always just a whisper away.

Perhaps he knew. Perhaps it was that knowledge

that made him look old, whatever defiance and strength he tried to project.

Some had argued that he should die anyway, just to avoid the risk. But there had always been humans who knew of the Kin, and they were managed, not murdered. Murder was a very human behavior.

Today would be Frederick Meloy's great test.

She followed them along the bustling street. Food smells from the stalls filled the air. Laughter spilled out from pubs. A dozen languages stirred every voice into a loud babble. She passed between countless people who did not know of her, and focused on the one who did.

In a quieter street, when Lilou judged the time was right, she drew close and whispered his name.

Meloy froze. Beside him Wheeler glanced around, startled, and locked his gaze on her ten feet behind them. His left hand delved into his jacket pocket.

Meloy saw her and reached out to hold Wheeler's hand.

"You," he said. His voice was lighter and higher than his appearance might suggest, that one word imbued with wonder.

Lilou let her shield slip, just for a moment. She became herself, a creature of desire and dread, a napaea whose natural allure could bewitch both man and woman and whose sole purpose had once been just that. Lilou had learned over the centuries to hold in her attractiveness, bury that purpose. Opening herself to the world was the best way of being known, and caught.

"Hello, Frederick," she said, closing herself off once again. That single brief glimpse had been enough. She felt a sliver of guilt, but also knew that she must use any means necessary to gain his attention. This was not a social visit. He would know that.

"It's fine," Meloy said to the big man beside him. Wheeler stared wide-eyed at Lilou, wearing an expression of naked animal desire. "Wheeler!"

"Boss?"

"I said it's fine. I know her. You can take yourself home."

"Boss? But I thought we—"

"Business can wait," Meloy said. "Everything can wait."

"We need to talk," Lilou said.

Meloy nodded. He blinked, looked around at others who were passing them by, and stepped closer to her. She could smell him, a faint mix of body odor and something older, like the dust of deep places. She wondered how long he spent down in his rooms beneath The Slaughterhouse, perusing his collection of relics.

"There's a pub around the corner," he said.

"Nowhere that anyone knows you."

Meloy tilted his head, and the arrogant sparkle returned to his eyes.

"A coffee shop?" she asked.

Meloy nodded. "This way." She walked alongside him, alert for any dangers from elsewhere.

They turned a couple of corners and then entered a small establishment. There were two tables on the pavement outside, one to either side of the door, and inside a dozen more tables and some bench seating. The place was buzzing, but Meloy led her through to two spare seats near the back. Framed posters of old movie stars hung on the walls, all of them signed.

A waitress stepped up and took their orders. Afterward, Meloy leaned in close. Lilou concentrated, working hard to hold back, inside. Meloy was hardly blinking. All of his focus was on her. She could almost feel the weight of his stare.

"You've been watching me," he said.

"Of course we have."

"I was afraid that Mallian... that thing... would want me dead."

"We're not murderers."

"Mallian is." His eyes darkened as red memories played behind them. "I saw him crush heads. Snap necks. It was..." He trailed off.

"No worse than some of the stories about you."

"My line of business, it's healthy to cultivate such myths."

"You're saying they're not true?" Lilou asked.

"If they were made up, and I revealed that, they wouldn't hold power anymore."

"So myths only retain their power if they remain uncertain and unknown."

Meloy blinked a few times, smiled, and leaned back.

"How are you?" she asked. "You know."

"It healed well enough." Meloy touched his chest through the tee shirt, tensing a little in his seat. "Still hurts sometimes, but that's fine. It's like a memento."

"We are grateful for your help," she said. "Rescuing the fairy was a good thing."

"And Angela's friend, of course."

"And Lucy, of course," Lilou said.

"So where's the fairy now?"

Lilou didn't answer. In truth, none of them knew,

and that was something that troubled Mallian deeply. The Nephilim had taken it as a personal slight that the fairy had vanished the moment they'd rescued her. Lilou had been secretly relieved. The fairy was the most powerful amongst them, and perhaps the most potent Kin still alive in the world. Imbued with old, forgotten magics and enchantments from the Time, she held their past and future in her grip.

Vanished for decades, her potential had always sung through their story, like a plucked string playing an endless tone. Mallian's plans for Ascent—revealing themselves to humanity once again, fighting them if necessary, rising to prominence—were beginning to frighten Lilou more than anything had scared her in centuries. It would disrupt every human belief system, and even without the turmoil Ascent would bring, their religions frequently inspired long and terrible wars. She and he had argued about it from his first mention of the idea. They still did.

The fairy was a big part of those plans.

"I need your help," she said.

"My help?" Meloy's surprise was evident.

The waitress came with their orders, and Lilou took a moment to sit in silence and look around the café. Though she was always alert and ready for trouble when she was out in the world, it didn't stop her from enjoying the experience. That was why she was asking Meloy for this favor, and no one else.

"There's a Kin-killer working in the United States."

She heard Meloy's sharp intake of breath.

"He or she has killed several Kin already, and they're only the ones we know of. Now the killer is working in a more confined area. Mallian's worried there's a pattern to their operation. He's afraid of what they're finding out."

"It's not another one like that Ballus thing?" Meloy asked. He'd been there when Mallian had killed the mad satyr Ballus, and had seen the abandoned pool awash with the corpses of dead Kin. It was a memory Lilou would never forget, and she could only imagine how awful it must have been for an ordinary man.

"We don't think so," Lilou said. "We think it's a human."

"More like Mary Rock, then."

"Maybe, but with her it was pure greed. With this one… we still don't know their goal."

"You want me to stop them?"

"I want you to come with me to the US."

"You?"

"We don't travel well," Lilou said. "It makes us vulnerable. I need a travel companion, someone who can look out for me. Someone who knows who I am."

"Can't the Kin over there sort this out?"

"No. They're… chaotic." She frowned and turned her coffee cup back and forth. "There's plenty you don't know about us, and much that you can never know. Here, in this country, there's some form of organization and communication."

"A hierarchy," Meloy said, and she knew he was thinking of Mallian, that amazing, terrible fallen angel.

"If you like." She nodded. "But in North America the Kin are much more scattered. In a way it's still very much old world and new world, and only in the old world is there still some sort of structure. Out there, they're much more wild. They used to think it would help them hide and survive."

"So if they're so disorganized, how do you know there's a Kin-killer?" he asked. "A psychic link? Some sort of supernatural message?" His eyes were wide, his speech speeding up, like a child asking about the moon and stars and whether there were aliens on Mars.

"Snapchat," she said.

"Oh… right." He laughed and took a drink of coffee, gazing at her through the steam.

"It's *because* they're scattered and vulnerable that I need to go," Lilou said. She didn't think he saw through the lie. The truth was, the Kin-killer was only part of the reason Mallian was sending her across the Atlantic. It would have been reason enough on its own—Mallian saw each Kin as precious, and a killer scything his or her way through their ranks was reason to take action. But there was something else happening in the USA that caught his attention even more. Lightning strikes on people. The fairy they had rescued and then lost again might have surfaced across the ocean.

It was the fairy he wanted more than anything else.

"And you want me as bodyguard," he said, interrupting her reverie.

"Partly, yes." She saw his expression light up as if reflecting her own. She understood the power she had over these people—more so with Meloy, who was already entranced by her kind. Yet she wanted his help to be voluntary. She could bewitch him into coming, make it so that he understood no other choice, but she wanted him fully there for her, an active presence instead of someone blindly following her scent.

"Partly?"

"More of a traveling companion," she said. "I haven't left these shores in a very long time."

"How long?"

She smiled. "Longer than anyone in this place would believe."

"I'd believe."

"Yes, I know. That's why I'm asking you."

Lilou could see that she'd tweaked his pride. He would go with her, of that she had no doubt. She also had to remember what a dangerous man he was. That, she must never forget.

"I thought you'd never come back," he said. There was a tone to his voice, a need that might have been perceived as weakness, and he'd never have revealed that to her before. He was a different man now.

"I know you've been looking for us," she said.

"Of course I have. You think I could forget?"

"No," she said. "But what about your business? Your world?"

Fat Frederick Meloy, perhaps London's most feared gangster, shrugged.

"I have people who can take care of things. For me, it was only ever about the relics."

"And now it's about us."

He did not reply, because the truth was obvious. His world had once been guns and drugs, women and money, and then he'd caught a glimpse of something wider and more fantastic, more wonderful. His collection of relics had been his most precious thing, and had become his primary reason for being.

Then he had seen a whole lot more.

"You'll come?" she asked.

"As if you need to ask." He stared at her, like a boy at his first love. "Even if I said no you'd make me."

"No," Lilou said. "This has to be all you."

"It's all me."

"Good. We'll be needing two plane tickets."

"For that, I'll need a name and a passport."

"I'll be in touch," she said. She was growing tired. It took a lot of energy, spending so long reining in her natural aura. She finished her coffee and stood to go.

"When?" Meloy asked, reaching out, not quite grasping her arm. She saw then that he was hers completely, and it was nothing to do with her being a nymph. It was simply because she was Kin. Whatever direction his life had followed before, now it was aiming somewhere else.

"Don't worry," she said. "It has to be soon. I have your private number."

"You do?"

"After what you did, what you saw, we know everything about you, Frederick."

She left without looking back, drawing herself in as she walked through the coffee shop and out into the Soho streets.

Lilou felt his gaze on her every step of the way.

She could not remember a time when she and her like weren't being persecuted, forcing them to hide, fade away from the world. Though comfortable in the occasional company of humans, she still mourned the fact that she had never known the Time, that period of history when humankind and Kin had existed alongside one another in relative peace.

Mallian told tales of that era. He was one of the few Time-born still alive and sane enough to talk about it, and she had seen him embark on long, nostalgic recollections of how he and their like had walked the wilds unmolested and free, each living their own particular and peculiar lives, carving myths across the bare canvas of time and establishing their own legendary paths.

She had never known that. Though inconceivably old by any human understanding, still her earliest memories were of conflict and pain.

Sad though she was, she never held a grudge against the humans. Time existed to flow from past to future. There had been Kin who could bend time and place to their own wills, and rumor had it a few still existed in the darkest places of the Earth. She was content, however, to ride the days, weeks, and years as they drifted by, continuing her own inevitable journey toward the great darkness that awaited one and all.

Although she had hardly known any different, she still did not feel a true part of the human world. It was ironic, really, that the safest place for them to hide was in one of that world's strongest beating hearts.

London had been her home for many years. Its roots as a human settlement were as old as Lilou, and her memories weaved in and around its establishment, its growth, and the remarkable changes it had undergone throughout its millennia-long history.

As she walked through the city now toward one of the few safe places left, a familiar feeling washed over her, a sense of history forming around her and trailing behind like a shadow. This often happened when her interaction with humans was intense. And it had been the case since Vince had rescued her from Mary Rock's killers, all those months ago.

Lilou had a long, deep past, and compared to her these humans were mere whispers in the breeze, carried away to nothing almost as soon as they were created. Sometimes their brief lives were lived brightly, but more often they bloomed like weak flowers, hardly ever approaching full potential before their autumns came and rotted them away.

The vagaries of time fascinated her. To humans she would appear almost immortal. To them her memories of the city—from when it was little more than a collection of hovels along the great river that would come to be called the Thames—would appear remarkable, almost supernatural. But even her own long life was nothing compared to the heartbeat of the world they lived upon, and beneath.

She often looked down on men and women because of their ignorance, yet sometimes that ignorance was a blessing.

She scanned her route constantly, all the way back to the safe place. Mary Rock was dead and gone, but there were still those who sought the Kin, and likely some who would hunt them, given the chance. The Kin-killer across the great ocean was simply one they knew about. There would be more, biding their time.

That was Mallian's argument. He called his cause Ascent because it involved the rise of the Kin to take their place once again beside or above humanity, like the grand, triumphant beings of old. If they did nothing, he posited—if he and his kind continued to exist in the shadows—then a time would come when memories were all they would be.

There were some among the Kin who were fine with that. Their time had been and gone, they said. Entropy carried them away, and what would be would be.

Lilou herself was on the fence. And with the two camps starting to polarize, the fence might soon be the most dangerous place of all.

6

Staring at his reflection in the water's surface, Gregor saw a man that should not be.

He ran his fingers through his hair, and hidden beneath the long locks he felt the nubs of horns stretching the skin of his scalp. Turning his face left and right, he bent lower to the water so that he could see the pale red irises of his eyes. His jawline was ridged and sharp beneath the skin, the contours partly hidden beneath his beard growth. Soon it would be time to shave his face and trim his hair, remove his shaded glasses, show the world who he really was.

Soon.

The riverbank was quiet, this tiny inlet hardly disturbed by the water's flow. The hard-baked silty beach where he sat had been used before. A few empty beer cans were scattered around, as were the remains of a fire, food wrappers weighed down by a stone. A couple of used condoms lay like the shed skins of unknown water creatures. No one had been here for a while. He was safe, for the moment, to spend some time planning his day.

On the river a few ducks squabbled, and insects buzzed and surfed the surface. There were no buildings to be seen from where he sat, and traffic noise was only faintly audible in the distance.

The phone in his right hand picked up a signal, and chimed. There were no messages or texts, no voicemails, and if Gregor ever used social media it was only to lurk and watch, never to post, never to interact. He opened the Internet, accessed a search engine, and scanned for news sites. Clicking on a national site, he began scrolling.

The Kin often revealed themselves in unusual patterns. Once, he had caught a werewolf in India by reading about the strange bleaching of trees in the area around a certain valley. Villagers had ascribed various theories to the markings, and the tale grew enough over the decades to merit appearance in an obscure volume about Indian legends. It had piqued Gregor's interest, and when he went and investigated some of the markings, he believed they might have been related to the Kin.

It was during the third full moon that he saw the beast. She was fully transformed, roaming the forests and leaving her scent sprayed on trees, marking the bark in elaborate patterns. In her wild monthly state, her caution was held at bay by pure moonlit instinct.

In accordance with instructions from the Script, he carried the third claw from each of her back paws in his pack. They continued to change with the moons and tides. And at times, when the moon was full, he could still remember her screams as he pierced her with a heavy wooden pike and hacked off her limbs.

Other patterns were less obvious. Whispers of sparkling shadows beneath a series of river bridges in the wild lands of Patagonia might have been elves, but six months of hunting had yielded nothing. Livestock stolen and found slaughtered around a riverside village in the Amazon might have been wild dogs or jaguar, but Gregor believed he had found the dwelling place of a chupacabra.

Four weeks into that search, the killings of cattle suddenly ended. Three men and four women from the village were found gutted, beheaded, and hanging from a tree. The murders were blamed on a feud, yet Gregor recognized a warning in the grisly remains. With the chupacabra frightened off into the vastness of the Amazon basin, he'd gone in search of easier prey.

He found it in Mexico City. A spate of disappearances amongst the city's poorest families was blamed on government-sanctioned death squads wiping out street children, but Gregor saw a more unnatural pattern. When he started finding the children deep down beneath the city, clean and healthy and possessed of a newfound vigor, he suspected the presence of a pombero.

When he found it and killed it, he felt not a moment's guilt. He took its tongue, and it remained with him now, shriveled and hardened into a thumb-sized knot.

His was not a simple life, nor an easy story. There were complexities. There was confusion. Only one thing settled his mind and heart, and that was the hunt.

He remembered very little of his life from before. Sometimes he dreamed of unidentifiable trauma in his childhood, and when he allowed himself to muse upon it, he thought perhaps he had lost someone close to him. His mind shielded him from whatever painful truth dwelled in the past. The turning point was meeting Jace Tan. That was when he became the person he was now.

Ever since Jace Tan, his life had been spent seeking, hunting, and killing. Gregor didn't even know his own age. The years drifted by, and his travels back and forth across the globe left the seasons jumbled, so he couldn't use them to judge the passing of time. Now, he used phones, the Internet, and other technology as much as he could, and he'd made sure that he was adept at digging his way through meaningless information to identify the patterns.

Gregor didn't waste time worrying about this lessening of his memory, this fog of history. He was an explorer of the future, not the past. A time would come soon when his current life meant nothing, and the endless years ahead of him would become his playground. Jace Tan had promised him that.

Browsing the news site, he chewed on a hunk of bread and some cheese he'd bought from a delicatessen in the local town, and drank water from a bottle. He never drank anything else. Being a man of simple needs meant that he could devote himself more fully to the chase.

In the year since he'd come up from South America, he had found and killed three Kin. That was a reasonable hit rate. His pack grew heavier, and the components he needed to fulfill the promises of the Script were being gathered. He wouldn't need many more.

His skin tingled at the thought. His senses sharpened, his heart hurried. Everything he had ever dreamed of came to this. He was almost tempted to remove the Script from its protective metal tube, safe in his jacket pocket, and read it one more time. But it was a fragile thing, and out here in the blazing sunlight wasn't the place. Each time he handled or looked at it, he feared an accident might take it away from him.

Every attempt to copy the Script had ended in failure. That alone was testimony to its provenance.

Old Man Struck By Lightning

At first he skimmed past the mention. It was unusual, but no more so than a hundred news items that never quite made the headlines, weird occurrences that possessed a twisted allure. He'd already moved on by the time his brain processed the headline. He scrolled back, read the article, and filed it away for future reference.

Then, minutes later, on a different local news site, another headline brought him up short and froze the breath in his chest.

Six Locals Struck
by Lightning
in Three Days

The feature went on to post sad comments about one of the people who had died, and then explore the surprise at what was far from a normal occurrence. Especially when, some of the time, the lightning bolts appeared to have come from a clear blue sky. This pattern had Kin written all over it.

It took digging to find names and locations, especially since some victims chose not to be identified. Yet there were always places to look. Social media was a foul stew of want and need, but for Gregor it was also a place where private information floated through the ether, just waiting for those with the know-how to pluck it away. He used optimum word searches, photographic filters, and a dozen other tricks to winnow down the names and addresses of some of the six victims. The dead one was easy to find and discount, the others only slightly more difficult.

The nearest one, a woman, was still in a hospital in Boston.

Gregor lay back in the sun and smiled. The familiar sense of a hunt settled around him, sharpening his senses and bringing the future closer. He had his backpack, containing as much of his history as he would ever need. He had the precious Script.

He had his knife.

For someone who spent much of his time alone, Gregor knew a lot about human nature. It was often essential in achieving his aims, and he believed that existing at a distance from society—if not physically, then psychologically—provided an objective view that offered an advantage.

As a result, he knew that the best way to act without drawing attention was to exhibit casual confidence.

He entered the hospital through the main doors, passed through the large lobby, scanned the floor map beside the elevators, rode up to the fourth floor, and strolled along the wide corridor toward May Ward. It was visiting time, and the ward was already busy with family and friends come to sit with their loved ones.

Even indoors he wore sunglasses and a baseball cap, and wouldn't reveal his true self to his target until he knew who or what she was.

His only problem now would be if she had visitors, but if that was the case he could always wait.

Patience was something he'd grown to embrace. Sometimes, the long wait before the catch was the most pleasurable part of the hunt.

The woman was in one of half a dozen small private rooms off the main corridor. She was sitting up in bed and reading from an e-reader, alone in the room. She was middle-aged, lean, and fit-looking. Gregor held back for a moment before entering, assessing what approach he'd take. Then, without glancing around— doing so might raise suspicions, if anyone was watching—he entered the room and shoved the door half-closed behind him.

If he needed to, he could lock it shut later.

Looking up at him, she raised an eyebrow, and took in his casual clothing and backpack. She blinked at the sight of the sunglasses and baseball cap.

Gregor paused five paces from the bed, beside the door to the small en-suite shower room. He frowned. He usually had a good sense of whether or not someone was Kin, even if their outward appearance was human. In this case, he thought not.

"Reporter?" the woman asked.

"*Herald*," he said.

"So I'm a big story now?" She sounded confident and in control. Her being at ease would make what he had to do that much simpler.

"Part of one, perhaps," he said. "Mind if I sit?"

The woman shrugged and nodded toward the chair at the foot of her bed.

Gregor sat and lowered the backpack between his feet. The knife handle dug at his hip. He could draw and use it in the space of a second, and he was one long step away from the woman. She wouldn't have time to scream.

"You're Marianne Francis?"

"That's me."

"Mind if I ask you some questions?"

She stared at him for a while, and in those few moments Gregor was uncertain just how this was going to go. She could press the call button beside her bed, and shout for help, but she'd only do that if she had something to hide.

He didn't think she did. There were no outward signs that she was Kin, and although he knew from experience that it wasn't always obvious, in this case he thought that betrayed the truth. However, he had to be sure. If she wasn't Kin, then there must be some reason why one of the Kin was using her. Six lightning strikes in such close proximity had to be connected, and he had an inkling of how.

Over time he'd heard and learned many stories of the Kin, and some said that lightning bolts were a favored method of remote attack by fairies.

"What did it feel like?"

"You're not going to write all this down?"

"Good point." Gregor smiled and opened a notes file on his phone.

"It was weird," she said, "like being punched really hard. A heavy, hard jolt. You ever touch an electric cattle fence? Bit like that, except a thousand times harder."

"Anything strange happen?"

"Besides being struck by lightning?"

"I mean anything you might not have expected."

She frowned. Becoming suspicious. He didn't have much time.

"How old are you?" he asked.

"Forty-two."

"Always lived in Boston?"

"Born and bred. When's this story going to run?"

"Are you Kin?"

"Huh?"

Her reaction was sincere—confusion, surprise. She didn't know what he was talking about.

Gregor stood and took a couple of steps closer to the bedside. The woman didn't look scared—not yet—but she was unsure.

"You want a photo of the markings?" she asked, and Gregor paused.

"Markings?"

She lifted her long hair from her neck and tilted her head so that he could see the patterns across her skin. A network of fine trails, like a river delta seen from orbit, or the fine tendrils of a feather.

Gregor lifted his phone and took a photograph.

"I thought you guys would be more interested in those who were hit twice."

His pause was hardly long enough to notice. *Nothing about that in the reports!*

"Yeah, sure." Admitting that he didn't know what she was talking about might blow any cover he had left.

"Cop who interviewed me said they're keeping it out of the news for as long as they can. Don't want panic to spread, but that's what I'm afraid of, tell the truth. Same cop told me most of those who're struck a second time are dead. What if I walk out the door and... *bam*?"

Gregor slid his hand beneath his loose-hanging shirt, and rested it on the knife handle. He was certain now that she wasn't Kin, but she was suspicious of him. To leave her alive might be risky. Yet to kill her would make him a murderer, and he had no way of disposing of her body. Hospitals were full of security cameras and potential witnesses.

As he turned to leave, she called after him.

"You gonna run the story?"

"When the police let me." He left and closed the door behind him, cutting off another question he only partly heard. He had to move. Head down, walking quickly, he left the hospital the way he'd entered.

Once he was outside and away he lost himself in the streets until he found a small, sheltered park. People were lunching there, some in small groups and many alone, and he bought a bottle of water and a sandwich from a deli so that he didn't look out of place. Then he pulled out his phone and started searching.

Now that he knew what he was looking for, he scanned social media rather than news sites. It didn't take long. More than a hundred people had been struck by lightning twice in three days, in incidents scattered over the northeastern states from Bangor to Pittsburgh. Many of them had died, but a dozen or so survived.

Ten of those survivors were missing.

Gregor thought he knew how to find them.

7

"We've got to get out of the city."

That was the priority. Everything else could wait.

"I missed you," Angela replied.

"People saw Claudette and that prick chasing you," Vince said. "They'll find her body. It's time to change…" He touched her short silvery hair, but he meant the whole package. It was time for Angela to re-imagine herself again. She had been so close to being caught, and if he hadn't been there—frantic in his search for her, arriving at the very last moment—he couldn't bear to think what might have happened.

This mad new world was the most amazing thing that had ever happened to him, but without Angela it would be no world at all.

"I wish this could end," she said.

"I think a cab would be risky, and buses have security cameras. We're best sticking to the streets, but off the main drags. Once we're somewhere safer, I'll steal a car."

"Vince, can't we take a moment?"

They paused on the busy sidewalk. Vince held her arm and edged her into the shadow of a bookshop's front canopy. His body prickled with energy, but he knew that Angela would need time to absorb and adapt.

He turned to her reflection. She hardly looked like Angela anymore, but he loved her more than ever.

He wished he could swallow the news he bore, and make it all go away. It wasn't cowardice on his part, it was good sense. When they were away, quiet and as secure as they could ever be, then he would tell her. It was important that they moved quickly.

There was already a weight persisting between them, an unspoken tension caused by the different directions in which they found themselves pulled. Angela, toward some distant and safe anonymity that he knew could never exist. Vince, pulled along with the wonder and terror of the Kin. He hoped their relationship was strong enough to survive. He hoped their love would spring back to its former shape.

"I've missed you, too," he said, "but we don't *have* a moment. Claudette might have been found already, and every second counts."

"We just killed someone, Vince."

"No we didn't."

"Who sent her?"

"No one," he said. "She was out on her own, looking for revenge. Against me."

"But she came for me!"

"You were easier to find."

"Because you're with them."

They locked gazes in the window reflection. He smiled, and he was pleased when she returned it. He'd missed her smile.

"Sometimes," he said. "Not all the time. But all that—*everything* else—can wait."

"Everything else?"

"There's plenty happening, and there's lots to tell you, but not here and now."

She nodded.

He turned and kissed her cheek. "If you want to stay alive, come with me."

"Movie quotes, Vince? Really?" She laughed, and that suited her so much more. He could see the fear she carried, but so long as it remained buried for a while, that was good. There would be plenty of time to be afraid.

They held hands and moved along the street, taking the first junction that steered them away from the park and the site of Claudette's death. Vince hadn't even considered the fact that she was gone, but it hit him now, the knowledge that the brutal, vengeful woman from London was no longer a threat to them. A chill ran through him when he realized just how close she had got to Angela—a trigger-pull away from exacting her revenge, a few seconds and several feet in a time that had spanned months, a pursuit that had taken in thousands of miles.

Yet he also experienced a measure of relief at the woman's death. If it weren't for information and help from the Kin, he would have never reached Angela in time.

Glancing across the street, he scanned the flow of pedestrians going about their business, the cars stopping and starting in heavy traffic, patrons sitting inside and outside cafés and bars. He looked for the wisp Ahara. If she didn't want to be seen, however, he would not see her. No one would.

"What are you looking for?" Angela asked.

"Just being careful," he said. *Get out of the city*, he

thought. *Get away, find safety, go to ground… and then I can tell her everything. About Sammi and her father Jim, and the Kin's fears. About Lilou.*

That was it, he knew. Lilou was the reason why he was putting off telling Angela the truth. The nymph was coming, and he felt a rush of anticipation at her arrival. And a flush of guilt at his excitement. He loved Angela first and foremost, above everyone and everything else…

But he still dreamed of Lilou.

The fact that he dreamed of her wasn't fair, and neither was his guilt. He was only human.

There was no sign of Ahara, but Vince knew that she was close. She was strange, even for Kin, a visage most of the time, less than a shadow, but when she did manifest and become something closer to his world, she was still a deep mystery. They could communicate well enough, though when she spoke her mouth moved just out of sync with her voice, like a badly dubbed movie. He sometimes wondered whether she actually spoke at all, or if her true voice was a whisper inside his mind.

"In here," Vince said. They ducked into a store and bought an I LOVE ALBANY baseball cap. Angela tugged it down over her dyed hair. It wouldn't be enough, but he'd grab every chance they had to make it out of the city.

In the four weeks since he had last seen Angela, he had learned much more about their situation. His earlier fantasy—that he could spring her from police custody and then make both of them vanish into the vastness of the United States—appeared to be just that. A fantasy.

Contacted by Lilou and instructed to keep him hidden and safe, Ahara and two other Kin had found him upon his arrival Stateside. They knew well enough how to hide, as did all Kin. But he and Angela were not like them. They were humans, and they could not avoid thinking and acting like humans.

There lay their potential downfall.

"Forget her," Ahara had whispered during his first long, lonely night in the basement of a derelict house close to Boston's docklands. Generations of immigrants had passed through those buildings during Boston's early years. Countless people might have spent their first night in America sleeping in that same place. Some had died there.

"I can *never* forget her!" Vince had replied. The mere thought was abhorrent to him. Ahara's smile, perhaps mocking, had made him even more determined.

He and Angela were both wanted by the authorities. For several days the massacre at Mary Rock's house in London had made headlines around the world. The dead had included a disgraced MP, a footballer who had once played at international level, and at least two businessmen who might have been called public figures. Rumors had built around the shockingly brutal murders and the burning of the big house, perpetuated and exaggerated rapidly across social media. They veered from reports of a sinister death-cult for the mega-rich, to a perverted swinging party gone wrong, to more imaginative tales featuring slave traders, mystical drug-fueled seances, and suicide pacts.

None of the speculation had touched on the truth. Vince still wasn't quite sure why Mallian hadn't begun feeding the speculation with rumors of the Kin. More than any of them, the Nephilim wanted exposure for his kind and a rise to their previous status in the world, a movement they called Ascent. In the wider Kin civilization, Vince knew, the general belief was that Mallian was mad, yet there were some allied with his cause—a core of supporters back in London, and scattered believers in other locations where the Kin persisted. Support for Ascent was growing every day.

The fact that Mallian hadn't used the attack on Mary Rock's house to begin the process of exposure meant he did not yet think it was time. That indicated to Vince that he wasn't mad, and that, in turn, meant that he was serious, determined. In a way that was more terrifying.

They passed into a network of back streets, busy commercial and residential areas where strangers passing by didn't attract attention. The further they moved out from the city center, however, the more they would be noticed. That was the last thing Vince wanted.

When they reached a large car park outside a massive strip mall, Vince grabbed Angela's arm.

"I'm going to steal a car," he said, keeping his voice low. "We'll drive out of the city, dump the car, then continue on foot."

"To where?"

"Somewhere safe."

"And where's that, Vince?"

He saw movement behind Angela and smiled.

"I want you to meet a friend."

Angela glanced behind her and saw the shape,

formed of sunlight like the glowing memory of a person.

"We've met... in the police station," she said. "Hello."

"Angela," Ahara said. She became more solid.

"Ahara helped me find you in time," Vince said. "We knew Claudette was closing in, but she was even better than we were at staying unseen."

Angela nodded. Vince thought he saw the memory of the woman's death reflected in her eyes.

"It was her or us," Vince said.

"I know."

"I'll find a suitable vehicle," Ahara said, and she faded away again, little more than a floating glow drifting ahead of them toward the first line of cars.

"You need to tell me what's going on," Angela said. "I've spent months trying to figure out how to remove myself from all this. From them. And now you come back and..."

Vince took a deep breath. *Now's not the time*, he thought yet again, but Angela deserved the truth, and he knew that she could take it. She was strong. Saying nothing felt akin to lying, and he had vowed never to lie to Angela again.

"Sammi's been taken," he said.

"Sammi?" Her eyes went wide.

"And that's not all. Jim's dead."

Angela took a deep breath. For a split second, the anger Vince saw in her frightened him to the core.

"Who took her?" Angela asked. "What do you know? Tell me everything."

They were driving along a Washington avenue

toward I-787, which would take them away from the city. Her thoughts were a raw stew, but she had a logical, ordered mind, and by the time she asked who had taken Sammi, it had all fallen into place.

I have to find her. That was her first priority, followed closely by her greatest regret. *We'll never get away from the Kin.* She believed that Vince was at peace with that dreadful truth, and even welcomed it. She wasn't sure she ever could be.

"They think it's the fairy," he said. "They tell me her name is something no human could ever say or understand, so they call her Grace."

"You mean the fairy we risked our lives to save?"

"They don't know why she's done it," he said. "Sammi was one of scores of people struck by lightning over a three-day period, most of them twice. Lots died. Sammi was one of those who lived. Jim must have been close by the second time she was hit, and…" Vince trailed off. He was driving carefully, keeping below the speed limit and doing nothing to attract attention. The fact that the car was stolen would do that soon enough.

Angela knew they shouldn't drive more than a few miles in a stolen vehicle. Highway cameras might pick up the license plate, and if the vehicle had already been reported stolen, an alert would go out to local police. If the system worked efficiently, she knew, no stolen vehicle would get more than a couple of miles once its report hit the wire.

The system rarely worked efficiently. In reality, they could probably drive all the way to the coast, but it wasn't worth the risk.

"Poor Jim," Angela said, and a deep wave of sadness

washed through her. She hadn't seen her brother-in-law in more than three years. She and her sister had never been close, and living in the UK had swallowed Angela's time, months ticking by, and then years. All the while she'd intended to travel back to visit family, yet there had always been an excuse not to. Maybe she'd been selfish in that, but she'd also sent invitations to all of her family to come and visit her in London. For the price of a flight they'd have had free—although cramped—accommodation in her maisonette, and an opportunity to explore one of the world's greatest cities.

None of them had ever taken her up on the invitation. There wasn't any unpleasantness, but theirs was simply a family with loose ties, love but perhaps not much affection. They'd all taken their own directions in life.

Her sister had died soon after she fled Britain. She'd heard about Sally's death several weeks after it occurred. Sitting in a cyber café, she foolishly Googled her family name. The stark words on the screen, a news snippet from their local paper, had smashed her like a hammer to the heart. She'd feigned illness to explain the sudden tears, drawing more attention to herself as she knocked a table and spilled drinks as she left.

That had been her darkest time. Lost and on the run in the country she'd once called home, she had tried to figure out how to contact her family, at the same time knowing it simply wasn't possible. It had been awful, knowing they might believe the stories about her being a murderer. The need to tell them the truth was almost overwhelming, but along with that came the certainty that if she did contact her mother, father, and sister, they would persuade her to meet, and that meeting would lead the authorities straight to her. Even if they didn't give her up themselves, the police would be keeping a close eye on her family.

She and Vince had stayed together for a while, a dark, depressing time when everything she treasured in life was being dismantled and weathered away to nothing. Her home was gone, her friends were gone, her ambitions were little more than echoes of someone else's past. Before Meloy, before the Kin, she'd been close to completing her doctorate. Now her research would be in the hands of the police as they investigated the massacre at Mary Rock's house.

Angela hated the idea of them picking through her studies, writings, and musings on subcultural theories, trying to attach significance where there was none, perhaps discovering coincidences that would excite them for a time as they followed nonexistent trails. She was comfortable in the fact that she wasn't a murderer, but knowing that others believed her to be one made her feel dirty, even guilty.

We can never give them up, she and Vince had sworn, and she was as committed to protecting the Kin as she had been on the day they left London. She understood their uniqueness, wonder, and splendor, but that didn't mean that she had to *like* them. It didn't prevent her from raging against their continued involvement in her life.

Everything she had understood about herself was in the past. Discovering her sister's death—after the accident, after the funeral, and not being able to even mourn with her close family—had been the most awful experience of her life. She was still trying to mourn, and being removed from the world of family and normality made it that much harder.

She'd seen her niece Sammi six times, the first three during the first year of the girl's life. She'd sent regular birthday and Christmas cards, and Sammi had always wanted to talk to "Aunty Angela" on those rare occasions when she and Sally chatted on the phone or online. A bright, gregarious child, last time they had met Sammi was already growing into a smart young woman. She was the love of Jim's and Sally's lives, and she'd had a bright future.

"One day I'll come and see you in London!" Sammi had said the last time they'd seen each other, a few weeks before Angela left for the UK, and Angela had really believed she would. Theirs was a fresh relationship, unhindered by age-grown troubles, the sort when the time span between meetings or chats meant little. Sometimes the bond between family was genuine and strong, honest and innocent, not a forced friendship.

She hated the idea that Sammi might think badly of her. How might that innocent young girl be suffering now? Her niece had been taken by the fairy, and her brother-in-law killed, and Angela couldn't help thinking it was all her fault.

"They'll never leave us alone, will they?" she asked.

"You know they can't," Vince said.

"I don't mean that. I don't mean…" She waved a hand over her shoulder toward the back seat, where Ahara sat, or perhaps not. "I know they'll always figure in our world, because they can't risk letting us go.

But they'll always be ripping our lives apart."

Vince had no answer for that.

"Why Sammi? We helped the fairy escape, so why come after me and my family?"

"None of them knows," he said. "They say Grace is unknowable, as if she's some sort of godlike figure for them."

"Or if they do know, they're not telling you," she replied. He glanced sidelong at her and she saw the hurt there, at the idea that his precious Kin were keeping something from him. She felt a moment of pity for Vince. She recognized the wonder of the Kin, but Vince felt the need to bury himself within it, surround himself. Angela was perfectly content to admire from afar.

"Oh, Vince," she said. Despair bit in for her poor dead sister and brother-in-law, and for Sammi, a sweet innocent girl snatched away from normality and thrust into this mad new world. Where was she now? Who was she with?

Was she terrified?

Was she dead?

"Help's coming," Vince said. Angela heard a strange tone in his voice.

"Lilou."

"Yeah. She's flying over. They don't like travel that much, so it must be important. She said—"

"Good," Angela said. She meant it. Vince's voice held a certain tone every time he mentioned the nymph's name, and Angela would never be able to convince herself that there hadn't been something between the two of them. Yet Lilou exuded goodness, and that had been a comfort. "I like her. She's familiar. It's good that she's coming."

"You're sure?" Vince asked.

"Maybe she'll be able to help us make sense of it."

"Lilou," a voice said from the back seat. Angela glanced back at Ahara, shimmering like heat haze in flickering sunlight slanting through the windows.

"Do you know Lilou?" Angela asked.

Ahara said nothing. Her image shimmered, like a television with bad reception.

"We have to find Sammi," Angela said. The car pulled onto the interstate and was swallowed by traffic headed out of the city. So many hundreds of people who knew nothing about the real world. She experienced a familiar disconnect, but also shame at the self-pity she'd allowed herself to feel. None of this was about her, and it never had been. Everything now was about Sammi, and Angela felt a curious hardening of her own edges, a strengthening of her foundations at this simple, terrible truth. She had a purpose once more.

Rescue Sammi, or die trying.

"That's why I came to find you," Vince said. "Claudette and her goon just happened to cross our paths."

"So we start with Lilou," Angela said. "She might know why the fairy—Grace—has taken Sammi."

"That's my hope," Vince said.

It was a good feeling leaving the city behind.

Sorry, Sally, Angela thought. *I'm sorry I wasn't there to say goodbye. But I'll save Sammi. I'll make sure she's safe.*

At the same time, the idea that she could do *anything* to rescue Sammi from a fairy who could summon lightning felt like a lie, as did any concept of safety. Though filled with purpose, she felt hopeless. Useless. She hated the feeling, but it was familiar in the shadow of the Kin.

"So is this our life now, Vince?"

"Things need to calm down," he said.

"And when they've calmed down, if they ever do, what about us? What about our life, having children, being together?"

Vince let out a low snort that might have been frustration.

"Do you even think about that anymore?" she asked.

"Of course I do." It was sharper than he'd intended, she knew that. "It's a different life for now, that's true, but it's life among the incredible, the remarkable. Most people have never known the Kin, and most never will. We're blessed."

"Blessed?" Such a discussion was pointless right now. It would serve only to drive the wedge even deeper between them.

"I love you," Vince said.

"I want to live our lives," she said.

They drove on in silence.

8

Over the years Gregor believed he had become attuned to the Kin. When they were close he could sense them in a strange, indefinable way. It was nothing physical, no goosebumps or shivers down the spine. Perhaps it was a sixth sense, or seventh, or eighth. It was a subtle vibration in his body, a nervousness that meant he could not sleep or settle. An excitement in his gut.

The nearness of Kin often meant that he would have to kill again soon, and that took him one life closer to the fulfillment of his own existence.

His body thrummed as if electricity was being passed through it. As if lightning hung in the air. He had never been so nervous or excited, and believed there was more than one Kin close by.

Behind the half-built house he sat on a set of timber steps and shrugged off his backpack. Pulling out several wrapped objects, he chose the smallest one he possessed, unrolled it and placed it in the palm of his hand. The feather came from an angel's wing, and it was the only such item he had acquired without first needing to kill. The relic collector in Mexico City had been old and forgetful, her dilapidated home protected by faux spells and charms that were powered by little more than local superstition. Gaining access had been easy, and stealing away the only relic worth owning had added a precious item to his growing collection.

The many years of pursuing his aims had imbued him with knowledge that went wider and deeper than the Script.

Placing the feather on its open cloth, folding one corner over so that a breeze would not blow it away, Gregor looked around for something to use. He found a plant pot with a wide, deep saucer resting underneath. The saucer was dark with mold, but it would serve his purpose.

Pouring some water from his canteen, he laid it down on the sun-warmed steps, swirling it around the saucer. It was around an inch deep.

Perfect.

Gregor waited until the water had calmed before placing the angel feather on its surface.

He had tried this several times before, and it had never worked. Always the feather had upended in the water, snapped quill pointing downward, feather aiming upward as if striving for Heaven.

This time it was different. The feather spun on the water's surface, left and then right and then left again, never falling still, as if strange currents turned it back and forth. Gregor held his breath as it continued spinning, reversing direction several times before becoming frozen in place. It happened so suddenly and certainly that the curved feather even seemed to straighten a little, its quill end lifting slightly from the water's surface as if pulled by a strong, invisible thread.

"It works," Gregor breathed, and he wondered at the

creature from which this feather had come. Even long dead, it still sensed the presence of its fellows.

Noting the direction the feather indicated, he packed the relics away once more, hefted the backpack onto his shoulders, and started following the Kin's trail.

He found the girl sitting out on her wide lawn, eased back in a recliner while an old woman fussed back and forth between chair and house, bringing drinks and food. About twenty yards distant, the girl seemed to be enjoying the attention, but she was tired. She dropped off to sleep in the midday sun. Her right arm slipped from the chair, hand hanging down. The skin of her upper arm was dark, a swath of patterns just like the woman in the hospital.

Something crouched beside her.

Gregor frowned, shifting position in the trees so that he could see better. At first he thought it was a shadow thrown by the girl in the chair, a strange trick of the light. Then he moved an overhanging branch aside, just a little.

The figure possessed the shape of a small child, crouched down with knees drawn up and arms hugging them tight. Its head was up, though, leaning over to the left. It appeared to be whispering to the girl. Motionless, she stared up at the deep blue sky, listening, frowning.

Gregor recognized the wraith for what it was. He did not consult the Script that much these days. Partly because it was old and fragile, and he could not even consider the chance of it being damaged or lost. Not only was it his driving force, it was a connection to the hazy past he still hoped to rediscover. Following the Script was his way of seeking the truth.

Another reason he rarely read it was that it had become so familiar, and he knew without looking which elements of the Script's instructions he still lacked. The remaining objects he sought spoke to him during the day and whispered into his ear at night, and sometimes he dreamed of them.

From this distance he couldn't quite discern the girl's true nature. What he was certain of was that she was Kin, otherwise she would have been running in terror from the wraith by her side.

He waited for a while, observing and planning his route across the garden to the girl. He was always cautious when he moved in for the kill. He had been caught in the act three times during his long journey—twice by humans, once by a fellow Kin—and each time he had been lucky to escape. His knife had found extra blood on those days. Being disturbed in his activities was time-consuming and dangerous, and he always strove to make sure the kill was clean, his escape clear and rapid.

He waited for more than two hours. Through a downstairs window he saw the old woman relax onto a sofa and drift into a troubled sleep. A radio played softly from somewhere in the house.

The girl barely moved, although the wraith that crouched beside her urged her to do so. That was strange. It was something he had never seen before, but the creature did not trouble him. He knew from experience that a wraith might touch him, might even be able to speak, but little more than that. They were old, forgotten, weak things, and whatever held this one tethered to the world was concentrated for some reason on the girl. During his long time hunting and killing Kin, he was used to encounters that inspired more mysteries.

Gregor made sure his backpack was secured, the metal tube zipped into his inner jacket pocket, and the curved blade gripped tightly in his hand. Then he left the tree cover and started out across the lawn.

The wraith sensed him first. Still crouching and hugging its knees, it turned to stare at him as he walked across the grass. He picked up speed, blade held down by his side.

She might be a witch, he thought. *She could just be.* One of the missing requisites of the Script was a witch's third ear and eye. He had seen a witch once in Guatemala two decades before, a starving, hunted thing that hid away in an old slaughterhouse on an abandoned farm, her skin darkened by old blood and horrible memories. She had forgotten herself, and her sloughed flesh had displayed no signs of the markings that might mark her as special. If she had once possessed a third ear and eye, it had long since withered and rotted away. She had been so pathetic that he hadn't even put her out of her misery.

This girl looked different, but as he closed on her and the wraith started to rise, Gregor felt a sinking disappointment as he realized his mistake.

The girl was doubtless Kin, but she was no witch. A nixie, perhaps. Her fingers were too short, her body too thin, and as she turned to look at him he saw the piercing blue eyes of a water sprite.

"Who are you?" she asked.

"A friend," he said. She smiled, but the wraith knew better. He recognized it now, or at least he knew its like. It was the remnant of an elf, member of one of the lesser elven clans from the forests of Europe. It posed no threat. It was faded and almost not there at all.

"And what are you?" he asked the wraith.

"Just a girl," the girl said, thinking the question was aimed at her.

"A disappointing girl," Gregor said. "All these patterns I follow, all this effort I put in, and most of the time I'm presented only with disappointment."

"Something strange happened," she said. "Are you from the news?"

"No," Gregor said. "I'm from somewhere else."

"Are you here about the lightning? It's strange." She glanced at the wraith. "She's asking me to go somewhere, she says it'll be better there, more peaceful than here, and…" The dead elf was backing away now, her face sad rather than scared, and Gregor thought she could see or sense his intention. She could no longer be harmed, but she must have wanted or needed something from this girl, and she realized her chances were dwindling. The wraith looked at the blade in his hand as if she recognized it.

Perhaps amongst the dead his reputation preceded him.

"Where is she asking you to go?" Gregor asked.

"She won't say."

Gregor knelt beside the girl and pressed the knife to her face. She drew in a sharp breath. He peered at the dead elf.

"Say," Gregor said. The wraith shook its head and backed away, fading into the sunlight and becoming opaque, heat haze across the sun-bleached lawn.

"I'm a secret," the girl whispered. "I've never revealed myself, I'm living with *them* now, aging with *them* and—"

"You're one of the deniers," he said. "I've met your kind before. Amazing beasts who wish themselves mundane."

"There's nothing mundane about humans."

"You'll never be human," he snapped. "Now say!"

"I told you, I don't know."

Gregor shifted the blade until it was pressed into her ear. A dribble of blood ran down the arc of curved metal. His heart barely increased its beat.

"It's a pity," he said, and he leant all his weight on the handle.

The girl, the denier, stiffened and thrashed a little before she died. As she faded away, so too did the wraith, shimmering into nothing as if it had never been there.

Gregor glanced toward the house, but there was no sign of the old woman.

The next time he tracked down one of these things that had been struck by lightning, a twice-struck, he'd try harder to find out where they were meant to go. He had a feeling that there, he might complete his collection at last.

As he left the garden and pushed through bushes back into the street, the old woman began to scream.

Soon he would rest and take out the angel's feather. It would spin once more, and then point. At the thought of following its lead, his heart began to beat faster.

9

"Gloria *Minogue*?"

"What of it?"

"Couldn't you have chosen a surname less likely to draw attention?"

Lilou shrugged.

"Jane Smith. Susan Jones."

"What's wrong with Gloria Minogue?" Lilou didn't like places like this. The airport was bustling with hundreds, perhaps thousands of people, snaking lines of them queuing in front of counters, many more drifting toward passport control and the departure lounge that lay beyond. The noise in the vast enclosed space was constant, with public address announcements adding to the cacophony. Children ran screaming and laughing, the *hum-hum* of wheeled suitcases vibrated through the floor, and wherever she looked she felt a hundred sets of eyes on her. She caught a man's stare, a woman's gaze, a child's frank glare.

Lilou had reined herself in as much as possible, because she'd known what this place was going to be like, but she could do nothing about her natural beauty. Her unnatural charm and allure was something she could control, to an extent, but the weight of her years, the depth of experience in her eyes and face, were parts of her she could not change.

"It's not the most innocuous of names."

"Why? I should be so lucky?" Lilou smiled at Meloy's quizzical glance. Just because she was Kin didn't mean she couldn't enjoy human culture. Music was close to her heart, and always had been from her early days when she enjoyed the entertainment provided by traveling minstrels and wandering troubadours.

"Oh, right," Meloy said.

"What if I told you she was a fairy?"

"Huh?" His eyes went wide. Shock relaxed his features, stripping away a surface sheen that helped her see more of the real him. She couldn't help but like what she saw. Meloy was full of bluff and bluster, a veneer that hid a deep air of menace, but at his heart he still possessed the wonder of an innocent.

"Joke," she said.

Meloy chuckled. She liked that about him, too. After all he had seen and been through, he could still find lightness in life. He held his chest and groaned a little. Echoes of the knife wound would likely trouble him forever.

"Still, you're sure?" he asked, quieter now that they were about to be called to check-in.

"Trust me," Lilou said. She projected confidence, but inside she was nervous. She had not flown for almost thirty years, and many things had changed in that time. Security here was tight. She couldn't allow any foolish mistakes to trip her up. "Anyway, what's *your* name?"

"You know my name," Meloy said. "Best way of getting into trouble is making one up. Eh, Lilou?"

"The name is Gloria," she said. She looked down at her feet. Everything about this was strange, but she had brought it upon herself. Out of the small group allied around the fallen Nephilim Mallian, she was the one best suited to travel, and the Kin most comfortable in human company. She didn't like to dwell too much on how tied in it was with her *raison d'être* as a sexual creature, a nymph whose basic instincts were to seduce.

This much human company was only stressful.

Other than a twitch at the corner of his lips, the man behind the desk didn't react to Lilou's pseudonym. She waited while Meloy was checked in, then they passed through to the departure lounge. He went into the Duty Free shop to buy a bottle of Scotch, while Lilou found a quiet corner to sit. She turned her back on the large seating area and faced the floor-to-ceiling windows that looked out onto the tarmac.

It was a blazing hot day, and there were thousands of passengers arriving from around the world or departing for every continent. It made her realize how contained her own existence was. It made her appreciate that, too. The closer it came, the more her journey across the sea frightened her.

She was glad of Meloy's company.

Taking out her mobile phone, she rang a number that only existed in her memory.

"Lilou," Mallian said in her ear.

"Gloria," she said. He did not react. Mallian wasn't known for his sense of humor. Lilou sighed and continued. "We're boarding soon."

"All is well?"

"Yes."

"Meloy?"

"He's fine. Keen to help."

Mallian grunted.

"So is there anything more I need to know?" she asked.

"A little. There are now over a hundred cases of victims being struck a second time, all within a two hundred mile radius of Scranton. Ninety have died, most of the rest are missing, including the girl."

"Most?"

"Two have been found murdered."

"Gregor."

"I'm sure of it."

"You still think she is responsible for the lightning strikes?"

"It wasn't the weather, Lilou."

"What can she be doing?" She watched a massive aircraft lift from a distant runway.

"I don't know," Mallian said.

"Really?"

"You're questioning me?" His voice was deep, and more and more these days it was tinged with anger and impatience. They were friends, but she had always feared him, and his ambitions frightened her. Perhaps being at a distance made her a little braver.

"You don't always tell me everything, Mallian."

Another grunt. "In this, I do. Ever since the Time, fairies have used lightning strikes to rid themselves of enemies."

"The ones who died were her enemies?"

"I don't think so. I think in this case she might have been looking for someone."

"Who?"

"More Kin."

Lilou frowned.

"And the girl? Angela Gough's niece?"

"That's still a mystery to me," Mallian said, and she heard his frustration.

"I'll find her," Lilou said.

"The Kin-killer has been drawn to this," Mallian said. "It's the sort of pattern that attracts him, and he appears more knowledgeable than we give him credit for."

"Which is why he's still out there killing us, after all this time."

"Find him, or the girl. Either one will lead you to Grace."

"And then we'll see," she said. It had been a long discussion, about what would happen if and when she found the fairy. Several times they'd met as a group, something that had been rare since the massacre at Mary Rock's house. The gatherings had occurred late at night, at one of their safe places high above the London streets.

Thorn the pixie had been Grace's friend for centuries, and after believing her dead for some time, he had jumped at the opportunity to free the fairy. Yet she had fled the moment she was released, and he had sunk into a deep sadness. She hadn't even said goodbye.

The old witch Jilaria Bran had believed the search a futile effort, and in her ancient eyes Lilou had seen traces of fear. They all knew how powerful and dangerous the fairy could be, perhaps Jilaria Bran more than most. In private, Mallian had hinted at a history between the two of them, but he had refused to elaborate. And Mhoumar, one of the more mysterious of the Kin with origins even Mallian could not guess, had simply stated that the fairy's path and fate were her own choice.

It was only Mallian who wanted Grace, for the sheer power she represented. A proud being, and older than them all, he had never shirked from admitting how much more powerful the fairy was even than him.

Back in the Time there had been magic, and to a greater or lesser extent many of the Kin had wielded it. To some it had come as naturally as breathing, and had been an integral part of their existence. When the Time began to fade away into the mists of history and the annals of myth and legend, the magic had faded, as well.

Mallian believed that the Kin had let it go, understanding that to possess such talents in the more prosaic, logical world of the humans would mark them as different and make their integration even more difficult. On occasion he blamed the lessening of their magical powers on a form of evolution—the thinning of their race over time, the rise of the human world smothering the Kin, fear turning to hatred amongst the humans.

The Kin falling from a position of power to scampering in the shadows, fleeing, hiding, and their magic doing the same.

With the fairy it was different. She was as removed from the rest of the Kin as they were from humanity, a being from a world not quite in line with this one. Her old magic obeyed laws that few in this world understood. She could bend existence to her will. Though during the Time there had been many calling themselves fairies, Grace was one of the few who had truly carried that name.

And Mallian wanted her for Ascent.

He knew that on his own, however many Kin he could call to his side would not be enough to achieve their aims, and rise once again to a position of prominence. Reveal themselves to the humans. Begin a new Time, fresh and recharged.

Having the fairy on his side might tip the scales in their favor. Unfortunately for Mallian and Ascent, it seemed that the fairy had her own ideas. This threw Mallian into deep depressions, and sometimes raging angers, but in her quietest, most private moments, Lilou wondered if it was for the best.

Ascent would change everything, for humans as well as Kin. She couldn't bring herself to believe that change would be good for anyone.

"Yes," Mallian said, pulling her back to the present. "And then we'll see. Safe travels, Lilou."

"I'll be in touch." She disconnected, and moments later Meloy sank into the chair beside her. Her own seat lifted slightly as his weight displaced it.

"Beats the hell out of me how those things stay in the air," he said as another huge jet took off.

"Thanks for that," Lilou said. "Just what I needed."

Meloy glanced at her and smiled. Always in his eye there was that look of wonder and disbelief, but it was a calm look, not manic. He'd seen and done things that had brought him close to the Kin. So close, in fact, that they could never let him go.

He was here to accompany Lilou, but at the same time she was keeping an eye on him.

"So tell me about this bastard," Fat Frederick Meloy said. There wasn't anyone sitting next to them. Nonetheless, she glanced around.

The aircraft thundered along the runway, acceleration pressing them back into their seats. They'd been lucky to get two seats by the emergency exit. If pushed, Lilou might have admitted letting her mask slip, just for a moment, when she asked at check-in if these were available. Soon they would be able to stretch out their legs and relax into the journey.

If she could relax at all.

She gripped the seat arms, shoulders tensed, jaw clenched. When she glanced sidelong at Meloy he was smiling at her.

"Just give me a minute," she said.

"It'll be fine," he said, leaning a little closer. "I'll look after you." It was spoken with such sincerity. He loved her, but only as much as he loved all the Kin he had met. Meloy was a gangster, perhaps responsible for some reprehensible crimes, yet since their clash with Mary Rock and her organization, he had been like a child discovering that his favorite superhero characters really did exist.

The plane lifted off the tarmac and her stomach lurched. Lilou closed her eyes, holding her breath. It was a long time since she had been away from London, and even longer since she had flown anywhere. There was a familiarity and a sense of safety that came with proximity to her friends. With every second that passed she was moving further away from them.

Meloy tapped the back of her hand and she opened her eyes. He nodded at the window beside her.

Lilou looked, and the sight saw away some of her fears. Below them lay London. The Thames snaked through the city like a dark fault line, and on either side lay the heavily textured world of tower blocks and streets, parks and squares, swaths of housing and the sites of larger, grander buildings. There was home, laid out before her, and given time she might even be able to zero in on places she knew—their several safe places, both above and below ground. The parks where she sometimes walked, dreaming of the true wild. Meloy's nightclub in Soho. Even though she was leaving, she found it a comforting sight.

Clouds wisped past and obscured her view as the jet climbed, and at last Lilou began to settle into her seat. Her hands unclasped, her shoulders relaxed, and she started to breathe more easily.

"There have always been those who want us dead," she said. "From the Time and down through the ages, the Kin have had our enemies. We're not totally innocent in that, of course. We're as good at making enemies as you humans, if not better."

"I wouldn't know," Meloy said, and Lilou couldn't hold back a snort of laughter. He raised his eyebrows.

"We made enemies of humans, and enemies of our fellow Kin. I've heard tales of conflicts and even wars between factions stretching back ten thousand years or more. Never in my lifetime, though." She looked at her hands, stroked her fingertips together, needing somewhere to focus. "In my lifetime it's been more of a hunt. There are those who are afraid of what they don't know or understand, and more often those who want to profit from it. You saw that with Mary Rock."

"She was... *eating* your people," Meloy said. He shook his head as if unable to comprehend.

"They're not my people, Frederick," she said. "You need to understand that about us. There are as many differences amongst the Kin as there are amongst humans. Probably more." She kept her voice low. They leaned in close so that she could speak, he could hear. Anyone looking might have thought they were lovers.

"But Mallian," he said. "The group who freed the fairy."

"We come together when we need to, and yes, Mallian and I are part of a small group in London who spend time together. Some Kin are loners, others like company."

"Just like humans," he said.

"But unlike humans, it's easy for us to find somewhere to be alone."

"Six billion of us," he said. "How many of you?"

"I have no idea." She wasn't lying. As far as she knew, no one was aware of how many Kin were left in the world, nor even how widely their proliferation had spread.

"So the one we're going to find," he said. "What about him? If it is a him."

"We think it is," she said. "Our quarry is known as Gregor, though no one knows if that's his true name or not. Likely not, or he'd have been found by now. He's become something of a myth amongst the Kin, as we are to most humans. He's our bogeyman. Unlike Ballus, his aims seem more focused. He's more of a... collector."

Meloy flinched a little. "Like me?"

"You collect old relics," she said. "This collector takes from living Kin, and murders them for what he wants."

"Takes what?"

"Various body parts. Corpses have been found over the years, here and there. Some in Asia, a couple in South America, and now in the States. For every five bodies found, the number that never will be found might be much greater. It could be awful.

"At one time we didn't even think he existed. We thought it was a group or organization among humans committed to hunting us down, perhaps spreading tales of this 'Gregor' to frighten us into lowering our guard, exposing ourselves. But he's real enough. He's been seen, spoken to. There are a few Kin alive today who wouldn't be, if they'd been on his list."

"List?"

"There appears to be some sick method to his madness. An aim to what he's doing, although no one can even guess what it might be. Perhaps it's no method, and only madness."

"He's met Kin, but always escaped?"

"Not all Kin are strong. Most of the ones you've met have been, but that's because it's the strong ones who aren't so afraid to reveal themselves or take action. The weak ones sometimes hide away, and some of them have been hiding for centuries. In deep places, dark places. There have been efforts to find and kill him in the past, but he either disappears for long periods, or those who go to find him are never seen again.

"There are as many rumors about who or what he is as there are Kin to tell them. As for his victims, he usually pursues them out of sight and away from civilization, where some of the more independent, lonesome Kin choose to hide. Most recently he's been below the equator. Now, though, something seems to have changed. He's come north, into places where more have made their homes."

"And places where he might be hunted down." Meloy's expression hardened, the danger simmering within him shining through.

"Yes, that too," she said. *Should I mention the fairy?* she wondered. Part of her wanted to, but it felt like a deeper secret, mostly because it was to do with Mallian and Ascent, and nothing to do with Meloy.

Not yet, she decided. *If Mallian has his way, all humans will know of the fairy, given time.* Lilou could not imagine how that would happen, and what the results might be. Best to mention nothing, for now. If the time came, and they managed to find their way to the fairy—via the Kin-killer or otherwise—that would be the moment to tell him more.

"I have a few contacts in North America," he said. "Some who might help."

"No," Lilou said. "It's important we keep this close, and quiet. Spreading panic won't help, and Mallian doesn't want any more human involvement than necessary."

"Right. So no one has any clue why this bastard's collecting?" Meloy asked.

"Perhaps it's just a fascination."

"If you're fascinated with something, you don't kill it," he said, and he was staring at her.

"Tell that to butterfly collectors." Lilou reclined her seat and leaned back, feeling the last tenseness leaving her shoulders, closing her eyes and ending their discussion. She knew he wanted more, but they had a long flight, and plenty of time together. As yet, she didn't feel totally at ease in his company.

Even on a plane full of people, Lilou needed time to herself.

10

At the house by the sea, Gregor let his caution slip. He felt close to something, sensed a change in the air, a pulsing potential that lured him onward as if tied to some point ahead. The string used to tie him was being pulled. Every instinct told him to go with the flow, but he needed a moment to pause and take stock.

He needed a rest.

As he approached, evidence of the lightning strikes was still apparent. Gregor passed by the two sites with a strange mixture of awe and fear, and decided to first examine the dwellings. He couldn't storm ahead blindly. He had to take his time.

Across a wide lawn from the main house, a small summerhouse was located close to the river inlet, and its door was not locked. Inside there were several wicker chairs and a low glass table. Pictures hung on the wall, showing a couple and their child in various holiday poses. The child was the local girl in the news who had been struck twice, and had since gone missing. The man was the dead father. The woman, so the news items said, had died in a tragic accident several months before.

He stored that information, ready to retrieve it if an occasion warranted. It was all about the patterns.

The low glass table was perfect.

With care and reverence he opened his backpack and started to remove the wrapped items contained therein. He placed them in two lines along one edge of the table, not so close to the edge that they might tumble off. He kept them wrapped for the moment, even though he knew what every package contained. He knew each by touch, by smell, and even by weight.

These were the relics with which his future would be assured.

Next he took out the Script. He kept the metal tube in his pocket, so close to him that he could usually feel it through his jacket's inner lining. It was still warm from his body heat. The screw at the end was tight, but he flipped up the small handle and strained, feeling the familiar surge of excitement as it twisted open.

He tipped the tube onto the table. The rolled and tied script slid out. He breathed in the faint aroma of time and dust, shivering at all it implied.

Not only time, but the Time, he thought. *Not only dust, but the dust of wonderful things.*

Gregor stood and backed toward the open summerhouse doors, never taking his eyes from the objects on the table. He felt the sun on his back, a breeze cooling the perspiration around his neck, and he heard the gentle mutter of a boat's engine. At last he tore his gaze away from the relics and glanced around, inside and out, making certain he was alone. The lawns were well maintained, the house small but neat, sad in its emptiness.

No one had seen him arrive.

No one was looking at him now.

His shadow cast across the table, he stared once again at the items he'd removed from the backpack. Before him lay his lifetime's work. It was rare nowadays that anyone carried their life's efforts with them, but these weren't things that could be backed up and copied, nor could the relics be stored anywhere that was safer than with him. He had considered what might happen if someone else got their hands on his treasures. He would fight to the last, of course, and Gregor was a man not afraid of fighting.

If that fight ended badly, then a victor might root through these objects, wrapped in fine microfiber cloth, and wonder what the hell they had found.

He'd also considered what might happen if one of the Kin found him. They likely knew about him now, what with all that he'd done. Some of them were strong, vicious, and better at fighting than he was. He had the scars to prove it.

One package contained a fragment of skull from a piskie. He'd found the creature in Buenos Aires, where it had lived in the basement beneath an old abandoned school. For a time he and the piskie had talked, and he'd even managed to befriend it. Far from its traditional Cornish home, it had seemed lonely, tired of its secretive existence in deep, dark places. It told him it was two hundred years old, but Gregor had decided it might have been six hundred or more. It told him tales of old times—though none of the Time, because it was far too young to know of that firsthand.

He'd spent several weeks earning its trust and allowing it to relax in his company. It didn't get to know many humans, it said. Most of them feared or hated it on sight, or coveted it. Gregor had replied that he was not like most humans.

On the day he'd taken its life it had sensed something was wrong, and he'd realized his own mistake in regarding this small, melancholic Kin as anything other than dangerous.

It had put up an heroic fight, slashing and cutting, fighting back as he tried to kill it. Even as his blade punctured its heart, his own blood had been spewing from a wound in his throat, spattering the screeching creature's face as it drew its final few breaths. Its claws had missed vital arteries by a whisker, and before he butchered the corpse Gregor had cleaned and cauterized his own wounds.

Then he'd taken the Kin's small head and left the rest of its corpse for the rats. He'd fled the city before cleaning the skull and collecting the portion he needed, in strict accordance with the Script.

The scar of that meeting remained, a knotted reminder of his lack of caution. There were others. A badly knitted bone in his left foot from the werewolf encounter in India. A rash of scar tissue across his right hip from his three-day chase and conflict with a faun in Norway. Other wounds, scars, and broken bones were as much a reminder of his mission in life as were the objects lined up before him now.

Such scars should have urged more caution, but Gregor was growing impatient. He wasn't sure how old he was, but he had gray hairs on his chest and head. His limbs ached on damp days, and the promise of the Script drew him on toward triumph. His old enemy, time, flowed around him and carried him onward. His great purpose was a rock in that flow of which he might grab hold, and if he managed to succeed in his aims, *he* would become the rock.

He had never once doubted the outcome of his journey.

Gregor knelt again beside the table and reached for the rolled Script. He untied the two bows and let it partly unfurl, rolling it delicately with his fingertip until it was open all the way. Ten inches long, six wide, the Script was treated leather on which a series of instructions had been inscribed. He had read these instructions many times, struggling at first to understand but, over the course of many years, finding that each reading brought him closer to a clear and concise translation.

Its origins remained unknown. Jace Tan, the ancient creature who had bequeathed it to him, had been vague in his suggestion of the Script's provenance. Gregor's memories of that time were also vague, shadowy moments that skirted his memory like names on the tip of his tongue. What he *could* remember was Jace Tan's words after he handed him the script.

You may have to search the world, because I no longer can.

Gregor had decided long ago that the origins of the Script did not matter. Whether or not the creature whose pale hide had been used as a canvas was alive when it was written, it was surely dead now. He passed his hand above the ancient symbols, left to right and then top to bottom, and whispered his own familiar précis of their directions.

*"Gather the parts, keep them close, wrap them
well. The claws of a creature of the moon. The
skull of a Cornish elf, the genital pelt of a
faun..."*

He listed other relics, and then passed over a couple
of lines that he did not know so well. Many long days
and nights had been spent looking at these symbols,
imagining meanings but never quite knowing. Perhaps
there would be a blending of the parts, a bringing
together. Maybe they would need to be set apart in a
particular pattern.

His plan was to ask the final Kin he had to kill,
offering the false promise that he would spare its life
if it translated for him.

What he did know was that there were only two
parts left to gather. That was why he sought out
patterns, and why the strange patterns of these
lightning strikes attracted him. Four Kin in two days.
They hadn't given him what he needed, and he felt a
deep frustration growing inside. He had to rein it in,
though, because it might lead to panic, and that might
cause him to make mistakes.

*"Keep them dear, keep them secret, absorb their
closeness while they absorb yours. When the
pattern of them falls into place, they will shape
your life, and you will become..."*

Gregor shivered as his fingers passed across those
final symbols and he recited their meaning. Pleasure,

fear, and the sweet anticipation that had been his driving force for so long. He repeated them.

"And you will become Kin."

"And I will live forever," Gregor whispered.

He blinked his pale red eyes and remembered the tattooist's needle in that San Francisco backstreet. He rubbed his hand across his scalp and felt the nubs of horns that had been implanted beneath his skin. Affectations. Falsehoods. The foolish adornments of a man searching for who he really was, or might become.

It was time to follow the girl who had disappeared. Once again, he took out the angel's feather.

11

The thing kept scratching at its chest. That's what convinced Sammi that it was real, and not just a quirk of her imagination.

Her mother had always commented that she had a great imagination, and Sammi enjoyed giving it free rein, writing down stories or simply telling them to herself. Since her mother had died it had become a kind of release for her. Sometimes. Other times it was no release at all.

At first she thought she was making this up while she lay on the lawn, knocked out by the second lightning strike—

From a clear blue sky?

—her father hunkered over her and awaiting the ambulance.

That was yesterday, she thought. The shape had come from nothing, arriving and helping her to her feet and whispering in her ear about her mother. She might have imagined that. Then it had guided her from the garden and out along the road, to take her to her mom. She could easily have imagined that, too.

It was tall and thin, and not-quite-there.

She felt a pressure on her arm when he held

her—she was pretty sure it was a "he"—but not the warm pressure of a solid, living hand. Her ability to sometimes sense the presence of someone close by was more than a feeling. It was built from subtle tweaks on all her senses—body heat, the sound of a heartbeat, a flicker of shadow or light, the hint of someone else's breath on the air—

There's none of that here, though.

—and her companion's presence was undeniable, though he still wasn't *solid*. She might have imagined that, too. Built him from nothing, a guardian angel guiding her away from the pain and out toward somewhere her mother might be waiting.

That, most of all, Sammi could have imagined, as she had countless times since her mother's senseless death.

I'll walk around the corner and she'll be there, sitting in a garden chair, she would think. *I'll open the front door and she's walking across the lawn from the summerhouse, bare feet whispering through the grass.* All these things were dreams and fantasies, yet every one of them was precious as anything real. *I'll look across the garden and see her hand curl around the gate to unbolt it from the inside. I'll pass an aisle in the supermarket and she'll be there, choosing which brand of cookie to buy for an evening treat.*

Mom is everywhere.

But this scratch, this itch, this weird habit of a being that shouldn't exist, that was... strange. That was odd. Sammi didn't think she would have ever imagined that.

"What's wrong?" she asked.

"Old itch," the thing said.

"Is that your name?"

It stared at her, frowning.

"Don't you remember your name?"

It looked away, troubled, hand clawed, fingers raking back and forth across its chest.

"That's what I'll call you then," Sammi said. "Old Itch. It's better than nothing."

They sat in a small patch of scrubland that had once been the garden of a large house. The house was dilapidated now, tumbling down, its story old and most likely forgotten. Fading memories at best. The garden had grown wild, with clematis plants subsuming the house's sad remains and rose bushes bulging out from their ordered borders and beds and spreading across the lawn. Grasses grew long, weeds sprouted in delight at their freedom. It was the world carrying on when there was no one there to notice. It was beautiful.

"Let me see," Old Itch said again. At first Sammi had been afraid he was some sort of pervert, but his interest was in the patterns on her shoulder, arm, and neck, and nothing else. That was the only time his eyes had really come alight.

She'd already forgotten that he'd appeared only-just-there when he'd guided her from the garden. Yesterday, or maybe two days ago, she wasn't sure, there was something about the days and nights... something about their ebb and flow... She was tired and awake, alert and dozy. The world was several steps away from her, and her dead mother felt closer than ever.

She slipped the tee shirt from her shoulder and turned so that he could look.

The bus journey had been strange. With every trundle of its wheels she was being taken further from her father, but Old Itch comforted her whenever she thought about it, as if he could read her mind. He probably couldn't, although there were things about Old Itch that she thought *were* pretty unlikely, and in some cases downright impossible. She guessed she'd discover more as time went by.

"Your mother sent me," he would say. *"We're going to see your mother. Don't worry, your father's fine, he's okay with all of this."*

Looking away from Old Itch as he examined the fern-like marks on her skin, she thought of her father and hoped that he really was well. Surely he would understand what she was doing. He would want her to find her mother.

"Closer," Old Itch said. Sammi turned and he was so close that she should have been able to feel his breath on her shoulder. He was tracing the markings with his fingertip, never quite touching her skin, yet she could feel him. Maybe his fingers were stroking the fine hairs there, even though most of them had been burnt away. "We're getting closer but… it's still moving."

"What is?"

"The Fold." His eyes flickered up to meet her gaze, then back down to the fine tendrils and sprays on her skin. "Here," he said, moving around so that he was examining her back again. He grabbed the neck of her tee shirt and pulled it further down, lifting her arm with his other hand so that he could examine where the markings spread beneath it and across her armpit.

Insects buzzed, a summer sound she had always loved. A bumblebee droned across the garden, skimming the long grasses and seeming to pause inches from Old

Itch. It hovered for a moment, approached his head as if mistaking it for a flower. Then it zigzagged away, buzzing angrily and disappearing into a large rhododendron bush.

One... two... three. He touched her, tapping just beneath her left shoulder blade. His finger was cold, so cold that she flinched, a violent movement that caused muscles to spasm in her back. So cold that it almost burned.

Like lightning, she thought, and for a moment she felt portions of skin across her back, shoulder, arm, and chest shifting slightly, those fern-like patterns swirling like oil on water.

"We should move," Old Itch said. He sounded more confident than before, and she wondered whether this was the first time he'd had a real destination in mind.

"Mom is in the Fold?" she asked.

"Mom is in the Fold." He itched at his chest again, a rhythmic *scritch-scritch-scritch*. This time the movement pulled aside the loose shirt he wore to reveal a flash of pale skin underneath. She saw ugly scars, and festering sores.

"What's wrong with you?" she asked, shocked.

"It's where they killed me," he said.

Sammi's eyes went wide and she pulled away, and Old Itch mirrored her expression.

"*Tried* to kill me," he said. "Where they *tried*. But... your mom made it all well again."

"She did?"

"Yes." Old Itch nodded, and the smile he tried on didn't suit him at all. It exposed his teeth. Some of them were too long. "She's a good woman."

"She always makes it well again," Sammi said, and Old Itch blurred for a while in her vision. It might have been because she was crying. She was looking forward to seeing her mother again.

It is almost the place, almost the Time, but not quite yet. Not until she is ready to bind and tie the Fold. Before she can do that, she has to be certain that she is ready. Leaving the world, however much she has grown to hate it, will be a major step.

She follows the borders of this new land. It still echoes and pulses with traces of the magic that formed it—deep, distant booms, shivers through the ground that transmit into her feet and legs. It's as if the place has a breath, a heartbeat. She's not troubled because the magic is hers, and she knows that its ripples will fade over time. As the Fold becomes better established, the magic will grow more stable. When she binds it closed and removes it completely from the old world, it will be self-sustaining, and barely even magic anymore.

The Fold will be another place.

She enjoys walking, and follows the edge of the Fold around a deep, steep-sided valley. It's very beautiful, and parts of it remind her of the Time. That's why she chose this place. Above her runs the ridge line and the edge of the Fold, and down in the valley a narrow river snakes through from west to east. The river has formed this landscape over eons, and she can relate. She and it are both timeless. From this high up she cannot make out its flow or surface detail, but she knows that parts of it are as still as a lake, while other parts are churned into white-water by sudden dips in the riverbed and protruding rocks.

That's another way that the river reflects her own life. Some peace, some tumult.

She doesn't like thinking about the bad times, but one of them is so close in the past that it still pains her. It feels like yesterday that she was released from the cell in the woman's attic. She feels gratitude toward those who freed her, but the Kin are as distant as the humans who helped. She can't understand the relationship between them all. There is nothing holding her to the world, no desire to remain, and the Fold is something she has been considering for several centuries.

Freedom has given her the impetus to seek it out.

The possibility of the Fold's creation was always at the forefront of her mind, and she always knew that she could make it work. It took some effort, but in a way the woman in London did her a favor by keeping her imprisoned, allowing her mind to settle and the magic to build within her, build until it was strong, rich, capable.

Those other things to which she was subjected... the tortures, the cutting, the slicing in an attempt to remove parts of her... they still echo and pulse like the magic in her land. She doesn't like thinking of them. It makes her head itch on the inside where she cannot touch, like a bad memory taunting her from out of sight.

In the Fold, she will be out of reach. Yet there is still some small part of her that wants company.

She walks down the hillside, enjoying the rough terrain. It's a beautiful valley, and she will be here forever.

The hillsides are swathed with greens, blues, and deep purples, heathers and grasses providing a palette of colors and shades that will change through the seasons. Once the Fold is closed she will need to shift the seasons herself, but that lies well within her power, and such a task will fill some of her endless time.

Sometimes she thinks she will make it autumn forever.

The valley slopes are rugged, criss-crossed with paths trodden by animals that are no longer here. Rocky outcroppings provide fixed points on which she can concentrate as she works her way down toward the bottom, and in the shadow of the hillside she can look across and see the far slopes bathed in sunlight. Beneath one rocky promontory there are shadowy recesses that might be caves. She extends her senses to probe into the darkness, then withdraws again, coming back into herself and feeling a chill of sadness that whispers right through her flesh, bones, and blood.

I should save that for another time, she thinks, and the prospect of forever hits her hard. This place is not large enough for forever. She can see the Fold's limits all around the valley, north to south, east to west, and she could probably walk a circuit of the whole Fold in a day. This will be her world. This will be her eternity.

She closes her eyes and sighs deeply, and there she finds comfort. Reality takes hold. It's not about a place or even a time, it's all about her. She has seen and done so much that being at peace is what she has sought for a long, long time. Longer than she can recall. The potential inside her mind is so much greater than a valley, a country, even a world can ever be. Though she will leave those caves for another time, the real exploration will take place within.

Other than the river, the valley is almost silent. There are a few lonesome birdcalls, some agitated insect scratchings, and the occasional rustle of small mammals and reptiles in the undergrowth, but already their numbers are shrinking. These creatures of the wider world will never survive in such a closed environment. Perhaps here and there are the corpses of those that have already died, caught within the Fold, and discovering them might give her some other distraction. A sickly treasure hunt. She will make a necklace from their bones.

If it weren't for her old magic, over time the place would wither and die. Trees and shrubs, flowers and heathers, they would all go the way of the animals, but she does not wish that. She wants this place to be home, and for that it has to *remind* her of home. The old, ancient home where she was perhaps born, even though the mere concept of birth is so far in the past that it has become entirely abstract.

Much like death.

Yet she hopes that over time, this place will become more like the Time she left behind. Its plants will change to mirror the ancient world she once knew. Creatures will be birthed from the magic, and she will recognize them from long ago—winged things, crawling things, animals that hunt by heat and sound, glorious and dead for many millennia. Giving the Fold a hint of the old magic will also give it the facility to recreate aspects of the past. She hopes it will be wonderful.

Once on the valley floor she crosses the flood plain

toward the river, and soon reaches the area close to a bend in the flow where she plans to build her home. She hasn't started yet, because she's in no hurry, but she knows that this will be the perfect place. The river is narrower and faster here, and she likes the idea that her long, long life will be played out to its watery tones. Her intention is to form echoes of the Time in buildings, as well as in nature. The architectures of her memory will feed that intent, and over time she will build a low, fantastic structure of wood and glass, rock and soil, which will be reminiscent of the great ground-homes of her Kin from millennia past.

She closes her mind and imagines everything this place will one day become. It is glorious. It's everything she has wanted for many centuries, and even more so over the past couple of hundred years, when humanity has multiplied like a virus unchecked. Their presence smothers her, their noise deafens. Their civilization has tainted the world far beyond redemption.

Yet for all her dissatisfaction with the world of Kin and human, she cannot be alone as she stares eternity in the face. This has caused her something of a dilemma—now that she has stepped out from the world, she cannot bear to enter it once more, even for something so important. So she is working on a solution. Soon, if those pathetic wraiths are effective and gather her selected companions, others will start to arrive.

Then the time will come to close the Fold and forget about the world.

The good, the bad, the humans, the Kin... all of it.

This is her new world, and soon she will call it home.

12

They met at a roadside diner. There were several big trucks parked in the lot, a neon sign with a raised arm above the main doors exhorting people to come in, and a menu board advertising STATE'S BEST CHILI propped beside the entrance.

It was almost dusk, and the lights inside showed that many window booths were taken up with individuals, couples, or families sampling the legendary chili or other food. The place was called Annie's Good Rest, and as they walked toward the entrance, Angela only wished she could.

The old gas station next door was abandoned and boarded up, and a car sat up on concrete blocks, rusting slowly into the ground. A loose shutter flapped in the breeze, letting out a regular *thump, thump*.

"Which movie am I in?" Vince asked.

"In your head, all of America's a movie."

"Yeah, well, remember that time in New York when—"

"You saw your first steaming manhole cover," Angela said, smiling. They'd only been to the States together once—before now, at least—and they'd done many of the tourist things she'd never done on her own. She still recalled his delight as the taxi had driven them through the dark, rain-swept streets of Manhattan and they'd pulled up at a traffic light. The steaming manhole had been just along a side street. She'd told him there was a laundromat beneath the street, and he'd believed her until they checked into their hotel room.

"This is a different movie," he said. He pointed across to the darkened gas station. "That's where the guy with the knife and hockey mask comes out." Even though his idea was a dark one, Vince still seemed enlivened by what they were doing. Excited, even.

Angela glanced at the door, fully expecting it to open and someone to emerge, but the person or thing she imagined didn't carry a knife.

Claws, perhaps. Or six-inch teeth.

"Food," she said. "What time are they due?"

"She said they'd be here within the hour," he said, glancing at his phone again.

He has Lilou's number, Angela thought. *They text each other.* She hated the cool jealousy that idea seeded in her, because jealousy was a base, useless emotion. She wished she could shed it and believe that Vince was hers and hers alone, and if Lilou was just another woman she could. But Lilou was supernatural.

She walked on ahead, and Vince caught up and held her arm.

"We'll have to be careful," he said. "I'll go in first in case..." He let the sentence hang because they both knew what he meant. Angela had taken off her glasses and bought another baseball cap, discarding the I LOVE ALBANY cap because it recalled the scene of the crime. Claudette's body had been found, meriting a mention on a couple of Internet news sites, but little more. One of the reports talked of an animal attack. Angela remembered those gremlins, vicious little creatures that had disappeared afterward into the trees.

She wondered where they had gone.

"She'll know what to do, won't she?" she asked as they approached the diner's front door.

"I hope so," Vince said. "More than us, at least."

"So where's Ahara?" She'd first noticed the wisp's disappearance a couple of hours before, as they'd been driving southwest from Albany toward Danville.

Vince remained silent. He reached for the door and pulled it open a crack, letting loose a hubbub of noise—voices, music, the clanging of cutlery and crockery.

"Vince?"

"I don't know," he said, shrugging. "She comes, she goes. It's not often I know what's happening."

"Oh, great." She pushed past him and entered the diner. Instantly the smells inside reminded her how hungry she was. They found an empty booth past the counter in a corner toward the restrooms, and a waitress came to take their drinks orders. Although she craved something stronger Angela stuck with coffee, while Vince took a beer.

"Sammi's not Kin," she said.

"You don't know that for sure." He stared at her, and she felt a flush of surprise, and realization. He knew, of course, as did she, but it wasn't often she let herself even remember the fact that Sally wasn't her flesh and blood. They had grown up together, their parents treated them both alike, and as her only sibling Sally had been an important part of her childhood. She couldn't even remember the moment when knowledge had dawned that her sister had been adopted, because it meant so little. Their drifting apart as they'd grown older had nothing to do with blood. Angela had never had reason to question her sister's true past. Until now.

"We'd have known," she said. "I'd have known."

"How?"

Angela frowned and thought about her little niece. "What would you have looked for?" Vince was pushing and she didn't like it.

"Whatever," she said. "Why would the fairy come after her? It makes no sense."

"Not much does," he said. "Not anymore." He spilled some sugar and swirled it around with his fingers, making patterns on the tabletop. He tapped the tabletop, eyes flickering around the diner. At first Angela thought he was nervous, but then she realized it wasn't that. Lilou was coming. He was excited.

She looked around. A family across from them were biting into burgers and vat-sized colas. In the booth beside them, two big men ate pie and drank coffee, guffawing at unheard jokes. Other customers continued in blissful ignorance of the real world, safe within their own, and Angela wished for the thousandth time that she had never heard of the Kin. Knowledge of them had ruined her life, and though it was her choice to accept the task of protecting them, it had set her on the run as a wanted woman.

It was Vince's fault, really, but she would never allow herself to blame him.

"I found you," she said. "I'll find Sammi, too."

Vince reached out and grasped her hands, and she

was surprised to see tears in his eyes. Maybe he was remembering Ballus and what that mad satyr had done to him. He still carried the physical scars, and the mental ones bled screams when he was asleep. Of the few nights they'd spent with each other since coming to the States, she had felt and heard Ballus haunting his nightmares during most of them.

"*We'll* find her!" he said. "Lilou will help. That's why she's coming."

"I thought she was coming to find another Kin-killer," Angela said, unable to hold back the bitterness from her voice.

"She'll help," he insisted. "It's all linked. The lightning strikes, the Kin-killer. She said there are patterns."

"You think she'll tell us what they are?"

"Yes."

The waitress came with their drinks and took their food orders. She didn't even catch Angela's eye, and as she hurried away Angela sipped at her coffee. It was good, hot and strong, but she couldn't relax.

"We shouldn't just be sitting here," she said. Guilt urged her to get up and run outside, but run where? She could walk this country for a thousand years and never see the same place or person twice. She'd found Vince when he was missing in London, true, but she'd had clues to follow, and it had been a place she knew so well. Here, in the country where she'd been born, she felt lost.

"This will be our best chance," Vince said. "You know that. Follow the trail, right?" She'd used that phrase a few times before everything had gone to shit, when she'd spent long days studying in their maisonette while Vince went out to work. Sometimes Vince would text during the day and ask what she was up to, and she'd reply, *Following the trail.* Researching a particular point or event sometimes felt like that, especially online research where one page led to others, one click to more. It was like building new synapses in the giant brain of the world. Digital trails, though nebulous, were just as easy to follow as physical ones.

The front doors opened and Angela glanced up. Then froze.

"What the fuck?"

Vince turned around. "Oh. Right. I didn't expect that."

Lilou walked into the diner. She saw them right away and headed for them, head lowered, and Angela knew that she was trying to hold herself back. Dressed in loose trousers and a shapeless shirt, still she cut an imposing figure, and many sets of eyes followed.

The person behind her attracted even more attention.

"Angela," he said, standing close to the head of their table. "Vince."

"Boss," Vince said.

That cut through the tension, and made Angela laugh.

Lilou told them everything she had told Meloy about Gregor, the Kin-killer. She talked about the patterns he followed and left behind, and how the murders of the lightning-strike survivors were undoubtedly attributable to him.

"So we just tell the police," Vince said.

"Much as I've no love of the law, I suggested that one," Meloy said.

"We can't do that," Lilou said. "They're involved enough as it is. If we set them on the trail we have to follow, it becomes too crowded. Too messy." She looked from Angela to Vince and back again. Vince's eyes were wider than normal, pupils dilated, brow unlined. Angela looked worried and nervous. They were the reactions she'd expected from them both. She was becoming adept at reading humans.

"So when do we get on the trail?" Angela asked. "That's my niece missing somewhere out there."

"Yes, about that—" Lilou said.

"She's not Kin."

"She survived two lightning strikes."

"So did four people who were subsequently murdered," Angela said.

"And they were Kin," Meloy said.

"Huh?" Vince asked.

"Deniers," Lilou said. "Much more prevalent over here than in the UK, they're Kin who have integrated into society and rejected their heritage."

"But... post mortems," Angela said.

"They'll pass," Lilou said. "I don't know much more about them myself, only what Mallian told me when he sent me along this path. Long ago, Kin began mating with humans, shedding their past and looking to the future. Over the years their bloodline has been thinned. They still carry the history of Kin in their blood and bones, and in their collective memories, but on the surface they're human. There are many descendants of deniers who don't even know what their ancestors were."

"They must know somehow," Angela said.

"Probably they have strange dreams," Lilou said. "Trouble fitting into society. I'm sure you know many troubled people."

"But surely not all of them are deniers."

"Probably not, but you understand how easy it would be for bloodlines to get watered down and eventually lost."

"So the fairy struck them with lightning and found them again," Vince said. "What's that all about?"

"Something else I'm here to find out," Lilou said. She hid the lie well, she thought. She was used to hiding things. Grace and her plans were *all* she was here for, really. Anything else was incidental.

"And this Gregor scumbag is targeting them how?" Vince asked.

"He has some way of tracking them."

"And now we need to find a way of tracking him," Meloy said. "That's where you come in, Angela."

"Me?"

"Sure. You found this troublemaker, didn't you?" He clipped Vince around the head, and although Vince smiled, there was something about the gesture Lilou didn't like. It reminded her of someone ruffling a dog harshly behind the ear. It spoke of ownership.

"Not alone."

"You're not alone now," Lilou said. "We're here to help."

"You're here to find Gregor," Angela said, her voice cold.

"Yes, but finding Sammi might lead us to him," Lilou replied. "And you're a friend."

Angela blinked, then smiled. Lilou felt a tension

within her ease a little, because Angela believed what she had said.

"We should get going," Meloy said. "Places to go." He stood, and Vince and Angela followed suit. Lilou stared at the big man's back. She'd asked that he come with her as a form of protection, but she was beginning to worry about bringing him along. There was something about his attitude that had changed, somewhere over the Atlantic. He was still in awe of Lilou and her kind, but there was an eagerness about him now that she did not like. An impatience to get on the trail of the Kin-killer.

Fat Frederick Meloy was still a collector of relics.

13

"We have to get there soon," Sammi said. "My father will be worried. He'll be home, waiting for me to go back. I went to get Chinese. He'll be hungry." She frowned.

Deep down she knew that wasn't right, because days had passed since she'd been struck down again and brought back up by Old Itch. She didn't know how many days. One? Three? Surely not more.

"He'll be worried."

"Your father knows," Old Itch said. "I've told you that." Over the course of the morning she'd seen a change in Old Itch. He'd become more impatient, even angry. Whereas before he'd been simply a presence, steering her along their route to wherever, now it was as if he was a shadow growing into a whole person, taking on personality even as he became more solid. Before his touch had been like being kissed by the wind. Now she could feel his fingers pressed into her arm when he held onto her.

"I want to speak with him."

"I don't have a phone."

"What sort of person doesn't carry a phone?"

Old Itch glared at her, then sighed. "You need to eat."

The thought of food made her stomach rumble and brought on hunger pangs, and she was thirsty, too. The sun was high and hot today, and it might well have been the hottest day of the summer so far. She should have been sunbathing out on their lawn, or running down to the river and along the wooden dock with her dad, racing each other to the end and seeing how far out they could jump. He usually won, because he had longer arms and legs. Then they'd have a "best leap" competition. She usually won that because she had more grace.

Her mom had always won, too, because her dad said she was as graceful as they come. *Like a gazelle*, he'd said once as he and Sammi watched her mother swimming up the river, then down again, doing her daily mile. *Like a swan. Like an angel*.

"Mom was an angel," she said.

"No she wasn't!" Old Itch scoffed, as if she'd meant it for real.

They were in a small town. She didn't know its name. She'd seen a dozen places like this, and the anonymous main street had McDonalds, Arby's, KFC, and Dairy Queen, but she homed in on a Starbucks. She wasn't so keen on their coffee, but she liked the muffins they sold. Right then, the most important thing in the world was a muffin.

Once inside she ordered, and when Old Itch went to pay she saw his hand pass over the contactless terminal. It beeped, the barista frowned, then she went to prepare her hot chocolate and cake. Old Itch hadn't ordered anything.

"How did you do that?" she asked when they'd taken a seat in a corner booth.

"Do what?"

"Pay with your hand?"

"I need to see the map," he said. He seemed agitated, uncomfortable being inside. He kept glancing around.

"Where's my mom?"

"Soon. Near. Let me see." He reached for her sleeve and tugged it up. She pulled away.

"You said soon…" *A while ago*, she thought, but she wasn't sure how long. That troubled her. Time seemed fluid, like the flow of tears.

He reached for her again, knocking the table so that it scraped against the floor, grabbing her arm and pulling her closer. Sammi knew it was wrong. They were in public, in a café with forty other people, and Old Itch had no idea how to act in front of them. He'd looked at her burn patterns half a dozen times, each time muttering to himself as he tapped her arm, shoulder, back, until he seemed satisfied and they carried on moving. They'd taken two bus journeys, one of them almost five hours long. They'd walked. Wherever they were going, it was further away than she'd thought.

She still didn't know what or where the Fold was. She had never heard of a place with that name, and it was strange that Old Itch didn't know, either. Especially as her mom wanted Sammi to go there.

Good girl, Sammi, she heard, and the voice was a soothing balm, filtering into her mind, easing her perception and senses, like her mother's hand on the back of her head when she was a little girl.

"Everything okay here?" The voice was deep and gruff, with an accent she couldn't quite place. It brought

Sammi back from whatever hazy place the words—her mother's, perhaps imagined, or maybe whispered into her ear—had taken her to.

"I'm fine," Sammi said. "We're fine." Old Itch was still leaning toward her, his sharp nails hooked into the neck of her tee shirt.

"Doesn't look fine," the man said. He was very tall, bearded, arms knotted with muscle and tanned a deep mahogany. "You her dad?"

Old Itch looked up at the man, surprised. *He's not all there*, Sammi thought. She wasn't sure whether or not she'd spoken those words, and she knew suddenly that they were true—not in the casual way they were sometimes used, but literally. Old Itch wasn't all there, although he had spent the span of their journey fitting himself into her world.

That's okay, that's fine, the voice said. It might not have been her mother after all. Sammi sometimes panicked when she forgot her mother's face or voice, but they always came back. Hearing these words didn't bring the comfort the voice usually possessed.

"I asked you a question, pal." That voice. British. A clean accent, but the threat was apparent.

"Mind your own fucking business," Old Itch hissed.

"You attacking a young girl in public is my business," Beard said. He reached between them and grasped Old Itch's arm, clasping it so tight that Sammi thought she saw his fist close into the skin, his flesh. Beard's eyes widened with surprise at something he felt, and then Old Itch stood and reached up for him, curving his hand around the back of the man's neck and pulling him down, closer.

Sammi tugged free and slid off her chair. She felt the attention of the whole place on them, and tried not to panic. Several people began to stand up. *Stay calm*, the voice that might or might not have been her mother said. If she ran she'd be lost. *You'll be lost.* She was safer with Old Itch. *He'll keep you safe.*

Old Itch and the man moved closer, and for a moment it looked as if they were about to kiss. They grasped each other's clothing, tensed, pushing and pulling, a conflict that saw neither of them give ground. Then Old Itch pulled Beard's head down onto his shoulder, opened his mouth, and pressed his face into the man's neck. Sammi could no longer see their features.

Violence sizzled in the air, a bloody potential that silenced the café and brought pause to its customers. Several people were frozen, half out of their seats, as if thinking again about their instinct to help. An old woman held her coffee cup in front of her face, lips puckered ready to accept the rim to her mouth. A child sat in a high chair, staring wide-eyed at the scene playing out just a few steps away from it, a line of spittle drooping slowly from its mouth to the floor.

At any moment Sammi expected Beard to lash out and send the shorter, thinner Old Itch flying.

Beard stood upright again, frowning. His hand went to his neck and rubbed, as he looked past Old Itch at a wall of posters advertising local music and poetry events. He was searching for something, trying to massage a thought back into his head.

The baby started crying.

"We're leaving," Old Itch said. He reached for Sammi, then paused, glancing around at the other patrons without moving his head. "Please," he said, lower. It was a quiet order, not a plea.

Sammi stood up and walked to the door, and her companion followed. She felt many eyes watching her go, and she smiled at a middle-aged couple close to the front door, as if to say, *It's fine, he hasn't taken me or anything.*

Although she was no longer quite sure.

"What did you say to him?" she asked when they were back on the street. Old Itch led them down an alley between buildings.

"Say?" he asked. "Nothing. A gentle bite was enough."

"You bit him?"

Old Itch didn't reply. She followed him across a large stretch of concrete that must once have been the floor to a long-demolished warehouse of some kind, and on the other side they came to a canal. Ten minutes along the towpath he stopped and turned to her.

"The map," he said.

Sammi thought about running.

"We need to see," he said, and his words were frantic, troubled. "Your mother's waiting." She realized for the first time just how old he looked. In sunlight his flesh was almost opaque, skin hanging loose. She thought back to when she'd first seen him, barely more than a shadow.

"Are you really real?" she asked, and Old Itch simply scratched at his chest again, shirt moving aside to reveal the weeping wounds beneath. His smile was wan, exposing his too-long teeth.

"Let me see," he said. He reached for her sleeve, started examining her markings, and she hoped her mother would be in the Fold.

I'm there already, the voice said in her head. *It's beautiful*.

"Close," Old Itch breathed. He sounded excited. "Very close. Tomorrow we'll be there, and then..."

"And then?"

"Things move on."

14

"If he looks for patterns, then so should we," Angela said.

"Follow the trail," Vince said.

"Right."

They were heading west. Meloy had hired a big Jeep Wrangler, and he drove while Lilou sat in the passenger seat. Angela and Vince were in the back, and several times since setting off Angela had looked around for Ahara. She was nowhere to be seen.

Perhaps she knew Lilou was coming, she thought, looking at the back of Lilou's head. Even from behind the nymph was beautiful. Meloy's devotion to her was obvious. Vince's still troubled Angela, but she was growing to believe it was more fascination than a sexual bond. Lilou amazed him. In truth, she amazed Angela as well.

She'd been surprised to see Meloy, but there was a strange comfort to him being here as well. He was confident and capable. He was also dangerous, but she was no longer really afraid of him. It was those who hunted and hurt the Kin who should be afraid.

Meloy had come to the USA with more than ten thousand dollars in cash. Enough to have him stopped and questioned at border control, without a doubt, but he and Lilou had apparently breezed through. Angela didn't like the way that made her feel jealous. If she attempted to leave the country she'd be caught, arrested, and spend the rest of her life in jail. An upside of Meloy's cash was that they could afford the technology to do what Angela planned. He'd handed over a grand without a flicker, and she suspected that ten grand wasn't much to him at all.

The laptop balanced on her knees was as light as a paperback book. The map function was so clear that it almost felt like being in a satellite, able to target in and zoom down on individual houses, and with a definition high enough to probably identify individual people. Perhaps some of the people in these composite images taken from orbit there were Kin, caught out in the wild when they thought they were alone and safe.

I wonder where I was when these pictures were taken, she thought. The map was dated the previous year. She'd have been in London then, and if these images were taken on a sunny afternoon, in London it would have been early evening. She and Vince might have been sitting in their garden sharing a bottle of wine and waiting for a couple of steaks to cook on the barbecue. It was strange to look at the image of the world as it had been back then, and wonder where people had been at that moment, what they were doing. It was a moment frozen in time.

"And the last one?" she asked.

Using his phone, Vince checked reports about lightning strikes, those victims who had been struck a second time, and the four survivors who later had met a grisly end.

"Little town outside Boston."

"Right. That's all the strikes plotted, including second strikes and the four murders." She reduced the map a little so she could include all the plotted points. "The murders all took place over the past thirty hours, and all within about a hundred miles of Hartford."

"What about times?" Meloy asked. "If Gregor's on the move, they might indicate direction."

"There's nothing in the reports," Vince said.

"Even if there was, they wouldn't release anything that accurate," Angela said.

"Hack the cops' computers," Meloy said. "Remember, they're looking for this bastard too. We use their resources, as well as our own."

"First, it's not easy to hack a secure system, even if you're a computer wizard," Angela replied. "Are you one, Meloy?"

"Not me," he said. "I have friends back in London, though."

"I don't think that will help," Lilou said. "We have an advantage because we already know motive. We know much more of what's going on than the police. Any faulty intelligence we glean from them might hinder us, more than help."

"So we're on our own," Angela said quietly. She looked at the points plotted on the map, blue for double strikes, and four reds for the murders. The horrifying idea came that there might be a fifth body within the scope of the map, just waiting to be found.

"What about the scars?" Vince asked. He peered at his phone, swiping and enlarging.

"What scars?"

"These scars." He held it out for Angela to see. "Most of the strike victims reported them. They look like ferns."

"Or river deltas," Angela said. "Send me the link." A minute later she called up the image on the larger screen.

"Oh," someone said. Angela glanced up. Vince looked around, and Lilou had frozen, turned around in the front seat.

"You didn't tell me you had a wisp," she said.

"Oh, look," the voice whispered again, and the air between Angela and Vince started to haze. Angela shuffled across the seat, moving closer to her door.

"Vince?" she asked.

"I thought she'd gone," he said.

Lilou's reaction shocked Angela. "I don't like wisps! Why the hell didn't you tell me, Vince?"

"I told you, I thought Ahara had gone!"

Ahara had not gone. She manifested between Angela and Vince on the back seat, blurring in like a double exposure, then more solid. She leaned slightly to the left so that she could look closer at the computer screen.

"What do you see?" Lilou asked. "Something about that?"

"Quiet, nymph," Ahara said. "Let me look."

Lilou's lips pressed together. She stared at the newcomer.

"What's the problem?" Angela asked.

"Kin stuff," Lilou said. "It isn't your business. Don't bother yourself with it."

"It's my business if—"

"I said *don't bother*!" Lilou shouted. The car swayed a little as Meloy jumped. Angela had never heard Lilou raise her voice, and Vince seemed taken aback as well.

The nymph's mask slipped through her anger, and her sensuous influence swept through the vehicle like a surge of power. As if they had been struck. It was such a primal, powerful sensation that Angela felt sick, her insides churning.

Meloy kept glancing at her, and reached out for her, giving her more attention than the road, bewitched as never before.

"Meloy!" Angela shouted. *"Lilou!"*

"And so the nymph plays her games some more," Ahara said. Lilou hunkered down, lowering her face, lifting her shoulders, and soon Angela felt the effect bleeding away. Vince and Meloy breathed heavily. The crime boss focused on the road ahead.

Ahara reached for the computer screen, and as she touched the image of the lightning burns she drew in a deep breath.

"It's the map of a fairy," she said.

"What does that mean?" Angela asked. "Can you read it?"

The wisp said nothing. She traced her ambiguous fingers across the screen, and when she touched, the image was dragged along as if following the contact.

"Ahara?"

"It's moving," she said. "A map of movement. Yes, I can read it."

"Then tell us where to go," Meloy said.

"Lilou?" Vince asked. The nymph remained crouched down in the passenger seat, making herself so small that Angela could only see an arm, her shoulder, and the side of her head.

"Yes," Lilou whispered. "If the wisp can read it, we follow."

"We're all in this together," Vince said.

Lilou laughed, a loud bark that didn't sound like her. There was no sensuality about her reaction this time. Only bitterness.

Angela held the laptop to the side as Ahara examined the image of the skin markings more closely.

"I can't see it all," Ahara said after a while. She passed her hand back and forth across the screen, as if trying to turn the arm pictured there.

"Can't you see enough?" Vince asked.

"Some," she said. "West."

"How far west?" Meloy asked.

"West... until we get there."

"No riddles," Lilou said. "No wordplay, wisp. West is away from the sites of the murders."

"I'm not playing," she said. "A fairy map is a living, changing thing, not something I can read from an image. It's as if trying to hear what someone is saying from a single photograph of them talking. So... west, and when we're closer, perhaps I will see more."

"It's toward the center of the spread of lightning strikes," Angela said. "And we've got nothing else." She took a screenshot of the image, saved it, then started searching the news reports for more information.

They all fell silent.

Vince drifted off to sleep, Ahara faded away to a mere haze, and Lilou slowly sat upright again, brushing hair over her ear and staring ahead. Angela couldn't be sure, but she thought she saw a single tear form at the corner of the nymph's eye before she casually brushed it away.

* * *

Only a few minutes later she saw something that clasped a tight fist around her heart. A certainty grabbed her that they were already too late. She clicked on the pop-up news link and scanned the report, searching for a name, a place, a photograph that would sever whatever tenuous links she still had to her old life.

"Another murder," she managed to whisper, and then she sobbed when she saw a name she did not recognize.

"Angela?" Vince said, stirring from slumber, instantly alert and as terrified as her.

"Not her," she said. "Not Sammi." *Someone else*, she thought. *Another daughter, another sister, another dreadful loss that a strange family will never recover from.*

"Not this time," Lilou said. "He's moving faster."

"Then so should we," Meloy said. "I'll kill the fucker with one hand." His threat filled the car and chilled Angela like a cool breath.

Good, she thought. *I hope you get to kill him before he harms another soul.* She looked at the clock on the laptop's corner. Time seemed to be moving quicker.

He is used to living in darkness. In the deep past, the dark was given to him as a punishment. Over time he made his own light, and during the Time he became comfortable living in both day and night, and made them his own.

This is not true darkness. Weak daylight filters in, and beams drift back and forth across his body like questing fingers. He can almost feel their touch. The movement and the arcing light makes the air around him feel fluid, and he imagines drifting up from the soft padded floor and floating, weightless, while the illumination explores his body. Perhaps it will be surprised at what it finds. Perhaps only sad. Long ago he gave up worrying about what others thought of him.

The swaying, the movement, the constant sense that everything around him is changing, provoke a sense of nostalgia. A desire for those times long ago when he would wander, walk, and explore. Too much lately he has spent long periods of time hidden away from the gaze of those who could never understand him. Or if they did understand him, they would never accept.

That is what's wrong with the modern world, he thinks. *Acceptance is too rarely given to that which confuses or confounds.* An important sense of wonder has vanished. The irony frustrates him. Confronted with more stories, myth, and wonder than ever before, humanity has drawn in on itself and welcomed in ignorance like an old friend.

His aim is to wipe away ignorance. Reintroduce that missing sense of wonder. Make it so that he can emerge from the shadows, rise from the stillness, and wander the steppes and plains of the world once again, even if those places are now fields of concrete and escarpments of brick and glass. Whatever future he might forge will never quite live up to his fond, aged memories, but that will not stop him from trying.

Anything will be better than this.

He sees a fly crawling across his stomach. He doesn't know how it made it in here. He splays one hand on his hip and the fly crawls between his thumb and forefinger, then onto the back of his hand. He lifts his hand slowly, turning it so that the tiny creature remains in a shard of light. Dust motes drift like snow around the fly's wings.

He blows, a soft puff of air that sends the fly fluttering into the shadows. It has nothing to fear. He won't hurt it, because the fly has done nothing to warrant being hurt.

In that, at least, he is fair.

The journey is long, and away from home he feels unsettled. There's a sense of safety around the idea of home, and he knows he has to shed that if his ambitions are to come to fruition.

At least he has not come alone. He cannot see them, because they are separated by walls, but his friends are close by. He is old and wise, and knows that he can never become so proud that he will turn help aside. He takes comfort from the closeness of his companions.

The gentle movement, the drifting beams of light, carry him further from home and closer to the future he has craved for a hundred years.

15

Though his deep past was a vague, shadowy place, Gregor still experienced occasional flashes from childhood. Because the memories were so clear and powerful, he never doubted that it was his own life he was remembering, and not some memory manufactured from the purpose his life had taken on. They inspired emotions and assaulted his senses like dreams or make-believe never could. And he should know, because make-believe had been at the center of his life forever.

His parents are in the back yard of their modest home on the outskirts of New Orleans. His mother is sitting in a comfortable chair, long hair gathered by a flowery band, coffee skin glimmering with perspiration. The summer has been hotter than most, and he can smell the aromas of the neighborhood sweltering in the still, heavy air. She is smiling in a strange way, and Gregor—he's not sure that's his name back then, although he knows no other—thinks it's to do with the music playing from the wireless. The wireless is propped in the open kitchen window, and a singer named Elvis is telling the world how he is "all shook up." Gregor can't help being excited by the music, as he knows his mother is. He sees that in her uncertain smile, and in the way she seems to be shifting slightly in her seat, as if swept up in the heat haze.

His father is cooking on their outdoor grill, a big metal drum sliced in two and filled with dried wood and charcoal. The fish is freshly caught. Gregor breathes in the scent, and it washes away the smells of the overheated and tired neighborhood.

His mother's foot moves in time with the music. His father uses a wooden tool to turn the fish, then taps it against the grill. He's smiling. Sweat drips from his chin into the grill with a sizzle, and his bare back flows with muscle.

Later, though part of the same memory and loaded with the same music and smells, Gregor is in the large field behind their street. He's getting older now, almost ten, and last summer his father and mother had a discussion with him about how he must play here safely, if they are to allow him out here at all.

He runs past the old tumbledown shack that most of the neighborhood kids say is haunted. Gregor has yet to work up the courage to go inside, and sometimes if the sun is just right he can see right through the place, in one wall and out the other, and as he watches he's sure a figure shifts back and forth in there, like an ancient occupier forever drifting from room to room searching for some forgotten thing.

Across the fields past the shack, he approaches the marshy area before the stream. It's this place that he loves the most. The smells and sounds are all different here, and if the wind's right—blowing across the fields toward the edge of town, rather than carrying dregs of the town out this way—he can hunker down and hear only wilderness. There's an age to that sound that he finds thrilling and terrifying. It's like the breath of the land as it sighs, remembering a time before humankind came and made its indelible mark. No stench of vehicle exhausts and sewage here. No touch of sharp metal and severe angles. No rock and roll.

He steps across the marsh, picking his way with care. It soon becomes a confusion of water and islets, heavy reeds hiding both safety and danger from view, but Gregor knows his way. He also knows that there are gators out here, but he hasn't seen one for some time. It's part of the danger, part of the thrill.

He's sitting on his favorite little island in the middle of the stream. It's thirty steps from side to side, but there are several trees growing there, and reeds and undergrowth, and a space at its highest central point where he can sit and look out without being seen from the shore. It's his secret place, and Gregor has come to discover that he likes being hidden away from the world. He likes being a secret.

Sometimes he fantasizes about living here. He could bring supplies over the space of a few weeks, and then one day just… vanish. He'd dig a hole in the ground between the trees and cover it over, making his home doubly hidden from anyone who comes searching. He'd expand it, with maybe a living space and a bedroom, and he'd bring food and water enough to last him a couple of weeks. He knows how to fish, and he could boil water from the river to drink.

Just him, unknown and eventually forgotten.

Of course, he loves his parents and could never leave them. But it's good to dream.

Sitting with his back against one of the trees, at first he thinks the commotion in the water is a gator. He freezes, a surge of fear mingling with excitement. Peering through the leaves, he sees something slick and gray slipping from the water and up onto the island's shore. It's small, perhaps the size of his leg, and for a while it remains so motionless that he wonders if it's just a log. But the stream doesn't flow fast here, certainly not enough to wash a log this size up onto the island.

Gregor reaches forward and grabs an overhanging branch. As he pulls it he loses sight of the thing for a moment, and then when he holds the branch aside he sees it again. It's sitting up and staring right at him.

His world changes in that moment.

The creature is propped up on two strong arms, blond hair wet and matted, pale skin slick from water and mud, breasts perfectly proportioned to its small, human body.

It has the face of a woman, only smaller than any woman he has ever seen.

The tail of a fish.

"Don't fear me," the thing says. The branch slips through Gregor's hand. Panicked, desperate to see the creature again, he leaps forward past the overhanging tree and toward the shore. He hears a hurried slither and a splash, and once clear of the branches and leaves, resting on his hands and knees just feet from where the thing emerged, he realizes he is alone once more.

The ripples in the water are already echoing from both shores.

"Come back!" he shouts. He breathes in deeply, but smells nothing unusual. He crawls forward into the water, his hands sinking in the mud, and he even dips his face beneath the surface. He opens his eyes but sees nothing. The water is heavy with silt.

He resurfaces, spluttering filthy water.

"Come back!" he shouts again. "Please."

The creature does not come back, that day or the next. Gregor comes to that place for the next seven days, sometimes at the same time as before, sometimes at dawn or dusk, waiting for the strange thing to emerge from the river again.

He looks in his father's books and figures out what it is he has seen. *Mermaid.* Too young for true romantic love, too old to forget what he has seen, Gregor is tortured by her non-return.

Then on the eighth day he is joined by someone else.

"I may have a use for you," the old voice says. "A course for you to follow. When I finish writing it, I'll give it to you."

Gregor cannot make out the man, because it's close to dusk and he hides in the undergrowth. Something about the way he hides forbids Gregor to approach. He's scared, but also drawn by what the man says.

"Who are you?"

"My name is Jace Tan."

"Are you... like her?"

"I'm Kin, yes."

"Just you? Her?"

"We're two of many. I've been watching you for a long time, Gregor. I think you might be the person I need. Listen to me, follow my script, and you'll come to know us much better. I have a great journey for you to undertake, a great project to fulfill, and more."

"More?" Gregor asks.

"Much more. I've seen you watching for us. I've sensed your sense of wonder. I taste your thirst for knowledge, and I can see the shades in your mind… the shades where the shadows of the Kin fall. I'll pull those shadows from your eyes. I'll let you see it all. You're someone who can help me, and for that I'm willing to help you."

"Help me how?" Gregor asks. He isn't sure why, but the sound of this voice is like a song from a larger, wider world, one which Gregor realizes he has been seeking all his young life. It is only natural that, offered some glimpse into this world, he will ask for more.

The man pauses for a moment as he looks into Gregor's soul, and when he replies there's a hint of humor in his voice.

"Help you see more. My great project is a meeting of worlds, a bridge between the world of Kin and humankind. And the only way it will succeed is for your eyes to be opened. Your fate to be changed. For you to *become* Kin."

16

"I want to speak with my mother."

They were waiting at another bus station. Old Itch said they had to head into the hills, although he'd ceased examining her scars so much. He was becoming more and more agitated the further they went.

"She speaks to me, in my head, but now *I* want to speak to *her*." A dawning fear was clouding Sammi's mind. A deep realization, filled with danger and threat.

"We'll be there soon," Old Itch said.

"That's not good enough anymore, Old Itch," she replied.

He winced. She could see he didn't like the name, but his hand went to his chest yet again, scratching at the wound visible there. It was unchanging. It neither healed, nor grew any worse.

"We have to see this through," Old Itch said. "She demands it. If we don't—"

"My mother?" Sammi asked.

"Yes, your mother." But Sammi could tell by the pause that he hadn't meant her mother at all.

She was ready to run. Every instinct told her it was the right thing to do, and since taking a seat in the corner of the bus station's open waiting area, she had worked herself up three times to the point where her muscles quivered and she imagined sprinting toward the exit.

Soon, very soon, her mother's voice whispered. *You'll see me soon.*

These were the words that kept her from running. Her concerns persisted, concern for her father remained, and she felt more like a prisoner with every hour that passed. Yet her mother's voice whispering in her ear, in her head, prevented her from taking action.

She's dead, she thought. *You're dead.*

You'll see me soon, her mother said.

A dozen times, a hundred, this silent exchange stirred her doubts and desires. And though deep down she knew it was impossible, she grabbed at any slight chance of seeing her mother again.

Old Itch sat and scratched, looking down at his feet, so it was Sammi who saw the old man first. He walked slowly across the waiting area, and the woman who held his hand reminded Sammi so much of Old Itch. She was the opposite sex, much younger, dressed very differently, but there was something in her eyes that echoed her own companion. A hollowness. A desperation.

Sammi caught her breath when the old man saw her watching. She saw herself in him. He looked both confused and hopeful, wearing the expression of someone seeking something they had previously believed out of reach.

It was a warm day, and on the man's bare forearm she could see the tattoo-spread of scars from a lightning strike.

"Just like me," she said, and Old Itch looked up.

As the man paused and frowned, Old Itch rushed across the paved area to meet the woman. It was a strange encounter. They stood close but did not touch, and despite hurrying together they didn't seem pleased to see each other. After a brief conversation they parted again.

"We have help," Old Itch said. For the first time ever he exuded an emotion other than vague concern. It might even have been subdued excitement. "Come with me."

"Who are they?" she asked.

"Friends."

"She didn't look like a friend."

"We'll help each other find the way," he replied. "Come on. The two of you together."

Sammi stood, and again almost bolted for the door. She was ready. Her own inner voice was starting to outweigh the voice that might or might not have been her mother's.

Something's not right here, she thought, *and Mom would want me to take care.*

Then she saw the same look of restrained fear in the old man's eyes, and she realized that Old Itch might have been right. She really might have found a friend.

She left Old Itch behind and approached the man.

"Were you struck?" she asked.

He nodded, looking at the spread of veinous patterns on her neck, shoulder, and arm.

"I'm Sammi. He says he's taking me to my mother."

"Jeff," he said. "It's Mary she's taking me to. In my head, I hear her…" He trailed off, frowning.

"You hear her telling you to carry on," Sammi said. "It's lies. They're lying to you, to me, and I think we have to—"

A hand closed around Sammi's arm and moved her away. It felt too cool, cold, not lifeless but shorn of life. The woman holding her—Jeff's companion—was an image projected onto the scene, fuzzy around the edges and two-dimensional. She had small pointed ears, sharp features, thin arms and legs too long for her body, and her eyes were tiny specks in the unhuman landscape of her face. They looked as empty of life as her touch.

"This is our bus," the woman said. Her lips were out of sync with her words.

As Sammi and Jeff were led onto the bus, they were far enough apart that they couldn't talk. When they boarded, Old Itch and the woman guided them toward the back, sitting them together on the back seat, Old Itch on Sammi's right, the woman on Jeff's left. It felt good, the heat of a living person. Jeff reminded Sammi of her father.

She felt tears threatening, but then Old Itch and the woman leaned forward and started talking past them, ignoring their presence.

"We're close," the woman said. "Forty miles, maybe sixty."

"Yes, I see that too."

"And here," the woman said. She grabbed Sammi's arm and pulled it forward, exposing the marks on the inside of her elbow. "A more detailed location, don't you think?"

"He has that?" Old Itch asked.

"On his back. Right shoulder, exactly the same."

"Good," Old Itch said. "Good."

"Where are you taking us?" Sammi asked.

"To Mary," Jeff said.

"No, not to Mary!" Sammi said. "And not to my mother!" Her voice rose, and she caught a warning look between the people—the two *things*—who were accompanying them. Because something had slipped. In Old Itch's excitement, at drawing closer to his destination, and meeting the woman, he had let go of whatever fugue he maintained around or inside Sammi's mind.

She still heard whispers of her mother's voice, but now she could feel them rising from her own memories, not implanted by someone or something else. For the first time since the lightning strike, it felt like her dead mother really *was* talking to her. That's what memories were, Sammi knew, because she and her dad had often talked about them.

Her mom was talking to her from the past and telling her that things were wrong.

Dusk was falling. The bus was moving. They edged out onto the freeway and headed west, sunset splashing across the distant hills and smearing the clouds with a palette of soft colors. Sammi eased back into her seat, knowing that there was nothing she could do right now. With doubts seeded, however, they began to bloom. Jeff and the promise to find his dead wife… it was so similar to Sammi being taken to her dead mother.

We were both twice-struck, she thought. *What does that mean? What are the chances?* She glanced at Jeff sitting beside her, and perhaps it was because Old Itch and the woman were there, but she noticed that Jeff also didn't look quite right. There was an angular strangeness about his head, as if it had been melted and reformed, flattened on the sides and protruding on top.

Who is he? she wondered. *What is he? And what is she?* The woman with him had grown still, vague, almost-there. Just like Old Itch when they'd first met. *I could see through him then, and I'm starting to see through him again.*

Sammi closed her eyes and envisioned her father as she'd last seen him, standing outside their riverside house and waving her in for their Chinese meal. She would get back to him soon. She would escape and run home.

Though she feigned sleep, she remained awake and alert. After a time she heard Jeff snoring softly beside her, and then she sensed a presence by her side, leaning forward across her lap. She dared not open her eyes.

"She'll be pleased," Old Itch whispered.

"Of course she will."

"She'll let us go."

"Set us free."

"Yes."

"Yes."

Their voices grew quieter and then faded to nothing. Sammi concentrated on the movement of the bus, road lights passing over her closed eyelids, the weight of Jeff sleeping beside her.

She made her plans.

"I need the bathroom," she said. She stood and yawned, stretching, and walked toward the small bathroom at the back of the bus. She didn't dare look back to see if Old Itch was watching, or even following, because that gesture would warn him of her intent.

The bathroom was small and cramped, hot and smelly, and as Sammi entered, she glanced across at the emergency exit. The door was closed and locked, but if she had timed her visit well—if the signs she'd glimpsed through the side windows were correct, if the bus had a regular scheduled stop in the next town—she'd have time to open it and slip out. Soon.

She closed the bathroom door and leaned against it. She really did need a pee, but she didn't want to start in case the bus stopped earlier than she'd anticipated. So much relied on chance. Would Old Itch be expecting her to run? Would he and the strange woman be blinded to the danger by their eagerness to reach whoever they were trying to find?

Sammi had attempted to read what they saw in her markings, but she saw only weird, beautiful patterns, and the only memory they inspired was of her father and the doctor joking in the hospital.

Am I a superhero now? she'd asked, and she wished she could fly. Pass through walls. Make herself invisible.

"I *will* fly," she murmured. "I'll run so fast that I'll become invisible. Run, pretend to hide, run again, get away from them, lose them."

The bus changed gears and she fell against the wall. It was slowing. She opened the door a crack and peered out, and she could see roadside buildings flitting by, and then a wide-open space with cars and trucks parked in ordered ranks. A roadside rest area, with diner, gas station, a row of small local shops. And a bus stop.

She waited until the bus was drifting to a halt before

leaving the toilet and lying low on the back seat. Crouched down, she waited. If Old Itch came to check on her she was ready to start shouting, but the memory of that confrontation in the coffee shop was fresh, how he'd whispered into Beard's ear or... or bitten him. With those long teeth the likes of which she had never seen before.

The bus stopped, hydraulic brakes hissed and clicked. Sammi leaned on the handle and the emergency window cracked open. She held her breath, waiting for an alarm. There was none.

Without looking back Sammi jumped down to the pavement. Directly behind the bus was an open area scattered with benches, and beyond that a row of small shops, most of them closed and dark. She ran for them. No shouts rose from behind, no calls for her to stop. A few people threw her strange looks, but she smiled at them and that seemed to calm their nerves. One of them even smiled in return.

When she reached a little ice cream parlor she paused to glance back. There was no sign of Old Itch, Jeff, or the woman with him. His guard. Just like Old Itch was her guard.

He's a vampire, isn't he? she thought with new clarity. *I've got to face that. A dead one, itching forever at the wound that killed him.*

For some reason, that fact didn't surprise or scare her as much as it should.

Sammi coughed a loud, barking laugh and darted for the space between two shops. She wouldn't stop. She'd disappear, pretend to hide, run again, jig left and right, lose herself to lose her pursuers. As long as they hadn't noticed her absence, and were still on the bus when it started again, she'd have a good chance to get away.

She leapt over a pile of refuse bags, turned a corner, startled a couple of young women smoking cigarettes outside a restaurant kitchen's open door. Muttering an apology she ran on, emerging into a small staff parking area. She dashed across a wide concrete parking lot that ended with a small road leading off between houses, shadowy and unlit, then risked another look back.

There were no signs of pursuit. Past the block of buildings she saw the freeway, and seeing the bus edge itself back onto the road, she felt both a rush of excitement and a terrible, hollowing loss.

I'm alone now. She went to speak, to call her mother's name, when the shadows beside a nearby house began to stir. A shape emerged and came at her, faster than should have been possible, utterly silent. It flowed like the night, and Sammi took a few faltering steps back, heels connecting with the curb and sending her sprawling. She didn't hit the ground.

Hands clasped her shoulder and right arm, and the coolness bit in as it had before. The wrongness. Hands didn't feel like that, and she knew why. People like Old Itch didn't exist, because he wasn't a person. He was a ghost. Knowing that should have given her power over him, but she was still terrified.

"Let me go!" she shouted, and Old Itch pulled her upright. He didn't look angry, but afraid. She wondered what he had to lose, but didn't care. He was misleading her, and taking her somewhere false, somewhere to do with him, not her and her dead mother.

"Don't shout," he said. "Don't be afraid, come with me because your mother—"

"She's dead!" Sammi shouted, and she lashed out with her right fist. It connected with his chest but she felt little pressure. He shifted back a step or two and she surged forward, punching again, connecting again. Her mother had always been against violence, but her father had taught her how to fight if she really had to. *"A kick to the balls and a fist to the face,"* he'd said, and she tried that now, kicking between Old Itch's legs, punching him in the mouth.

It was like kicking and punching water. He shifted around her blows, flickering in and out of shadow and then manifesting again slightly to her left or right.

"Please come with me," he said, and the plea surprised her. His eyes were dead and flat, and filled with lies.

Sammi reached for his chest and punched him in the wound he always scratched. He gasped and fell back, and his shadow smeared like a smudged ink sketch.

"Leave me alone!" she shouted again. Lights came on in a couple of houses. A door opened. Sammi stood over Old Itch where he lay on the sidewalk and glared down at him.

"Please," he said. "She'll never forgive me. She'll never let me rest."

"Who?" Sammi snapped. "Who is this all for?"

"You'll get to know her," he said. "In the Fold, you'll have forever to know her."

A brief flicker of doubt and sympathy lit inside her, but then Sammi shook her head.

"You took me away from my father," she said. "Days ago, I don't know how many. I've been confused, *you've* confused me. But I know you now, Old Itch. I know what you are and what you were. You don't scare me anymore."

"Your father's dead," he growled, voice filled with bile and hate, and she had never heard him sounding so alive.

A chill ran down her spine.

"Hey, miss, are you okay?" a man asked. He was approaching slowly along the sidewalk.

"I'm just leaving," she said.

"Maybe you should—" the man began.

"Don't go," Old Itch said, but Sammi knew that he wasn't strong, only persuasive. A ghost could have no hold over her.

"Mom?" she said as she ran into the night. There was no reply. "Mom?" Silence. Sammi sobbed once. Her mother was dead. Whoever had been speaking to her since the lightning strike, it hadn't been her mother.

She had to get home.

17

Gregor knew he was close.

His backpack sat on the passenger seat beside him. He could not remember a time when it had been more than six feet from him. He felt more whole than he ever had before. His corners were established, the edges of his life were solid and defined. Just a few more missing pieces, and he would be complete.

Those pieces were close by, and he had to be careful. He had to ensure that everything went well. He welcomed his instincts and senses, but he had to trust in the science of things, though that science was strange.

Pulling off the freeway he parked by the side of a quiet road, climbing out and leaving the car's passenger door open to keep the dome light lit. The road headed through a forest, and trees on either side whispered at his intrusion, the gentle breeze chilling him after he left the warmth of the car. He stood and urinated, looking up at the sky where a few stars peered through wispy clouds. The sunset had been amazing, and driving into the foothills he had sensed the wide expanse of wilderness awaiting him. Of course, this was where it would end. It would be in the wild, the silence, the places where few people ventured.

He zipped up and took the small bowl from the car, placing it on the graveled roadside. Filling it with water from a plastic bottle, he delved into the side pocket of his backpack and brought out the feather once more. Careful as ever he uncovered it, lifted it with an unconscious reverence, and placed it on the water's surface.

As it began to spin, there was the mutter of another car's engine. The vehicle's lights came into view and caught his car, casting it in shadow and splashing through the windows.

Gregor remained crouched down. Some people might stop to offer help if they thought he had broken down, but most would pass by a mysterious parked car in the woods, especially at night. He wasn't afraid. Fear played little part in his life, and he was confident of his abilities to protect himself.

The vehicle slowed. He raised himself a little, looking through his car windows at the approaching lights. They stopped, remained on, and he heard the unmistakable squawk of a radio.

Cops. Gregor grunted in frustration.

A door opened. Boots crunched on gravel.

He turned back to the angel feather, now so still in the water that it might have been frozen there. It pointed further along the road and up into the hills, and he felt some small satisfaction in knowing that he was heading in the right direction. As he reached for the feather, eager to hide it from view, the voice came from much closer than he'd expected.

"Please stand and step into view, sir."

Gregor paused.

"Please, sir!" The cop was serious. Gregor knew that tone.

"I just need to—"

"You need to stand and do as I say."

"Problem, Chris?" The second voice came from the parked cruiser.

"No problem." Chris punctuated his statement with the unmistakable cocking of his piece.

Gregor stood and leaned against the car, still looking away from the cops. The bowl and feather remained by his feet, and he wondered how he might explain them. He wondered how he might explain a backpack filled with strange items, including body parts. The possibility of being arrested had always troubled him, but he never believed it would be like this, a chance meeting in the dark.

"I'm feeling a bit sick, that's all, officer."

"I'm sorry to hear that, sir. Please keep your hands in view and turn around, nice and slow."

"Car's a rental," the other cop said from their vehicle.

"Okay, Cam. Gentleman's just feeling sick. Been drinking, sir?"

"I don't drink." Gregor did as he was told, turning to face the cops, hands held up at chest level. The first cop, Chris, stood by the car's trunk. He was short but athletic, and he seemed very comfortable pointing his gun at a man who was doing nothing wrong. "Do you really need to aim that at me?"

Chris did not reply. He looked Gregor up and down, then took two steps to his right and looked at the ground behind him. He saw the bowl, but in the poor light he probably couldn't make it out.

"What's that?"

"A drink. Water."

"You drinking like a dog?"

"I'm not doing anything wrong." Gregor tried to inject confusion and fear into his voice, but inside he was assessing, and trying to work out how the situation had gone so wrong.

"Cam?" Chris asked.

"Hang on."

Gregor frowned. The cops were acting strangely. Chris took one more step to the side and Gregor tried to see past the cruiser's glaring headlamps to Cam. He was still inside the vehicle, and impossible to make out.

"I have my license," Gregor said. "Just let me—"

"Hands where I can see them," Chris said. He was very much in control.

The trees whispered as if in cahoots with the two officers, muttering their suspicions of what Gregor was doing, perhaps sharing the knowledge they had of him. Places like this had seen him before, hunting, stalking, killing. He had taken a leshy in South America, and perhaps that tree spirit's death was known throughout every forest.

"That's him," Cam said, and everything shifted. This was more than a random stop, and Gregor was in far deeper trouble than he'd suspected.

Chris tensed, his whole attitude hardening.

"Hands on the car roof, lean forward, legs back and apart." Behind him another door opened and his partner joined him, a taller, bulkier shadow also holding a gun.

"Who do you think I am?" Gregor asked. "My name's Philip, I'm a football coach at my son's school, I'm heading out to join my family camping, I had to stay behind for a while because I had some work to finish up, I don't know why you're treating me like a criminal, I feel sick and I was having a drink and..."

All the while he was doing what Chris asked, but slowly, very slowly, turning and placing his right hand on the car roof, and as he turned he plucked the blade from its sheath on his left hip and held it curved against his forearm.

"Just do as you're told, dickhead," Cam said.

Head down, Gregor placed both forearms flat on the car roof, careful not to knock the blade against the metal. He felt it against his skin, cool and keen. It was almost a part of him, and as Chris approached and tapped his left foot to spread his legs some more, Gregor took a deep, slow breath and let the knife do its work.

He swept the blade down and back, pivoting on his right foot and turning left, feeling the blade enter flesh. It was a familiar sensation, as was the gasp of warm breath against his neck as the cop gasped his shock and surprise.

"Chris!" Cam shouted.

Gregor knew he had no more than a couple of seconds to act. Blade wedged into Chris's side, he tugged on the handle to swing himself behind the cop, wrapping his other arm around the man's chest and holding him upright. Though still conscious, Chris just grunted in pain, and offered no resistance.

The other cop was ten feet away.

"Put the knife down!" Cam shouted.

Gregor started pushing Chris forward. He was strong, the cop was small, and even though he'd been stabbed, Chris's automatic response was to walk, not slump down. The blade in his side prevented him from doing anything else.

Eight feet away.

"Stop, let him go, get down on the ground!" Cam shouted, but there was no way he would shoot. Even if he thought of himself as a crack shot, he wouldn't risk blowing off his own partner's head.

Four feet.

Chris still grasped his gun and he brought up his right hand, waving the weapon uselessly.

Gregor paused, tugged the blade from the man's side and shoved him forward into his partner, following his falling body and dropping behind it, lashing out with the blade, feeling and hearing the satisfying *slick* of razor-sharp metal through flesh.

Cam tried to cry out, but all he could utter was a wet gurgle as his neck opened and his life leaked out. He dropped to his knees beside Chris. Gregor shoved at the cops and rolled aside, coming up into a crouch. He was ready with the blade in case one of them lifted their gun his way. But Cam was too busy dying, and Chris squirmed into a fetal position, hugging the agony in his stomach.

Gregor's heartbeat had barely increased. He breathed deep and slow, alert for any unexpected changes in the situation, but he was confident that he was fully in control. As Cam bled out, he plucked up Chris's dropped gun and heaved it behind him into the trees. He'd never liked guns. The blade was his way.

When he knelt beside the bodies, Chris started begging, but Gregor paid no heed. One hard thrust of the knife into his right ear, a twist, and the man was gone. He wiped the blade on the cop's uniform, then hurried to the cruiser. Climbing in, he sat in the passenger seat and looked at the small computer terminal mounted on the dashboard.

There was a photograph of him on the screen. It came as a shock and he frowned, trying to make out where and when it had been taken. The white walls, paint flaking. The bland furniture. A hospital—and then he remembered visiting Marianne Francis. He had left her alive because he hadn't wanted anyone on his trail for her murder. She must have snapped a photo on her phone when he wasn't looking, and now this half-blurred image was available to every cop in the state, perhaps the country, as they searched for the serial killer of those lightning strike survivors.

So much for showing her mercy.

Angry in spite of himself, he switched off the headlights and slammed the cruiser doors. A couple of minutes to drag the bodies into the ditch beside the road was all he could spare. The feather still pointed, true and sharp, and his time was ticking down. He was close to success, and the end of this part of his life.

What came next would depend upon what he found at the end of his journey.

18

Vince knew that Lilou made every man feel special, but with him he believed it was true. He had saved her life, after all. Down in subterranean London he'd fought and killed Mary Rock's two goons to stop them from killing her, never intending to end that day a murderer, but never once looking back and regretting his actions.

He had been injured in the process, badly, so Lilou had helped him, hidden him away and introduced him to the world of the Kin. He'd already known about their dead, and had spent years collecting ancient relics from their time on Earth. Lilou had revealed to him that they were still alive.

And *how* alive. He had fallen in love with her, not knowing then quite what sort of creature she was. Even when he'd come to know more, it hadn't lessened his passion, but it had confused the guilt he felt. He had tried to rationalize it, and over time it had become something that he could deal with, even explain away if the need arose. Because his love for Angela was a solid thing, with foundations and history, a tactile fact. She was a huge part of his life, and he could trace his love for her from the moment they had met.

His love for Lilou was supernatural.

"What is it between you and Ahara?" Vince asked.

Lilou didn't seem to hear.

"Lilou?"

"Nothing," she said.

"Really." He felt anger rising, and didn't like her taking him for a fool. Her sigh meant that she knew she could not.

"It's not Ahara," she said. She brought her legs up and hugged them to her. They were in a large motel room, supposedly resting for a couple of hours. Angela and Meloy were out buying food. Ahara had vanished as soon as they drove into the parking lot. Meloy had offered to go with Angela, and when Vince objected, she said it was okay, that she wanted to catch up with the gangster.

Vince had felt a surprising pang of jealousy. It was ridiculous, especially compared to the tension between him and Lilou, though that was a tension that went only one way. It was in her nature to have men love her, and he often wondered what she made of relationships.

"It's all wisps," she said. "They're unreliable, treacherous. Of all the Kin I've known, other than the wraiths they're the least... *here*. You know what I mean?"

"Ahara comes and goes," Vince said, nodding.

"Comes and goes from this world."

"Where does she go to?"

Lilou shrugged.

"So you and the wisps have a history."

She stared at her feet. Sighed. "I've only ever been bewitched by one creature, and the bastard broke my heart."

"You've broken a few in your time," Vince said, and Lilou glared at him, such an alien, inhuman stare that his blood ran cold. Sometimes he had to step back and remind himself that he chose to associate with creatures that weren't human, however they appeared. Lilou's eyes had seen other worlds.

"His name was Ecclehert," she said, and her expression softened. She even broke into a sad smile. "I haven't uttered his name aloud in… a long time. He came to me out of the tortured northern lands after the French Bastard King took England for his own. Ecclehert brought tales of murder and rape, crop burning, cattle slaughter, and famine. He spoke of cannibalism amongst the human survivors, and even those words could not shock me. The power to shock had been smothered by his power to entrance me, completely and utterly, and he didn't even know what he was doing."

"He was a wisp, like Ahara?"

"Very similar. Sometimes barely there. That's why it surprised me so much. I'm used to being the subject of infatuation, not suffering from it. Ecclehert's appearance broke my life in half. There was before— those old times shortly after the Time, when I was born into and wandered a land growing ever more inimical to the Kin. And there was after—when I swore that love would never touch me again."

Vince sat on the edge of the bed. He knew what was happening. Even as Lilou talked about never lowering her defenses, her mask was slipping and the real nymph was showing through. His heart swelled, his groin ached, his soul pulsed with desire. He slipped from the bed and sat beside her on the sofa, and while every part of him screamed that this was wrong, Lilou's gravity drew him close.

"More than anything, my love for him came as a shock. I believed myself immune. Because so many loved me, I thought I knew all there was to know."

Vince reached for her, right hand stroking the back of her neck, left hand resting on her thigh. Lilou looked up at him and smiled, and she did not draw herself back. He craved her, groaning out loud at the pressure building at his center. She reached for him, her own eyes hooded and heavy, mouth slightly open, lips full and glimmering.

Vince's hand curved over her thigh and reached deeper, and then Lilou gasped aloud and stood, backing away from him with her hands over her face.

"Lilou…"

"Even now, Vince?"

"I can't… I couldn't…"

"I'm sorry. I'm sorry." She turned from him and took three heavy breaths. When she turned back she was only Lilou again. The nymph was reined in.

"Oh, fuck," Vince said. He leaned forward with elbows on his knees and his head in his hands. "Fuck!"

"Vince, it's not you."

"Of *course* it's me!" He rubbed his head, then sat back. "Finish your story."

"I'm not sure—"

"You started telling me, now fucking *finish*." His erection remained, and Vince drew his legs up so that she would not see. He hated himself for what had happened. He hated the fact that nothing *more* had happened.

"If you want." She sat on the other side of the bed, as far from him as she could, and looked down at her hands. "Ecclehert shunned me and left me. He made me feel like a child again, without control."

"I know the feeling."

Lilou turned her hands, examining them. "It was three hundred years later that I heard he had died. The news landed heavily on me. I believed he had stolen away a part of my life that would never again be complete. I carry a hole in my heart, and over time I've grown to blame Ecclehert the wisp for putting it there. They're flighty creatures, rootless and constantly adrift, and no wisp I have met since has found itself able to condemn Ecclehert for his actions. So I carried the injury close, telling no one—not even Mallian. Like any untended wound, it festered." She looked at Vince again. "You're the first one I've ever told."

"It's not Ahara's fault," he said.

"All wisps are the same."

"I'm sure there are Kin who believe all humans are the same."

She shrugged at that but didn't reply. Vince closed his eyes and tried to forget what had happened.

Angela and Meloy returned a few minutes later to find Lilou asleep on the bed and Vince surfing the Internet on the laptop. He'd been searching, but had found nothing to indicate where their journey should carry them next.

Angela had rented the room next door. She and Vince took it, and Vince was pleased that he felt not even a shred of jealousy at Meloy for staying in the same room as Lilou. He didn't care what happened in there, and likely he would never know.

He did care what happened with Angela.

They shared a bottle of wine and made love, and all the way through he was thinking of Angela, only Angela. Afterward as she lay sleeping curled against him, he spent hours staring at the ceiling trying to convince himself that would always be the case.

Angela woke and realized that she'd slept much longer than she intended. After making love they'd huddled close together, and she reveled in it, holding onto a brief moment of intimacy and warmth before rising to continue their search. Now it was time to return to that search.

Sammi was still out there somewhere, and the more time passed by, the more terrible the danger Angela believed her to be in. The story Lilou had brought of Gregor the Kin-killer was testament to that, and the murders were continuing.

Vince was sleeping on his back, snoring softly as he always did after he'd had something to drink. She raised herself on one elbow and looked at him. Light filtered through the curtains from the parking bays outside, and a red glow played across the bed from the alarm clock on the bedside table. Vince had changed so much from the man with whom she had fallen in love, but the passion endured, changing with time and events and molding itself to their new, stark reality.

She recalled with fondness their mornings waking in their flat in London, more often than not hearing their upstairs neighbors fucking like rabbits to see in their day. The flat was gone now, as were those comfortable, carefree times—part of the history of them that was being revised with every moment that passed.

Angela wished it was a less exciting story. She would have been content maintaining the routine—waking, Vince leaving for work, her studying at home, drinks with Lucy in the evening, dinner with Vince later on, TV or a walk or retiring early to bed to read or make love. Some people frowned upon such routine, and said it wasn't really living, but sometimes routine was perfect.

She wasn't sure Vince would agree. She'd never seen him so alive, so *involved*, as he was now. He had been passionate and eager last night, his lovemaking urgent, as if he'd been waiting forever. It reminded her of the early weeks of their relationship, when they'd disappeared from the world for days on end.

Angela didn't believe that Vince would want that life anymore. She was too afraid to ask.

She rose from the bed, dressed, and drank some water. Though they'd only shared a bottle, the wine was stale in her mouth, like a memory gone sour. Delving into the bag she and Meloy had brought back from their shopping expedition, she took out a few of the items and started working with them.

Since being sprung from her cell and dropping out of sight, Angela had worked hard to translate her theoretical knowledge of the criminal underworld into working methods that might help her and Vince survive.

From her studies on both sides of the Atlantic she knew a lot about the processes that would have been put into place to capture them. The authorities knew for sure that she was still alive, and they would assume that Vince was still at large, at least until they could prove otherwise.

The two of them shared a page and ranking on the FBI's Most Wanted list, and the information contained there was extensive. Their images would be readily available to police departments across the country, and their details were flagged at every border control point in airports, ports, and hard border crossings both north and south.

Once a criminology student, now she was a criminal.

Online accounts were an obvious target, and she and Vince had cut all ties with any social media accounts they'd once maintained, as well as banking sites and any website that required logging in with their old passwords. Between them they'd lost more than ten thousand pounds in several accounts, but it was a small price to pay for freedom.

Most criminals were caught through mobile phone records. She and Vince bought burners—a new one every few weeks—and on the rare occasions they did text or call each other, they never used names, real or otherwise. Angela had persuaded Vince to abandon any website surfing habits he'd had before. She had read several papers discussing the use of average search patterns, and the complex programs designed to identify them.

Before their lives had been upended, she might have spent her online time checking the BBC News site, retail listings for true crime books, a shopping site selling sexy underwear, ten minutes on Twitter, and half an hour jumping across YouTube. Repeating those surfing habits now would be begging them to be flagged.

Cell phone records, Internet searches, facial

recognition software, voice recognition technology... no matter how she looked at it, the odds were stacked against them. They could take basic measures to avoid capture—her altered appearance was a start—but since Claudette's slaying she would have to change that again, too. But habits were entrenched, sometimes subconscious.

Difficult to change.

To survive as themselves, they had to become new people.

Angela was troubled that he'd hardly taken her advice to heart. While she cut and dyed her hair, changed her choice of clothing, wore false glasses or color-altering contact lenses, Vince was still very much Vince. Tee shirt and jeans, a loose jacket if it was cool, leather boots. His hair was longer than before, true, but only because he hadn't bothered cutting it. The problem was he didn't seem overly concerned about surviving as himself. He wanted to survive as a friend of the Kin, first and foremost. They had become his whole world.

Where did that leave her?

She sighed and opened up the screwdriver set. The money Meloy had brought was proving useful, and within ten minutes she had murdered two phones and a digital radio and spread their guts across the small dressing table.

"Wassup?" Vince said from behind her.

"Doing some shit," Angela said.

He yawned and sat up, shifting across the bed, standing, and moving behind her. She welcomed his familiar scent, his hands on her shoulders. It felt like home.

"What the hell?"

"It's pretty simple really," she said. She connected wires, stroked a screen, and then on the radio she turned the dial up and down, passing through crackles and areas of white noise until she heard voices.

"They sound like..." Vince said.

"Police channels," she said.

"You never cease to surprise me."

"Doesn't mean we'll hear anything useful." She sat back into him and enjoyed the pressure of his hands on her shoulders, as his fingers worked at tensed muscles.

"That was nice," he said, and she knew what he meant. It was a while since they'd been together long enough, and safe enough, to make love.

"Yeah," she said. "Just like old times." His hands paused, then continued massaging. She sighed. She knew it could never be the same again, so why continue berating him for what had happened? She didn't blame him, not really. She hated that he'd lied to her. Yet deep down she was also grateful for the view of the wider world she had been offered, even though it had changed her life forever.

Now that wider world was a threat to her sister's only child, and if they didn't work quickly, Sammi might be the next one dead.

"What are you hoping to hear?" he asked.

"Something that might lead us to Sammi," she said. "Or this Gregor character. The cops will be searching for him."

"They're calling him the Lightning Killer," Vince said. "Why does every killer need a name?"

"Good for the TV series," Angela said. "I'm going to shower. I'll leave this on."

"Yeah, great, nothing like the disembodied voices of local cops to ease me back to sleep."

"We've slept too much," she said, standing and turning to him. "You need to listen while I'm showering." She put her arms around his neck and kissed him. He tasted of sleep, and of her.

"We didn't sleep that much." He smiled, raising and lowering his eyebrows.

"We need to go," Angela said. "Sammi."

"You found me," he said. "You'll find her... and we've got help."

"Yeah, a nymph and a gangster. That worked out well last time."

"Hey." Vince held her tight. "It'll be okay."

Voices rattled from the radio speaker, calm and flat. It sounded like business as usual out there.

"Sure it will," she said. "Make me coffee."

Angela took a quick shower, wishing for more than the weak, lukewarm flow. As she dried, she heard a commotion outside in the room. Voices. She covered herself with the towel and opened the door. Lilou and Meloy were standing inside the closed door. Vince was crouched over the radio, head tilted as he listened.

"Oh no," Angela said, because the scene she feared was playing out in her mind again and again.

"Not Sammi," Vince said.

"What then?"

"Two dead cops."

"Stabbed," Lilou said. "Gregor uses a knife."

"Do you know where?" Angela asked, alert and alight.

"Yeah," Vince said. "I know where."

19

At last they are starting to arrive.

From her vantage up on the hillside she sees the first figure. She has been walking the Fold, probing its boundaries and ensuring that the magic she cast is firm and rich. There is no reason to doubt, but she is going to be here for a long, long time. It's wise to make sure that this new world will function and persist.

Looking down the steep slope at the near end of her valley, she sees the remnants of the human road that once led into the place. It protrudes a little into the edge of the Fold, and already the majority of the artificial surface has been subsumed into the land, wiped away by her powerful magic and leaving behind untouched countryside, virgin soil on which she will make her own mark. The same has happened to the score of buildings that were contained within the boundary, so there are few traces of them left.

The fragment of road, the final remnant of humanity, has been left for the arrival of her Kin.

She's too far away to see the newcomer clearly, so she hurries down the steep slope, bounding from rock to rock like a young child, and not the ancient thing she is. Freedom is giving her such energy. Already she feels more alive than she has in many, many years, and the prospect of sealing off the Fold and making it hers forever is almost too exciting to bear.

As she reaches the valley floor and approaches the short ribbon of paved surface, she sees that it looks like a man, accompanied by one of her wraith servants. That is no surprise. The deniers are all very humanlike— it was a necessity for their incorporation into a world that would never willingly welcome them. Once he understands what has happened, the knowledge will enable him to re-embrace his true self.

"Welcome," she says.

"Mistress," the shape with the man says. It shimmers in the air, and bows, a vague presence that seems to pulse and throb with reflected sunlight.

"You've done well, Gradaal," she says.

"Thank you, Mistress!"

"My name's Jeff. Who the fuck are you?" The old man is agitated, looking around as if seeking someone else. "Where's Mary? I was told I was coming to meet Mary."

"And did you *really* believe that?" she asks.

The man's eyes flicker to the side, then back again.

"I don't know what you are," he says. "I don't know what this thing is that brought me here, but I want none of it. I want my old life back."

"And I'm giving it to you," she says. "This is your old life, here with your Kin. Not out there with those... *humans.*" She almost spits out the word, it's so distasteful.

"They're not so bad," the man mutters.

"Can I go?" the wraith called Gradaal asks.

"I'm giving you something they never can," she says to the man.

"What if I refuse?" he asks.

"I've fulfilled my purpose," Gradaal says. "As you requested, as you instructed, I did everything—"

"Go!" she shouts, surprising even herself. The shimmering shape, wraith of the elf Gradaal who died at the hands of human inquisitors over five hundred years ago—burned and cut, sliced and pulled apart— flickers away to nothing. As she vanishes again from the world, she leaves behind a long, low sigh of peace.

"What have you done?" the man asks, shocked by the shout, startled by the wraith's disappearance.

"I gave her peace, just as I promised," she says soothingly. "I'm offering you the same. Look at my world, the Fold in reality I have made ready for you, and for me, and for *all* of us. Look." She turns and gestures along the length of the valley. "It has a river and waterfalls, seven lakes, three areas of marshland, woodlands so numerous that they never begin or end. East to west, up the valley sides and through ravines, it leads to the hilltops from which you can see the entire Fold. Caves and canyons, hidden places, a hundred square miles to wander to your heart's content. And up, higher... look."

The man peers up into the sky, and he doesn't seem surprised that it has gone from daylight to night in the few minutes since he arrived. She can do that. Here, she can do anything.

"The endless stars," she says.

The man frowns. "I... don't recognize them. The constellations. The patterns."

"Didn't I tell you? This is a whole new world."

"Who are you? Why have you done this? I was happy."

"Your name is Hengle," she says.

"No. No. My name is Jeff." He appears shocked by his old, forgotten name. His reaction frustrates her, but she cannot let her impatience mar this moment. There is an eternity for things to sort themselves out, and become right again.

"Hengle," she says, quieter. "Four hundred years ago you lived in northern France, making a woodland your own. Two hundred years later you were living in London, married to a human wife. Since then you have denied your heritage. You're here to embrace it once again."

"Where's Mary?" he asks. "I was promised Mary. She's been gone too long, and…" He looks past her, deeper into the Fold. "She was never here."

"Mary is your dead wife," she says. "A human. I cannot raise the wraith of a human, not like Gradaal who brought you to me. And even if I could, I would not. I'm offering you eternity, Hengle. This place, my place, once it's sealed and becomes the Fold it will be a new Time for all of us. Kin only, no humans. No one forcing us to hide. No society to which you must submit or assimilate. You don't have to deny who you are anymore."

"I'm Hengle," he whispers.

"You are," she says, delighted. "Here, you can allow yourself to be Hengle the werewolf once more. How long has it been?"

Hengle smiles and cries at the same time. He reaches for his belt, zipper, buttons, and strips off the human clothing that has acted like a shield between his denier's life and the reality of who he really is. He looks up at the strange starscape, and she makes a moon appear, large and full, a face in the sky.

"A long time," he says. Naked, he walks past her and steps from tarmac onto grass. He squeezes his toes. Without looking back he starts walking, then running, as a change begins.

There's a sound behind her, footsteps on a hard, smooth surface. She turns around. A woman is approaching, hand in hand with the wraith of an old, short goblin. Both of them have the look of someone seeking something.

She can give them both what they want.

20

As they approached Danville in the early pre-dawn hours, Angela only hoped their plan would work. It had so many variables and unknowns that she felt a heavy, hot tension in her chest, with Sammi's wellbeing at its core.

The wisp Ahara was with them again. Angela didn't understand why and how she came and went, but the Kin seemed to be working to her own agenda. Vince had told Angela the reason behind Lilou's dislike of the wisp. She didn't care. The nymph's love life concerned her only so far as it involved Vince, and beyond that only if it affected their search for Sammi.

The girl was her focus.

In truth she was also Angela's distraction, a fresh purpose which gave direction to this new life spent running and hiding.

"Almost there," Vince said. He was driving the Jeep, Angela next to him. In the back sat Ahara and Lilou, with Meloy between them. The wisp was still looking at the image of the skin map on Meloy's phone screen. "You guys ready?"

"Ready," Meloy said. He had contributed the most to their plan, though it was shaky at best. Angela found herself trusting the gangster all over again. Fat Frederick

Meloy, reputation notwithstanding, had proven to be useful in London, and she hoped that trend would continue here. His fascination with the Kin helped keep him in line.

Several minutes later Vince pulled up close to Danville's small bus station and Lilou and Meloy jumped out. Lilou caught Angela's eye and nodded. She nodded back.

Ahara remained in the back seat. "Anything else?" Angela asked, turning to look at her.

"We go into the hills," Ahara said.

"We're finding Sammi," Angela said. "Gregor's looking for her, too. Find him, we find her. So can you help with that?"

Ahara peered at the veinous map on the small phone screen. "It's leading us into the hills," she said again.

"Fine," Angela responded. She turned back around and stared through the windshield as Vince drove them slowly along the main street.

"She'll help when she can," Vince said.

"Big help so far."

"She got you out of jail."

"Yeah, but I'm still not free."

"We're as free as they are."

Angela had never thought of it quite that way. She'd never compared herself to the Kin, not even since being on the run. There were people hunting her now, in the same way that there were always people hunting the Kin. Mary Rock in London, Gregor over here, others.

"Let's just look," she said. "You take the left, I'll take the right."

"Where would she be if she was here?"

"I don't know," Angela said. "I hardly know her." That stark truth only added to the guilt she felt at Sammi's disappearance, and the desperate need to find her and protect her from the Kin-killer. Whether or not she was Kin—and Angela had tried to shove that possibility from her mind—she owed her niece a duty of care, even if she'd shown little affection over the years.

Since losing her own life, family, and friends, she cared a lot.

Danville's streets were just waking up. Dawn lit the horizon, and the streetlights started to flicker off as early morning workers hit the streets. They all had somewhere to go, and several drivers overtook the Jeep as it cruised along the main drag.

"We can't do this for long without attracting suspicion," she said.

"Especially if the town's waking to news of two dead cops," Vince said. "The Feds will be swarming all over the place soon."

"Not the best spot in the world for us to be."

"If she's here, we'll find her before then."

"She probably won't even recognize me," Angela said.

"Sure she will!" Vince said confidently, but she wasn't convinced.

They reached the edge of town and parked by the side of the road. Vince dashed into a Dunkin' Donuts to grab a couple of coffees. Angela glanced into the back seat. Ahara almost wasn't there, and the wisp might have smiled at her. Or not.

She jumped a little when the door opened again, and Vince climbed in. Coffee in hand, they drove back along the main street, taking a left along the first of the side roads. Smart houses stood on either side. Gardens, driveways, back yards, paths heading off between buildings… they were looking for a needle in a haystack.

Angela dialed Meloy. He answered after two rings.

"Anything?"

"Nothing here," he said.

"Right."

"Angela, we'll find her," he said. "That's what we're here for."

"Lilou's here to find the killer."

"Yeah, well, that's Lilou. I'm here for you and Vince as well. I'm loyal to my friends."

Angela thought again about the stories concerning Meloy, the terrible things he'd supposedly done to people, the brutal crimes he'd perpetrated. She couldn't help but feel glad he was on their side.

"*What's* Lilou?" the nymph demanded.

"Angela's worried you don't care about her niece."

"We're here, aren't we?"

"I see you," a voice said. "I know you." Lilou stepped away from Meloy and looked around. Close to Meloy's side stood a thin, small man. She had to blink a few times to really make him out. It wasn't that he was uncertain, like the wisp, but that he was almost not there at all.

"Who the fuck?" Meloy jumped at the sight of someone so close to him. His hands came up in a reflexive defensive gesture.

"Who are you?" Lilou asked.

"I see you," the man said again. He snatched at a half-hidden wound on his chest, fingers like gossamer threads, mouth moving just out of sync with his words. Lilou knew what he was.

"I see you also," she said, "I'm sorry to say."

"Not as sorry as I am," the man said.

"So who is this?" Meloy asked.

Lilou looked around to see if anyone else was watching their exchange. Early commuters awaited a bus to board, and no one seemed to be paying them much attention.

"A wraith," she said.

"Like a ghost?"

"If you like, but brought up by someone with a purpose. Wraiths haunt unwillingly."

"She told me she'd set me free," the wraith said.

"Who told you?"

"I never knew her name. I'm not sure she could tell me. The fairy."

Lilou's eyes went wide.

"Fairy?" Meloy asked, looking equally shocked.

"Where is she?" Lilou asked.

"Somewhere close but... I no longer have the map," the wraith said.

"Did you lose the map?"

"The girl ran away. I wasn't as good as I should have been."

Meloy reached for the wraith, his hands moving close but not quite touching, as if he was afraid that he might touch nothing.

"Take us to her," Lilou said.

"What? No," Meloy said. "What about Sammi?"

"Sammi ran," the wraith said.

"Where is the fairy?"

"In the hills," Meloy said. "That's what your friendly wisp has been saying."

"In the hills," the wraith agreed. "But if I go there now, without my charge... without Sammi..." He looked and sounded bereft, wretched.

"Which way did she run?" Meloy asked.

The wraith pointed.

"How long ago?"

"Dawn."

Meloy grabbed Lilou. "She's close!"

"Okay," Lilou said, nodding.

Meloy grabbed her harder. "But what the fuck is this about a fairy?"

As soon as the man stopped to help her, Sammi knew she was in trouble.

"Hey, kid, need a lift?"

"Yeah, like I'd ever get in a car with a stranger." She was on the edge of town, tired from fleeing the bus station, hungry, thirsty, and wondering how the hell she would get back to her father. She'd gone to the police station, but when she'd arrived there things had been chaos, with people rushing back and forth, lots of cars in the parking lot, and a local radio station's mobile studio parked up on the sidewalk across the street.

The craziness had scared her away.

"Those marks on your arm," the man said. "You been struck?" He rubbed at his own arm as he asked.

"Yeah," she said. "You?"

"Twice."

Her hand went to the network of marks, smoothing over them for the thousandth time, reading herself like Braille. She wished it was a language she understood.

"Hurts, doesn't it?" He stared at her arm and where more of the pattern was visible on her neck.

Sammi frowned.

No, not really, she thought, and she knew he was lying. But why would someone lie about being struck by lightning?

"I can show you something," the man said. "I think you'll like it. I think it'll like you."

"Get lost, creep."

The man held up a large feather, holding it by the shaft.

Something about it entranced her, even though from this distance it looked normal. From a goose perhaps, or a swan. It was the purest white she'd ever seen, and it seemed to shift and twitch in his hand, even though there wasn't any breeze. It was like a living thing, striving to free itself from his grasp.

"You want to tickle me somewhere with that, perv?"

"It's not like that," he said, and he let the feather drop outside the car window. His eyes were wide, expectant, and she noticed for the first time that they were tinted a strange shade of red. She had never seen eyes like that before. She certainly hadn't ever met a man like this.

The feather swooped down, drifting back and forth as it floated toward the ground. The man's expression dropped, then the feather lifted once more and flitted toward her. He seemed happy again.

Sammi couldn't help herself. She took a step forward and held out her hand, anticipating the soft touch of feather against skin, reaching for it and wondering how such contact might change what had happened to her. She was lost, afraid, alone and unknown miles from her father and home, brought here by what she thought might have been the ghost of a dead vampire. It was all so strange, terrifying, yet somehow it didn't seem surprising.

As if she had been expecting this her whole life.

The feather crossed half of the gap between girl and car before drifting to the ground and staying there. It twitched left and right, then became still. Something about it seemed... pitiful.

"I don't understand," the man in the car said.

Sammi took a few steps forward and plucked up the feather, holding it by the quill. There was no weight to it at all. She held it up to one eye and looked through the fronds, and was amazed to see the vibrant colors of the world concentrated through it, all the edges sharper, everything revealed in a higher definition than simple reality.

"That's mine," the man said. He opened the car door and got out, approaching her with his hand held towards her.

She saw the knife he held, blade curved back against his forearm. Viewed through the feather it seemed different from everything else, older and more decayed. It was a dull, rusty red, stained by untold deaths.

Sammi turned to run. Something clipped her left foot out from under her and she went sprawling, still clasping the feather. She crawled forward across the gravel roadside and onto a grassy verge, kicking out behind her to try to ward him off. Getting ready to stand and run, she felt something grasp her belt and lift her clean from the ground.

"Mine," he said into her ear, and a big hand closed around hers. He squeezed tight, grinding her knuckles together. She let go of the feather.

"Help!" Sammi shouted, and then she felt something cool and sharp against her throat.

"One more time, and you'll never scream again."

She squirmed and struggled, looking around frantically to see if anyone had noticed what was happening. No cars passed by. This side road leading out of town was bordered on both sides by fields of fruit trees growing on timber and wire frames and an occasional lane leading to a farmstead, the road itself edged with a dusty verge and drainage ditch on both sides. Lonely telegraph poles marched toward where the road veered to the left, a quarter of a mile further on. Much farther in the distance, hills stood shadowed against the dawn sky.

They were alone. She should have never come this far out.

"What do you want?" she shouted, but she feared she knew exactly what he wanted. Her mother and father had warned her about men like this. Despite that strange stuff with the feather, and all of the weirdness about lightning strikes, he was just a pervert preying on a young girl alone.

She couldn't afford to think about what might happen in the future. Everything was now. First chance she had, she would kick him in the balls and sprint back into town.

"Stop struggling," he said, pushing the knife harder against her throat. "This blade's tasted a great deal of blood over the past few days. Most of it not human."

Sammi ceased her struggles. Fear bit in deep, ice around her heavy heart, a stone in her chest. The man pulled her upright and kept his arm rested on her shoulder, blade to her throat. She smelled his breath, stale and somehow meaty, like roadkill two days dead. Every part of her wanted to do the things her parents had told her to do in a situation like this, and the things she'd learned in the mixed martial arts classes she attended intermittently—rake her boot down his shin, stomp on his toes, kick him in the nuts.

She did none of those.

Most of it not human.

Whatever had happened to her since the second lightning strike, this man was part of it.

"I want my dad."

"Daddy's dead, kid." It was the second time she'd been told that, but she wouldn't allow herself to believe. She *couldn't*. After everything that had happened to her family, her life couldn't go that way.

"What do you want from me?"

"I'm not sure yet," he said. "You're not quite what I expected, but we'll go somewhere to find out what you are. Now, into the car without making a sound." He started to move. "Hungry? You hungry? I am. We'll stop for food."

"Hey!" It was a woman's voice, and she looked up and into the rows of fruit trees across the verge and ditch. A woman stared back at her. Behind her was a tall man, both of them readying as if to leap across the ditch. They looked like they'd been running.

Sammi's first thought was, *She's not human.*

He will lead us to Grace, Lilou thought. They had to rescue Sammi but let the man escape. She had no idea how to do that.

"Who the fuck are you?" Gregor shouted.

"Take it easy," Lilou said. She considered lowering her mask, because despite his affectations this man was human. But he was also a human who had known, hunted, and killed the Kin for decades, and he knew what they could do. If not immune to her charms, he might be ready.

"Yeah, take it easy, Gregor," Meloy said, stepping past her toward the ditch. He could be across it and onto the man in seconds. And in that time the man would slice the girl's throat.

Gregor's eyes went wide and Lilou sighed. *Now he knows we know him*, she thought. She wasn't sure how that might affect the situation, but it felt as if they'd given away an advantage. They weren't just passersby who'd wandered across the scene.

His gaze flickered back and forth between them, then settled on Lilou. He smiled.

"I don't need you, but I'll be happy to gut you anyway."

Meloy tensed and Lilou grabbed his arm, digging in with her nails. She felt the muscles there, solid and knotted, ready to uncoil. She had seen the rage this man could unleash, but Gregor's exploits were legendary. Here was the Kin-killer.

"Let the girl go," Lilou said. "She's no Kin."

"I'm not so sure," Gregor said. "And why does that matter?"

"You tell me."

"I don't share my secrets."

"'Course not," Meloy said. "Piece of shit like you—"

Gregor flicked the knife. Sammi squealed, then bit her lip and squeezed her eyes shut. Her left ear dripped blood.

"Leave her, and we let you go," Meloy said.

Gregor glared at him. "Why's this your fight, human?"

"As human as you, fuck face."

"See here!" Gregor said, pulling down his lower eyelid. "See here!" He swept the same hand through his hair, revealing the nubs of horns. "Does this look *human*?"

Meloy said nothing, for which Lilou was glad. Maybe he was learning a level of control.

"She's got nothing for you to take," she said.

Gregor didn't reply. He backed toward his vehicle and climbed in through the passenger door, pulling the girl in behind him. Keeping the knife at her throat, he scrambled across into the driver's seat and pulled her into the seat beside him.

"Shut the door," he said, and she obeyed.

Lilou leapt over the ditch, her movement light and graceful. The Kin-killer watched her every move, and behind her she sensed Meloy taking advantage of his distraction, slipping across the ditch and behind the car.

The engine roared and the car leapt back, clipping Meloy and sending him sprawling into the dust.

Lilou glanced his way as he rolled, and he came up onto his knees and nodded her way. Bumped and bloodied, he was not badly injured.

The car powered away along the road, throwing up a cloud of dust that hung in the still morning air.

"Now what?" Meloy asked.

"Now we call the cavalry, and hope we can catch up," Lilou said, and she thought, *Now we follow him up into the hills*. If the wretched wraith they'd quizzed was telling the truth, Gregor was on his way to the fairy, taking the girl along as some sort of prize.

21

Vince's phone rang and Angela snatched it from between his legs while he drove.

"Yeah," she said. Then, "Fuck!" She paused for a while. "You're sure?" Another pause. "Okay, we'll pick you up." She dropped the phone into her own lap.

"What?" Vince asked.

"Left here, head west. Lilou and Meloy spotted her." After a moment she added, "Gregor's got her. They're driving for the hills."

Vince dropped a gear and swung the Jeep around a corner, powering along the road and heading for the edge of town. They had been cruising Danville for over an hour, and the sudden burst of speed made him feel as if they finally were taking action, instead of treading water.

"Anything else?" he asked.

"He's holding a knife to her throat."

"Doesn't mean anything," Vince said, but he knew it was a stupid thing to say, and he cursed himself for it. It was as bad as saying, *Everything will be all right*, when he knew there was a good chance it wouldn't. Gregor was a cold-blooded murderer whose kill rate had increased drastically over the past few days. Only last night he'd added two police officers to his score sheet. He wasn't a man troubled by taking lives.

The cloudy issue here was whether or not Sammi was Kin, but even that might not matter.

"Faster," Angela said.

Vince knew he had to take care. They'd seen several police cruisers around town, and suspicions would be heightened by the recent murders of fellow officers. They were lucky they hadn't been stopped and questioned already. The town was small enough for officers to notice strangers, but big enough for strangers to have plenty of reasons to visit. Perhaps they had luck on their side.

Angela navigated using a map on her phone. She spoke in short, clipped sentences, and anxiety came off her in waves. Impatience, too. She knew that every passing second put Sammi in deeper danger, so Vince made sure as he drove that he grasped every moment.

A few minutes later they left town and headed for the hills, passing between rolling fields of fruit trees speckled here and there with distant farmsteads. They spotted Lilou and Meloy jogging along the road ahead of them, and Vince barely stopped long enough for them to jump into the rear seat.

Ahara appeared as a shade between them.

"Fucker's got her," Meloy said.

"Who is he?" Angela asked.

"Freak who thinks he's Kin," Meloy said.

"You saw through that?" Lilou asked.

"Of course," he said, as if offended. "He's as much Kin as I am."

"So what's the plan?" Vince asked.

"Catch them, stop him hurting Sammi," Angela said. She glanced across at him, eyebrows raised as if to say, *What else?*

"And then into the hills," Lilou said. "We have to protect the fairy from Gregor, too." Something about the way she said it troubled Vince. He looked in the rearview mirror, shifting slightly so that he could see Lilou. She caught his eye and looked away.

She was lying.

This wasn't about protecting the fairy at all. He didn't think her real goal was to save Sammi, either, or even stop Gregor.

"Into the hills," Ahara said, "and somewhere very different."

"Faster," Angela said. "Faster, Vince."

Vince gave it some gas.

Sammi had never been so terrified. Even that time at the hospital, when she and her father had arrived after her mother's crash, it hadn't been like this. They'd both known that something terrible had happened, and walking through the automatic doors the breath of the hospital had whispered the truth in sterile, bleached awfulness. The fear had been keen, the terror of what was to come, but they had faced it together. Hand in hand, hearts beating as one. The doctor's voice had barely matched his mouth.

Thinking of that time now, Sammi realized how alike the doctor and Old Itch had been. Both were harbingers of doom, in their own way.

She had escaped from Old Itch, though. If only the

words that doctor had muttered had been escapable.

Yet this was worse, because looming around the danger she was in were the doubts about her father. She wanted to ask this man what he'd meant when he said her father was dead. She wanted to ask if he had killed him. She wished she'd seen through Old Itch's lies earlier, shaken herself from the stupor, run home. She wished.

Sammi sobbed silent tears as the man drove with one hand, the other still holding the knife to her throat. Balanced on the armrest between them was a plastic bowl of water. The feather he had pointed at her floated there, and no matter which way the water slurped and splashed from the car's movements, the feather pointed in the same direction. Sammi couldn't help looking down at it. There was something otherworldly about it, as if it had a life of its own.

She couldn't plead with him. There would be nothing to gain. She had to keep her wits and watch for any advantage, any chance she might have of escaping him and his knife.

The blade still hovered close to her throat, but it was dipping lower now. The angle of his arm must be uncomfortable, maybe even painful. They'd been driving for five minutes, maybe more, and she hoped that her stillness was lulling him into a sense of control.

Trying not to move her head, she looked around the interior of the car. She hadn't heard the locks click into place, which meant that she would be able to open her own door. There was nothing she could use as a weapon. The man kept his eyes on the road, only glancing down at the floating feather when they came to a junction, a driveway, or a forest track. If she made a move, she thought she'd have a second or two to get her right arm up between the blade and her throat. He wouldn't see her moving her arm to begin with, and even if he caught the movement out of the corner of his eye, she would be quick.

Sammi couldn't help imagining the quick jerk of his arm, her skin parting, the cold metal slicing through flesh and opening her up to the outside. She might scream, or it might emerge as a bubbling gasp. She might be able to fight back, or perhaps the shock would freeze her, allowing him two or three sawing motions which would sever everything vital.

How long would it take her to bleed out, to die in this seat? Perhaps he'd open the door and shove her from the car while it was still moving. Would she feel the impact of her body hitting the road and rolling into the ditch? Would she land face up, or die lying face down in the dirt?

Dad, she thought. *Mom. What do I do now?*

It was the thought of her mother that brought out the fight in her.

Looking to the left without turning her head, she waited until he was staring ahead at the road before nudging the plastic bowl with her left elbow. It spilled onto the floor at Gregor's feet.

"Fuck!" he shouted. Still gripping the wheel, he moved the knife from her throat and leaned down, reaching for the feather where it swilled around on spilled water.

By the time he realized his mistake, Sammi was going for him. She slammed her fist into his face, scratched across his right eye, then grabbed at his hair and shoved hard, banging his head on the door. Twisting in the seat she reached with her right hand, closing it around his wrist as he brought up the knife from between his feet. She had the advantage, her whole weight bearing down on his arm.

The car jumped, skidded, and then she felt the moment of smoothness as the front wheels lost contact with the road surface.

Sammi's whole world shook as the vehicle slammed nose-first into the ditch beside the road. The engine revved wildly, then stalled and cut out. The impact caused her to lose her grip on Gregor's hair and arm, and she scrambled back across her seat and reached for the door handle.

Gregor stirred, blinking rapidly as blood dripped into his eyes from a cut across his forehead. The impact had slammed his head into the steering wheel.

It was lucky for Sammi that the airbags hadn't deployed. Maybe he'd disabled them. She opened the door and fell out onto her back in the road, kicking with her feet to get clear of the tilted car, imagining it bursting into flames and freeing her of the threat of that terrible man.

No such luck. He came for her out of her passenger door, a blood-smeared demon, snarling and still gripping the curved blade in his right hand.

Sammi rolled onto her hands and knees and went to stand, but something stood in front of her. A tall something with thick, heavily haired legs and the largest feet she had ever seen.

Cow, she thought. *Buffalo. Elephant*. But none of

that rang true. As she lifted her head to look a weight pressed onto her back and forced her down onto her stomach. It didn't push too hard, did not hurt, but she had the feeling that the life could be crushed from her in a matter of seconds. Breathing in a shuddering breath, Sammi smelled a primal, spiced aroma.

"Gregor," a deep voice said, rumbling down into her chest.

"Jace Tan," Gregor said.

And then he began to cry.

22

On his thirteenth visit to that small private island, Gregor sits at the water's edge despairing of ever seeing the water-thing or Jace Tan.

"The Script is here."

Gregor jumps and spins, but there are only deep shadows behind him.

"You can't see me," the voice says. It is deep and powerful, a vibration through the ground. Gregor suspects that there will be ripples rolling from the island every time he speaks.

"You came back," Gregor says, and he can't hide the relief in his voice.

"You're going to do something for me," Jace Tan says.

"I'm not sure..." Gregor trails off.

"You *are* sure. You've been sure from the first strange ripple you saw in the marsh. From the first shadows that passed across your dreams. From the first time you considered leaving home and finding more of the world, finding the world that few others know."

I'm not sure... if he's right, Gregor thinks, but there is no arguing with that voice. No questioning its weight.

"I'll leave the Script to you now, and you can take it and begin your journey," Jace Tan says.

"I want to see more," Gregor replies. "I want to know more. It's not fair, only being given a glimpse. It's not right."

"I agree," Jace Tan says. "Not fair, not right. You will see and know more, Gregor, over the coming months and years. You'll also have to take up a knife. A weapon for me, and for you."

Gregor shrugs uncertainly.

"Who are you?" he asks.

"I've told you my name."

Gregor pauses before asking the next question, not sure if he wants the answer.

"What are you?"

"Old. Too old. You have to travel the world, because I no longer can."

An object lands beside Gregor, a short metal tube.

"I'll return to you when it's done," Jace Tan says. "Perhaps then you can see me."

"But—"

A rustle, a flurry of movement, a heavy splash, and then the presence is gone, leaving a deep, dark hole in Gregor's life.

Gregor had imagined the owner of that voice a thousand times, building up an image in his mind of what such a great, powerful old man Jace Tan might look like. It was never anything like this.

The figure stood proud in the sunlight, naked but for a skirt of heavy red cloth. One great foot pressed the girl down onto the road. He stood nine or ten feet tall, his dark skin weathered by time and age, scarred and marked by conflict. In all his years hunting and killing Kin of all shapes and sizes, Gregor had never seen anything like him. He wiped blood from his eyes and stood, leaning back against the crashed car. He could only stare.

"My name is Mallian," the huge man said. His face was beautiful but severe, and Gregor imagined an age of rage having sharpened those soft features, drawing his brow into a vicious ridge, his eyes into deep piercing pits. He exuded anger. It was a pressure in the air, a gravity tugging everyone and everything toward him to meet the judgement he would hand out.

"Mallian," Gregor said, dropping to one knee. "My lord. My life."

"Is it finished?" Mallian asked. His lips might have twitched, but they would surely never smile.

"Almost."

"Almost," Mallian said. "The time is close. Closer than ever before… and you tell me *almost*."

"I… I've been trying my best." Gregor looked at Mallian's foot, so large that it covered the girl's entire back. She twitched, but couldn't move from where he had her pinned. He could crush her with one small step.

"You've had a rich few days," Mallian said.

"Yes. Richer than all the past three years, but I'm still looking for…"

Gregor's words trailed off as he noticed for the first time the shapes behind Mallian, both in the road and sheltered within the shadows of fruit trees and hanging vines. One was a small man with simple dark clothing and flaming red hair. Gregor would never forget his own run-in with a piskie. The man stared at him, and Gregor tore his gaze away, unwilling to become pixie-led.

An old woman stood in the road thirty feet behind Mallian, still as a statue but for the breath that misted at her mouth. She wore a necklace of pale objects that might have been bones. Beside the road, hunched down, was a large creature that resembled an otter. Between blinks it changed to a woman, an otter, a woman again, and the changes were so rapid that Gregor believed they must have been in his perception of her rather than literal. He had heard of the kooshdakhaa, one of many animal spirits of the North American continent, but this was his first time seeing one.

Hiding in the fruit bushes was a large hairy man, peering out between plants. Gregor couldn't quite distinguish his scale, but thought he was almost as large as Mallian. Sasquatch? Perhaps. Of all the Kin he had met and studied, it was ironic that this most popular of the mythical beasts was the one in which he had never found cause to believe.

"You've brought friends," Gregor said.

"We all need friends," Mallian said. He looked down at the girl beneath his foot. For a second Gregor thought he was going to bear down and crush the life from her, but instead he removed his foot and scooped her up, a single huge hand closing around her waist. He raised her to eye level, examined her, then approached Gregor with the girl hanging by his side. She was limp and unmoving.

"Do you still carry the Script?"

"Of course!" Gregor said. The idea of not having it with him was as ridiculous as traveling without his backpack full of Kin prizes… or his feet, or his hands. They were all an integral part of him.

"How close are you?" Mallian asked. "What else do you need?"

"Only two parts," Gregor said. "A witch's third ear and eye, and—"

"The blood of a fairy's second heart," Mallian said, nodding. "And that's so close."

"Up in the hills," Gregor said. "I was going there. I've been following the trail." He nodded at the girl. "She's one of the twice-struck, and she'll get me there."

"You've been doing wonderful work, Gregor," Mallian said. "I'm here to help you finish your task." He looked over his shoulder and muttered something. Though the old woman wasn't close, she seemed to hear his whispered words, tilting her head. Her eyes widened. She glanced left and right, as if assessing her position. Others closed in around her—the small pixie, the otter woman, now in human form. The hairy man emerged from the crops and strode over the ditch onto the road. He wasn't as tall as Gregor had first thought, but he was stocky and strong, muscles built on muscles. He wore loose trousers and a rough shirt. His face was leathery and inhuman.

"This is Jilaria Bran," Gregor said as the old woman came closer. "She has something of what you need."

The old woman came close, standing beside Mallian and looking down on Gregor with a sneer. He was far beneath her, a fly to a spider, shivering beneath her gaze. Sharp fingers probed and explored across his skin, scratching here, pinching there.

"He's worse than human," Jilaria Bran said.

"He's a friend," Mallian said, "and his purpose is important. You know that."

"As is mine," she said.

"As is *ours*!" Mallian said, his loud voice sending a vibration through the ground.

Gregor blinked and imagined himself as a small boy, back on that marsh island, ignorant of all the things the world contained and wishing to know more. Mallian had given him a purpose back then, a great destiny, to become Kin and bridge between worlds. He had a feeling he was about to have his perceptions widened once again.

"But I've lived so long," Jilaria Bran said, voice quieter.

"You'll be remembered as one of the greatest," Mallian said. He placed his free hand across her back and pulled her in close, crouching down and hugging her to him. She was half his height. He pressed his forehead to hers and they whispered to each other, words Gregor could not hear.

Engines sounded in the distance. Dust clouds rose around a bend in the road, and Gregor tensed, expecting the harsh blare of sirens at any moment. He would run into the fields. Mallian and the Kin would do the same, and he would lose the girl, this strange girl who he'd thought was Kin but might not be at all.

The vehicles that came around the bend weren't police cars. One was a small car, the other a truck with piles of raw timber in the back. They slowed as they approached the scene in the road, then stopped a hundred yards away.

A short fat man stepped from the car.

Mallian stood to his full, incredible height once more

and turned to face the new arrivals. Gregor didn't hear, but he saw the man mouth the words, *Oh my God.*

"Jeremiah," Mallian said. The hairy man disappeared into the fruit trees beside the road, and seconds later he leapt from the field closer to the two vehicles. Another man was leaving the truck. Jeremiah punched him to the ground, and Gregor heard the meaty impact as his fists connected. The fat man standing beside the lead car backed away, and a shape in the passenger seat slid down as if to hide.

"Bring them," Mallian called.

Jeremiah did as he was told, dragging the floored man behind him, clawing open the car door and dragging out a woman, nodding at the fat man to lead the way. The kooshdakhaa woman and the pixie went to help.

There was unbridled terror in the eyes of the newcomers. It was a look he had seen before, but never directed at him, because he was just a man with body modifications, a faux-Kin who dreamed that he was more. An oddity, a madman with a blade.

But soon I will be *Kin,* he thought, and he smiled at Jilaria Bran.

A witch's third ear and eye.

23

As they swept around the bend in the road and Angela saw the scene before them, her shock was echoed by Lilou's single breathed, disbelieving word.

"Mallian."

No one else spoke. The surprise was too intense, a palpable thickening of the atmosphere inside the Jeep.

Mallian turned and looked their way, and Angela saw the small shape in his left hand.

"Sammi!" she cried. "He's got Sammi!"

Vince powered along the road, skidding to a halt twenty yards from the car that was nose-down in a ditch.

"Angela," Lilou said, holding her arm. "Be careful."

"Careful?" All she cared about was Sammi. The girl seemed slumped in Mallian's grasp, held up off the ground by the giant Nephilim.

"Mallian has his ambitions," Lilou said.

"And aren't they yours as well?" Vince snapped.

Angela was confused, but she brushed it all aside. She and Meloy opened their doors at the same time, and as she jumped from the vehicle, Angela tried to assess the situation. They had arrived in the middle of something. It was a standoff of some sort, and Lilou's words rang back.

"Be careful."

A bloodied man stood close to the crashed car. Most likely that was Gregor, and she caught the glint of a blade in his left hand. Beside Mallian stood the witch Jilaria Bran, and behind them along the road was the pixie Thorn. She had last seen all three of them outside Mary Rock's burning house, that night in London, and finding them here in broad daylight was surreal, so much so that she blinked to clear her vision, doubting herself.

How the hell did they get here? And why?

There were two vehicles further along the road, both standing abandoned with their doors open. A man and woman walked in front of a big, hairy man. The hairy man dragged someone along the road behind him.

And there was someone else. A woman, or a creature, or both. The woman was naked and sleek, pale-skinned and with auburn hair and damp skin. The creature she might have been had brown fur and graceful lines. She changed constantly between blinks, and only when Angela caught her from the corner of her eye did her image settle into one or the other.

Somehow, for some reason, Mallian had come, and he had gathered North American Kin to his cause.

Angela picked up her pace and ran forward, Meloy close behind her. She heard Vince clamber from the Jeep and call her name, but she wouldn't stop, not even for him. She wouldn't stop for anyone.

Pausing by the crashed car, she circled around its rear end, keeping Gregor in view.

"Angela," Mallian said.

"That's my niece," she said. Her heart was thumping. She had never seen the Nephilim so clearly, so exposed to the daylight, and she could not help feeling that a line had been crossed. He wore only a scrap of clothing, but nothing could hide his size and inhumanity. He was a monster, his shadow cast across them all.

"This?" he asked, lifting Sammi in one hand. She stirred, but only a little. "She's well."

"Put her down."

Mallian stood taller. "You'd dare order me—"

"Put her the *fuck* down, Mallian!" Angela shouted. She heard gasps around her, and she didn't care if they were human or Kin. "Put her down and get out of my life!"

"I'm not in your life," he said. "You're in mine, and for now I need to keep hold of this girl." The figure in his grip squirmed.

"Sammi?" Angela said. "It's Aunt Angela, I'm here. I'm here to help."

The hairy man pushed a fat man and a woman to the ground behind Mallian, and then heaved the groggy person he'd been dragging so that he landed beside them.

"Keep watch on them, Jeremiah," Mallian said.

"Mallian, why are you here?" Lilou asked. "*How* are you here?"

"You didn't know he was coming?" Vince asked.

"Of course not."

"Well, if he wanted exposure, this is the way to do it," Meloy said. The awe in his voice was obvious. The fear, too. Angela didn't think she'd ever heard the London gang boss sounding so afraid.

She stepped forward. Vince held her arm but she tugged, and when he gripped tighter she turned and slapped his arm away, glaring at him.

"It's dangerous," he whispered.

"It's always dangerous," she said. Turning again, walking toward Mallian and the innocent orphaned girl in his grasp, she kept one eye on Gregor to her left.

"Jilaria Bran," Mallian said. "You have been my friend."

Still holding Sammi in his left hand, Mallian brought the witch to his side with his right. Angela saw a strange look in the old woman's eyes. Terror, and then a calm acceptance. Her expression softened, and she looked up at the Nephilim she might have known for five hundred years.

Mallian closed his huge hand around the back of the witch's neck, fingers meeting at her throat. She did not blink.

The scene froze, all movement ceased, and a gentle breeze brushing through the fields of fruit bushes dropped, as if the land itself was paying attention to this scene that should never be.

With one sharp twist and tug, Mallian ripped the witch's head from her body. She made a single sharp squeal as her neck stretched, then bones snapped and flesh ripped, and her body dropped to the ground at his feet.

Angela made a sound, something between a sob and a scream.

Mallian held the head in his hand and looked at it for a while, as if possessed of a deep, silent sadness. For that moment Angela believed the Nephilim to be on his own. Perhaps he was remembering old times, reliving old memories he had shared with the witch. Or maybe he was thinking only of the future.

"He's gone mad," Vince said. "He's insane."

"More than before?" Meloy asked.

"No," Lilou said, quietly so that Mallian could not hear. "He's moving on. This is Ascent."

"Gregor!" Mallian said, and he held out his hand. The man stepped forward and grasped the head by the hair, lowering it to the ground and kneeling beside it, knife poised.

"Stomp him!" Lilou shouted. "Mallian, that's the Kin-killer. Crush him!"

Mallian barely glanced at her.

As Gregor started carving into the head, Angela began to move again. She walked toward Mallian and her niece. This time Vince didn't try to stop her, but came with her. She was grateful to him for that. They had lived together, and when the time came she was sure that they would die together. Even if that time were now.

"I don't care about any of this," Angela said. "Just give me my niece and we'll go. Do whatever it is you have to do, Mallian. I don't give a shit."

"Oh my God!" someone shouted. "My God, help me Lord, my God!" It was the fat man from the car, grasping onto the woman he'd been traveling with. Behind him the other man was sitting up, dazed, face bloodied, and he froze in place when he saw what was happening. None of them could understand. The creatures, the headless woman, the terror.

"Mallian?" the hairy man standing over them asked. There was an eagerness in his voice.

"Of course, Jeremiah," Mallian said.

The violence that erupted then was brutal and shocking. Angela had seen its like before, in the house where Mary Rock and her sick group of diners had died. Vince and Meloy had seen it, too, and perhaps

Meloy had perpetrated such acts, even if some of the stories about him were untrue. Out here in the rich dawn light on a wide country road cutting through the heart of America, it seemed so much more shocking and unreal.

The blood looked much redder.

The hairy man fell on the fat man and his companion, pummeling them with his fists, stomping on them when they fell, and he seemed to have the strength of an ape, heavy fists swinging with dizzying speed, dull wet thuds interspersed with the sharp crunch of bone. He laughed as he worked, a high-pitched giggle that verged on hysterical.

The fat man was soon motionless, but the woman managed to crawl across the road and tumble into the ditch at the roadside. She left a trail of blood behind her. Jeremiah went after her on hands and feet, following the gory trail and jumping on her in the ditch, ripping and thumping. His giggle rose even higher. Angela was glad she could not see, but the sounds were awful.

The other man who'd been stirring on the road stood and ran back toward the vehicles at the sight of such horrific violence. He staggered as he went, still dizzied from whatever had put him down in the first place. He didn't get very far.

The shape that darted at him looked almost comical, but Angela knew that Thorn was anything but. The pixie tackled the man's legs and brought him down, then scrambled up his back and grabbed hold of his hair. Three heavy impacts on the road and the man was still, but the creature kept slamming his face into the ground. Blood splashed Thorn's clothing. He didn't care. If anything, he seemed to welcome its warm wet kiss.

"Give her to me," Angela said. Her heart hammered even harder as she looked at Sammi in the Nephilim's grasp. Her niece seemed limp and unconscious, but Angela saw what the Kin leader could not. She was feigning. The girl was looking right at her. Angela offered a vague smile, and Sammi closed her eyes.

She thinks Vince and I are killers, Angela thought. *Maybe she thinks we're with them.* But she couldn't let that affect her now. Whatever Sammi had heard about them, on the news or from family and friends, it was a lie. Angela would do everything in her power to make her understand that.

"Only I say what happens here," Mallian said. He gestured behind him at the murdered people. "You've seen that."

Jeremiah crawled from the ditch, and he had blood on his face. He was carrying something. At first Angela couldn't make out what it was, but when he lifted it to his mouth and took a gaping bite, muffling his mad laughter at last, she recognized a forearm and hand.

She gagged, turned away, and saw Vince staring pale-faced at what was happening.

Mallian looked, as well. "Oh, Jeremiah, that's disgusting." He sounded amused.

Jeremiah shrugged, swallowed. "I am what I am."

Mallian turned back to Gregor. "Time is short. There'll be more along soon, so you should hurry."

"Kill him!" Lilou shouted. She stepped toward the Kin-killer, Meloy with her. Gregor crouched above the witch's head like a dog with a bone, jabbing his knife at the air between them. Mallian put himself in the way.

"He's doing something for me," the Nephilim said. The nymph and the gangster stopped as he stared them down.

"Mallian…" Lilou said. "You could have trusted me."

"Should I have?" he asked. "You consort with humans."

"*He's* a human!" She gestured at Gregor.

"Not for long," Gregor said. He dug, cut, sawed at the head, and with a crack he opened up the dead Kin's skull, reaching inside and removing a slippery black object the size of a plum.

"What?" Angela asked. "What's he doing? What have you told him, Mallian?"

Gregor stood with the object and showed it to Mallian, smiling with pride.

Mallian nodded. "Close," he said. "You're close."

"Thank you," Gregor said. He nodded down at the girl in the Nephilim's grasp. "It would be much easier with her."

"No!" Angela shouted. As she stepped forward her vision blurred and then the naked woman was in front of her, image flickering as if caught between two frames of a film. Woman, otter, part of both, her nudity was threatening, her animal teeth sharp and yellowed with age and use.

Angela lashed out. The woman must not have been expecting trouble from this human. Angela's fist connected with her jaw and she went down, sharp teeth clashing, furred body striking the road. She grunted and was on her feet again, clawed hands raking the air as she came for Angela.

Angela ducked and punched again, but this time she missed as the otter woman twisted aside and kicked her legs out from beneath her. Then the creature was on her, smelling of sweat and stale water, and her mouth opened wide to display sharp teeth clotted with old meat.

The otter-woman screeched as she was shoved away from Angela, and then Vince was crouching at her side. He held a short knife in one hand, offered up to anyone who might attack them again.

Angela stood and brushed herself down.

"No more," Mallian bellowed. The Nephilim's thunderous voice was enough to halt the scuffle, freezing everyone in their place. No one could confront him and win. Tall, strong, proud, he had chanced the hazardous journey to North America for a reason, and Angela knew there was no talking him out of it.

Sammi was looking at her again, her eyes this time wider with recognition. Angela smiled and nodded, and the corner of Sammi's mouth flickered. But she had seen so much, been through so much, and now she was in the hands of a creature she could have never imagined and would never understand. Angela wanted to sweep the girl into her arms and protect her, and to take comfort from the contact.

She had been away from her family for too long.

"Why kill them?" Lilou said.

"Jeremiah needs to fuel himself," Mallian said. "Besides, it's too early to be exposed. Ascent has a way to go, but only a short way. You're still part of it, Lilou. Still my friend."

Lilou did not reply.

Jeremiah chewed on something plucked from one of the other dead people now, and the wet chomping sounds were audible. Angela's stomach heaved, but she swallowed down the bile. She wouldn't demean herself in front of these monsters.

"And I'm still your friend, Lilou," Mallian said. "Too many years to throw away."

"Friends trust each other," she said.

Mallian dropped Sammi at Gregor's feet. The girl stood, unsteady, and Angela dashed for her, but Mallian was quick, and she ran into his heavy arm. She had never been this close to him. She could smell his breath, feel his heat, feel the weight of this huge creature. She feared him, but that didn't stop her from hating him.

"You have no idea," she said, looking up into his big face. "No idea about love or caring for anyone else."

"I care for everyone who matters!"

"Like her?" Angela nodded past him at Jilaria Bran's headless corpse.

Mallian shoved her to the ground. She didn't even see it coming, and it was like being hit by a tree. Winded, dazed, Angela rolled onto her side and watched as the huge Kin waved to the others around him. Thorn and the cannibal Jeremiah vanished into the fields of fruit. The naked otter-woman was already gone.

Gregor grabbed Sammi's arm and dragged her past Mallian toward the murdered people and their cars.

"Please!" Angela shouted.

"Don't beg him," Vince said, kneeling by her side. "Don't plead. We'll follow, and we'll kill the bastard who has her."

Angela could only watch. She was aware of Meloy and Lilou standing close behind her, and the sense of hopelessness was profound and shattering. Four of them could not take on Mallian and win. Eight couldn't do it, nor sixteen. He held power over them, like a raised foot forever ready to fall on an ant. There was nothing they could do within his shadow.

Out of it, they might fare better.

Gregor pushed Sammi into the dead man's truck and got in himself, pulling the door shut, performing a rapid turn in the road, and then driving away. Mallian watched him go, leaning against the dead couple's car, tensing, and heaving it over onto its roof. He grabbed at the tires and ripped them into shreds, one of the wheels coming off in his hand.

"I hate you," Angela said as Mallian ran past them toward their Jeep. He glanced at her. He'd heard, and that was the only satisfaction she could take from this.

Behind them, she heard the sound of the Jeep being beaten out of action by the Nephilim. Then a few pounding footsteps, a rustle of branches and undergrowth, and he was gone.

"We've got to get the fuck away from here," Meloy said. "Now."

"What's four more dead bodies to my name?" Angela said. Then she spun on Lilou. "You've got some explaining to do."

"I *will* explain," Lilou said, "but not here. Just know that I'm sorry."

Hearing "sorry" from the nymph made Angela angrier than if she'd fought back. She started to spit out a reply.

"I can follow," a voice said.

Angela glanced around and Ahara was with them, standing behind Meloy at the edge of the road.

"How?" Angela asked.

"I have the Kin-killer's scent now. I can follow, but we have to hurry, because the trail won't last forever."

"We need a new car," Meloy said, looking around at the three wrecked vehicles. Bodies lay bloodied and mutilated in the road.

"Across the fields," Ahara said. "This way. A farmstead."

As the wisp left the road, glowing into the rows of fruit trees, Angela tilted her head to the sound of distant engines. "Someone's coming."

They jumped across the ditch and entered the trees. Hope was slipping away, but the recognition Angela had seen in Sammi's eyes meant that she had to grasp onto it with both hands.

24

He is shut away from the eyes of the world.

The brief exposure to American sun felt good, and even though only for a short time, it allowed him to sense the vastness of this land, the epic scale and scope of its landscape. The countless places there are to hide. He might never return to London—he has yet to decide—but if he does leave his longtime home behind forever, he knows that this new world will afford him a suitable place to continue his plans. Plans that are drawing toward an important juncture.

Meanwhile, though she gave herself to the cause of Ascent, he cannot help but mourn Jilaria Bran.

The van sways and rocks as it heads toward a safe place nearby, and in the darkness of its interior, he remembers some of their times together, both good and bad. They were not always friends. Once, he was more inclined to protect the humans than to harm them, and Jilaria Bran chided him for what she thought of as his weakness.

In troubled times along the borderlands between England and Wales, with French nobles building castles and probing into the Welsh mountains, Jilaria Bran plied her trade. Luring unsuspecting travelers, peasants, and French soldiers into her clutches with promises of salvation or revenge, she built a grisly store of human body parts with which to experiment in the magical arts. She fed and entertained them first, and made love to some, never letting them spill their seed inside her but collecting it for use in strange potions. After a time—sometimes hours, other times days—she killed them and took them apart.

Useful portions she treated and stored, pickling some in vinegar, curing others in a network of deep caverns that lay beneath her shack in the woods. Those remnants she could not use were fed to her pigs. She took pleasure in telling him how her bacon was renowned in the area for its richness.

The witch was, perhaps, the first relics collector, although one who gathered human body parts rather than Kin.

She was careful to hide her activities, and sometimes when the moon was but a sliver and the woods were darker and more dangerous than ever she would venture out, naked, and cast her spells. She never told him what those spells were.

"*We all have our secrets,*" Jilaria Bran said. "*My spells are mine.*" Now they would remain secrets forever.

He saw her sometimes, back then, when he allowed himself out of hiding to prowl the deep forests of those places. By that time he had been hidden away for millennia, too large ever to pass for a normal man. But he'd found remote places to stay—caverns, ruins, deep valleys where no humans dared explore. From there he still could interact with the world, from time to time.

He and Jilaria Bran argued about her activities. He

told her they were cruel, and would attract attention to her Kin ways.

"We have to stay hidden," he told her. *"Our time has been and gone."*

In return, she insisted that she wasn't about to be driven down into holes and hovels. Besides, she said, those who had cause to suspect she wasn't human tended to disappear. Their hides, heads, and hands hung in her caves.

Finally he left that place and headed north. He didn't see Jilaria Bran again for almost three hundred years. In that time she did not change, but he did. He sometimes thought it was she who planted the seed of his discontent, nurturing the ideas of rebellion that would eventually manifest as Ascent.

Now she is gone. That amazing witch, that murderess, that propagator of ideas. He asked her to give herself to the cause, and she did so without question. Mallian hopes that in her final moments she thought back to those earlier times, and recognized that she was always right.

The humans will never be superior to the Kin.

It is the Kin who are superior.

He closes his eyes and his head sways as the van rocks. He knows he will not sleep. They are too close to their goal, and he feels glad that Jilaria Bran will play a vital part in events.

But Mallian is not conflicted. He has let Gregor go, and will capture him again when the time is right.

Soon, he thinks. *That will be soon. Then I'll crush him like the stupid, gullible human maggot he is, and Jilaria Bran and all his Kin victims can sleep avenged.*

* * *

She is shut away from the eyes of the world.

This is what she has always wanted, and the final part of her dream is at last coming to pass. Yet a fairy is not a solitary creature, and with eternity to spend in this Fold she has created, she will no longer be alone.

Four Kin have come to her so far, all of them brought by the wraiths she tasked. She has let the wraiths free, as she promised. She understands that dragging them back from the beyond has meant a form of torture for them, but their joy at being released is enough to balance against that.

She is beyond guilt.

Joy, she can feel. Already the Fold is changing, and although there is a small route still open into and out of the real world, in here the rules and laws are flexing and adapting to her will. Time stretches and twists, and she has already been here for a hundred days. Landscapes grow and morph to her desires, and at the northern end of the Fold the rocks have stretched up into delicate arches, glittering with quartz and other fine reflective crystals, embracing a series of pools and waterfalls where a mermaid now frolics.

Her name is Shashahanna. Until recently she was Sasha, a young woman living and working in Boston who had been human for forty years. She had a boyfriend and many other human companions, and if her reality sometimes slipped, she pulled it back, denying her true nature. She has told the fairy about her human life as a denier. Although she began her time in the Fold missing the humans she professed to love, her reality has quickly changed.

She visits Shashahanna on occasion, watching from

the high hillsides as the mermaid dips into and out of the pools, leaping across the spits of land and swimming on her back, watching herself reflected in the stone bridges arcing across the water and reveling in her newfound truth. Sometimes Shashahanna laughs, sometimes she cries tears of joy, whooping and singing songs of water and air. She is happy, and the fairy feels the reflection of her happiness in her own ancient heart.

Further along the valley and higher up its side, a small cave has been opened up. Spread around its mouth and down the hillside are slicks of rubble and shale. She walks past from time to time, but she is content to let the dwarf Dastion do his work. It's been a long time since he has allowed himself to dig. She hears his singing echoing from the depths, and probing with her fairy senses she can feel down into the ground. The Fold goes deep—even she is not certain how deep, because she has allowed it to sink down and embrace depths she will likely never see—and her senses float her through the mines and hollows he has already formed.

An expert at excavation, Dastion has moved many tons of rock. Three tunnels twist and turn into the hillside, two sunken shafts are underway, and there are levels down there where he has discovered gold, diamonds, and at least four places where the teeth of dragons are still bitten into the ground. Their clasp is sure, even in death. Dastion has marked these areas as special, and the fairy understands that they will keep him occupied for a long time to come.

Perhaps one day he might even bring a dragon's tooth to the surface. That will be an interesting moment. No dragon's tooth has seen daylight since deep in the Time, and she cannot tell how such an exposure might affect the Fold.

Times have changed.

Dastion was brought to the Fold by the wraith of a mothman, taken from his home in a Chicago suburb. Dastion admitted to her that he was a denier, and had been for ten decades. Yet he has always been a sad dwarf, had taken to drink and drugs, his body wracked with sickness. Unhappiness marked every year of his denial, and she could not imagine a place less dwarf-like than a city, where even subterranean places crawled with the blight of humanity.

Dastion took to the Fold more naturally than any of the three Kin who arrived before him. He has been more grateful to her, and more ready to embrace the experiment she is overseeing. She and Dastion are already friends.

Fer the shapeshifter has taken longer to adapt. She is a fighter, and she struggled all the way into the Fold. Even after arriving she continued her fight, grasping onto her denial even as she shifted from human to beast, beast to human. Each change caused her untold agonies, and her screams echoed across the valley, bringing Dastion to the surface to see what was happening, causing Shashahanna to dive into her deepest pool so that she could not hear the sounds of distress.

The fairy took a whole day to calm Fer down. That night the shapeshifter cried, but the following morning she awoke to the most amazing sunrise, prepared by the fairy's magic and setting the eastern half of the Fold aflame with all colors of the rainbow, and some colors never before seen by humans.

This made Fer see the wonderful truth. For as long

as she had been a denier, her perceptions had been closed to such wonders. Her body had been human. Her true nature—the freedom to change and dance through countless permutations—had been constrained by the life she chose. The fairy understands the deniers and what they craved. However, acceptance and freedom in a world of humans meant *being* a human, or at least feigning humanity. It was a false existence.

Now Fer runs through the Fold, relishing her newfound freedom, her spirit given wing. From hilltop to valley, end to end, she sprints and calls out in whatever voice her current incarnation takes. The fairy has heard the howl of a dog, the screech of a bird, the cry of a deer, the bark of a fox. Sometimes Fer runs as a human, naked and free in a world she must have imagined only in her dreams, but which she never thought she would see again. Though not of the original Time, still Fer is embracing this *new* Time that the fairy has granted her.

Hengle the werewolf, the man who was Jeff, has also made himself entirely at home. He lives in a small building on the western slopes, its walls and roof raised from the ground by fairy magic. He has experienced one change here, and in that time he hunted some of the few animals that remained from the real world, to persist within the Fold.

He will need more food, however. The fairy will create it for him. She will look after all her new friends, because they are here to keep her company.

And more. They are here for something more. But the Fold is still young, and there is no need for her to reveal that other purpose. Not yet.

This Time is hers, and she can take her time.

25

The attack came from the place Lilou least expected it.

Still in shock at seeing Mallian, she was even more shocked at witnessing Jilaria Bran's sacrifice to his cause. She had known the witch for some time, and though they had never been close, like all Kin who lived in a loose group there was a bond between them. Born of survival and nurtured through danger, this bond was as instinctive as breathing. It wasn't something that could be easily forgotten.

She was dwelling on Jilaria Bran's death when the hands grabbed her and flung her to the ground.

"Answers," he breathed into her face. Meloy loved her, but Lilou more than anyone knew that love could also inspire pain, anger, and hurt. "We need answers, and now!" His weight forced her down, crushing the air from her lungs. She knew that she owed them all answers, and perhaps revealing the bigger picture might enable her to solidify her place within it.

"I can tell you everything," she said. "I will. Please get off me, Frederick."

He blinked down at her, almost close enough to kiss. She felt his breath. His anger was palpable, and she could feel him shivering. Letting her go, he stood and stepped back. As Lilou too stood, and brushed herself off, she met Angela's gaze. Then Vince's.

She felt a rush of shame for misleading them.

Lilou had been lying to them from the start.

"I'm going to steal a car," Vince said. "Easier on my own. You stay here and find out…" He looked at Lilou. "Everything." He kissed Angela and moved away, heading for a large farmstead they'd come across a couple of miles from the road. They had already heard sirens, screaming from town and halting at the scene of the slaughter. They had to move soon.

Everything depended on following Gregor's tail.

For now, however, sweating and panting from their run through the fruit fields, they were ready for the truth.

"I wasn't expecting Mallian to be here," she said. "He sent me with you, Meloy, to track Gregor, but only because he knew Gregor would lead us to the fairy."

"How the fuck did he know that?"

"Gregor is a Kin-killer, and he knows how to hunt us. Lightning strikes are a method fairies have used before for killing enemies, but in this case Grace was using them for something else. Marking Kin who have denied their heritage, it seems, then drawing them to her."

"Sammi's not Kin," Angela said.

Lilou shrugged. She didn't know the truth of that.

"But why is she drawing them to her?" Angela asked.

"Mallian believes she's trying to remove herself from our world," Lilou said. "Leave it all behind."

"Kill herself?"

"Fairies rarely die," Lilou said. "Mary Rock discovered that. No, it's more likely that she is making a Fold. An alternate pocket in reality, cut off from this world. There's a precedent for it. The story is part of Kin mythology, although there are a few still alive who remember it."

"Like Mallian," Angela said.

"Like Mallian."

"But why did he send you to find the fairy?" Meloy asked. "What's his interest in her? We rescued her, she fucked off. It seems pretty obvious she doesn't want anything to do with him, or with us."

"It was a mistake on his part," Lilou said. "A misunderstanding. Mallian hoped that rescuing Grace from Mary Rock would gain her trust and confidence. Instead, she fled and came here."

"But why does he want her?" Meloy asked again, more forcefully.

"Ascent," Angela said.

"Yes," Lilou said. "Grace might be the last of the fairies. The only one seen in many centuries. It was assumed that most had finally died, and those who did survive into the modern era have likely removed themselves, just as Grace intends to do."

"They're powerful," Angela said. "That's why he wants her. That's why he rescued her from Mary Rock."

"More powerful than you know," Lilou said. "Back in the Time, many of the Kin possessed forms of magic, weak and strong, elemental and transmutational. Even nymphs like me could spin spells and cast wards, though only weak ones. As time went on most of us lost the ability, and as humanity grew and cast their own spells across the world, our magic leaked away. I've still got a touch of it, as most Kin have. In me it manifests as little more than an instinct, an attraction. I have some control over it, but I'm a passive carrier rather than a wielder. I have little choice over what I can do, or how powerful it is." She looked at Meloy. "You've witnessed it, and felt it."

Meloy nodded. He looked grim-faced. "And Grace?"

"Fairies are the Kin that kept the greatest distance from the world of humans. As humanity grew, spread, and cast its influence wider and more powerfully across the globe, the fairies retreated. They found their way into hidden valleys and wild woodlands. They removed themselves, and when people started to venture even into those remote places, the fairies took themselves further. But they always kept their magic, and that's what Mallian wants."

"He can't accomplish Ascent without the fairy's magic?" Angela asked.

"I don't think so," Lilou said. "He's been talking for a long time about revealing ourselves to humanity, and taking a new place in the world. He's never been clear about what that new place might be, and he's always been one step away from moving forward with Ascent. As you know, he has his supporters. There are factions in Britain, and a few over here, just waiting for his word. At the first sign Ascent is beginning, these factions will reveal themselves."

"How?" Angela asked.

"In public. In the media. Some through violence. All from a position of strength."

"And you?" Meloy asked.

"I've spent a long time on the fence," Lilou replied. "Part of me wants what he wants, a life where hiding isn't our main concern. Another part of me understands that our time has been and gone, and seeks to accept it."

"Everything would change," Angela said. "Every religion, every belief system, it would all be challenged if the Kin really come to the fore. You can't just throw magic and myth into the world without expecting upheaval. It'll be *chaos*."

"Worse than chaos," Meloy said. "There's no way Ascent could be peaceful. Humans don't work like that. We strike out against what we don't know and what confuses or scares us. We don't welcome it. It won't be chaos, it'll be war."

"That's why he wants Grace," Lilou said. "With the fairy and her magic on his side, humanity wouldn't have any choice."

"Even though she's made it clear she just wants to vanish into this Fold," Angela said.

"For a long time that confused me," Lilou said. "I always thought Mallian was full of grand plans that would never see fruition. Before we knew Mary Rock was holding Grace, finding and joining with her was just a dream. And even after we knew, and were planning to rescue her, I never thought he'd get Grace on his side. But I think Gregor has something to do with that. Gregor and the relics he's been hunting, stealing from the Kin all these years."

"For what purpose?" Meloy asked.

"For a spell," Lilou said. "Mallian still has a touch of magic himself, and his is stronger than most. I think he set Gregor on this course long ago, and the relics he's gathering will form part of a spell that will control Grace."

"Gregor's being duped."

"Of course. He's a gullible human. Mallian is using him, and lying to him."

"But what if the fairy gets into her Fold?" Angela asked.

"Mallian and Gregor will follow. Until she closes it off, it's still part of this world, though hidden away. There will still be connections, a few narrow, ill-defined routes."

"Why here?" Meloy asked.

Lilou shrugged. She could offer no answer, and she was glad to see that they accepted her lack of knowledge.

"But if Mallian does manage to draw Grace to him, using whatever spell he might be conceiving... everything will change," she said. "The whole world as it is now will change. Meloy's right, it could be catastrophic. Ascent..." She shook her head, feeling the pressure of forbidden knowledge striving for escape. *These are only humans*, she thought, but at the same time she realized a solid, comforting truth. They were also her friends.

"We cannot allow Mallian to control Grace," she said. "It's all happened before."

"What has?" Angela asked.

"Ascent," Lilou said. "A form of it, at least. There are stories. It was a long time ago, before I was born, and it didn't end well for anyone."

"What about Sammi?" Meloy asked.

"She's Gregor's route to Grace," Angela said, "and Mallian will follow. So tell us the stories, Lilou. Tell us everything you know. Until Vince gets back, we've got time."

Not much, I fear, Lilou thought.

* * *

Vince edged his way behind a large red barn. The area was used to store old and broken farm machinery, and he had to work his way over and around rusting equipment, trying not to make a noise, alert for movement. He'd spied on the farmstead for a couple of minutes before moving in, and made sure no one was home. Or if they were, they were in the big house, and not outside working.

They'll have heard the sirens, he thought. *They'll be wondering what's happened, and if they come out to see they might spot me. And like most farmers and a lot of other Americans, they'll have guns.*

The thought froze him to the spot, leaning against a car-sized machine that looked like a cross between a thresher and a baler. He was already trespassing on their land. If they had heard about the incident on the road they'd shoot first and ask questions later. Which made it even more important for him to find a car and leave, quickly and quietly.

Moving around the end of the barn and into a wider yard, he kept another smaller building between him and the main farmhouse. The ground here was scorched grass, dusty and dry, and he trod carefully to avoid making too much noise.

Three vehicles were parked across the yard, two trucks and a big car. The car was a Ford, decades old, so it would be easier to hot-wire. It was also furthest away from the farmhouse. He glanced around, then hurried forward, trying to look as though he belonged here.

Something growled.

Vince stopped, hands in his pockets, acting casual, but he thought of Mallian and the hairy man who had eaten human flesh, and his skin crawled. There was movement to his left. He glanced that way and saw a dog, a scruffy retriever with gray around its snout and a round body testament to a lifetime of treats.

"Good boy," he said, holding out his hand, palm up. He liked dogs, and generally they liked him. He knew that farm dogs could be very different, workers rather than pets. This one might bite off his hand as soon as look at him.

It growled again, crouching a little on its outstretched front paws.

If he ran, the dog would bark and run after him. It might have been old, but it would still catch him within a few steps. If the barking didn't bring the farm owner, his own shouts would as the dog attacked him.

"Good boy, good lad. Come and see, eh?" Vince took a risk and went to one knee, hoping to present a less threatening figure.

The dog tilted its head and started panting, its big tongue drooping from one side of its mouth. Then it trotted over to him and sniffed his hand.

Vince tickled the dog beneath the chin and breathed a sigh of relief. It grumbled as he scratched, turning its head and licking at his hand.

"No time to waste here, mate," he said. "Come on then. You coming?" He stood and walked away, afraid to move too quickly in case the dog thought he was playing and started to bark.

Ten steps from the Ford the dog scampered after him. It stayed by his side as he tried the driver's door and found it open, reached beneath the steering column. Locating the nest of wires, he prepared to tug them out and rip out the connectors. Then he saw the key fob hanging in the ignition.

"Small mercies," he said. With one last glance around he climbed into the car. The dog whined. He gave it a last stroke, then closed the door and started the car.

He drove quickly from the yard, looking in the mirrors and ready to duck down if a gun-toting farmer appeared from the house. But no one seemed to have noticed. All he saw in the rearview was the lonely old dog, watching him go with tail raised as though certain that his new friend would return.

Mallian told me about a previous attempt to rise. It was doomed to fail from the beginning, but he always took hope from the stories. He wasn't there himself—he knew nothing about it until long after it was all over—but he met kin of Kin who *were* there, gathered their stories, became a collector of tales. He studied what happened and took from it what he could. He always told me it was like a Kin myth, handed down from old to new, but remembered by those like him who live long, long lives.

I think it's more like a fairy tale.

It happened during the first of the Crusades. While Palestine was aflame and Jerusalem was under siege, a warrior king came out of the east and marched on the Crusaders with a small but powerful force of his own. His name was Eophorus, and he had been assembling the force for thirteen years.

Eophorus was a centaur, proud and strong, scarred from many conflicts with humans and carrying a dark memory. The love of his life had been staked to the ground and left to die in the sun, called a beast and a monster. He never got over his lover's death, and his plan to rise up against humanity was as much about revenge as it was pride in being Kin.

The army he led were not all Kin. Eophorus had spent most of those thirteen years forming alliances and making promises. Warriors, mercenaries, lost armies looking for a new war, he brought them all and launched them into the greatest battle being fought at the time. His enemies were everyone else—the Turks, the Crusaders, and all parties allied to both sides, bound by faith and the promise of riches.

Eophorus knew that if he defeated these warring armies and took Jerusalem for himself, his name would echo around Europe. He would become known the world over, and the city would be the base for the expansion of the new Kin, and their new Time.

At the head of his army marched a fairy.

No one knows her name. Lost in the mists of history, erased by failure. Eophorus brought her like a figurehead, mounted on the grandest horse his army possessed. He was proud and confident, and knew that no power could match the fairy's magic. When she faced Jerusalem's bloodstained walls and those wretched soldiers battling there, her smile would rip open the sky, and her whisper would sweep all enemies before it with cleansing fire.

The fairy did not whisper or smile.

All combat paused as Eophorus and his forces approached. For a moment there was disbelief, and the soldiers on both sides must have thought they were confronted by demons. Imagine... an army comprised of many Kin, facing people who only knew of them from stories, or local legends, or fleeting glimpses in distant forests and deserts. It should have been a moment of power and glory. It should have been the moment when the story of Eophorus and his ascent truly began. Instead, defeat was seeded in that silent pause on a vast battlefield.

The fairy fled. Vanished. No one saw her leave, and Eophorus was left at the head of an army without its greatest weapon. Shocked, confused, he did the only thing he could to maintain face. He ordered a charge.

Hooves and feet, wings and claws, two legs and four, human faced beast and the battle commenced.

Thus began three days of fighting and dying. It's said that with every thrust of his pike and slash of his sword, Eophorus grinned through a mask of human blood, certain that his fairy was working her magic and would appear to take control close to the battle's end.

The battle ended.

She did not appear.

Eophorus was captured. His surviving troops, Kin and human alike, were massacred, their corpses gathered and burned until their unbelievable faces and bodies were nothing but heat and dust. Then after the Crusaders completed their task and took Jerusalem, Eophorus was staked out in the sun and left to die.

26

The car Vince had stolen had no working air conditioning. With four of them inside, and Ahara sitting between Angela and Meloy in the back seat like some strange haze, they had to keep every window down just to try and stay cool.

"The way he had those people killed..." Angela said. "I had no idea he could be so brutal."

"You saw him at Mary Rock's place," Vince said.

"Yes, but those people were *eating* the Kin," she replied. "He hated them."

"To Mallian, all humans are the same," Lilou said. "He'll crush any that get in his way. He wants to kill you, or rule you. There's no in-between. That's why he's so dangerous."

"Charming friend you have there," Meloy said.

"He's been my friend for hundreds of years," Lilou said, and she sounded so sad that they fell silent.

Angela couldn't shake the memory of Sammi, hanging there in Mallian's hand, helpless and seemingly lifeless, her eyes lighting up only when she finally recognized Angela.

She didn't think I was a murderer, she thought. *Sammi must have thought I was there to save her. But I let her down again. I've been letting her down all my life.*

Now she was in the hands of a human madman, being dragged toward some unknown fate, surrounded by monsters. Angela couldn't bear to imagine what the girl must be going through.

"We're going to need help," she said. "They'll be following Gregor, making sure he finishes whatever it is Mallian's started. The Nephilim's too powerful, especially with those new Kin he has with him. We can't fight him."

"Not on our own," Ahara whispered.

"Can you still follow them?" Angela asked the wisp.

"Moving quickly, but I still have his scent."

"Maybe I can help," Meloy said.

"You?"

"I'm more than just a pretty face."

"How can you help?" Vince asked from the driver's seat.

"I've got contacts," Meloy said. "From my days as a… you know, relic trader." As he said it, he looked nervously at Lilou, but she didn't respond.

"How reliable are they?" Angela asked.

He continued to look uncomfortable. "There's one woman I dealt with for years. Never met her, but I'm pretty sure she still lives close by. We're heading into a million acres of forest, and this region's rich in relics. She also knows…" He didn't finish.

"Knows what?" Lilou asked.

"She knows that you're not just artifacts."

Lilou twisted around in her seat, angry. "You *told* her?"

"She already knew. She also knows how to keep a secret. So that makes her reliable, right?"

"She might be another Mary Rock," Lilou said, and there was a hint of menace in her voice. As subtle as it was, it sent a chill down Angela's spine.

"No," Meloy said. "She'd never do anything to hurt the Kin."

"Why didn't you tell me about her before?" Lilou asked.

"Because of the way you just reacted. I didn't want to give her away, or put her in danger."

"Right. You, worried about putting people in danger."

"I have my loyalties," Meloy said, voice low. "You know that."

"How can she help us?" Angela asked.

"She offers protection to Kin," he said. "She's built a network. She has people."

"And she told all this to you?" Angela asked. "A stranger?"

Meloy shrugged. "She hardly told me anything. You know as well as anyone that the information is out there, if you know how to get it and what you're looking for."

"What will her allegiances be?" Lilou asked.

"I can't know that for sure."

"You have to know before we ask her for help."

"Ahara," Angela said. "We can send Ahara, and if the woman proves dangerous, she can just…"

"Wisp away," Ahara said. Angela had never been certain she could trust the wisp, but the more time she spent with them, the more Angela believed she was on their side.

"Where?" Lilou asked. "How close?" She turned to peer at Meloy. "While we drive there, we need to know everything you know about her."

Meloy pulled out his phone and accessed the net. "We should probably swap cars, too," he said. "Just saying."

"Great," Vince said. "I'm becoming a professional car thief."

Lilou employed her charm to buy a used car from a dealership in a small town called Castanea. They left the stolen one in a sports center parking lot and headed out again.

Every minute they weren't pursuing Sammi put Angela more on edge, but they had to be ready. Confident of success.

After three hours' driving, they arrived at the agreed meeting place for Meloy's contact just before dusk. He had contacted her by phone and filled her in on some of what was happening. Relayed on loudspeaker, to Angela the woman's concern had sounded genuine. They were placing a lot of trust in a stranger, but they had little choice.

Ahara directed them into the hills of the Susquehannock State Forest in central Pennsylvania, first following well-kept roads, then narrower routes that headed up into dense forests and rugged countryside. Eventually these tapered down to single-lane roads, hacked into the landscape and fighting to retain their grip on the land. Trees edged into them, and branches met in places to form a foliage canopy. Grasses and weeds broke through the surface in a slow-motion assault from below.

"End of the line," Vince said as they pulled into a large, open parking area. It followed the slope of the hillside, an expanse of gravel like a dull gray scab over a wound in the land. Theirs was the only vehicle there. He parked and switched off the engine.

As they left the car, the relative quiet was startling. Birdsong was the only sound, a constant background chatter from the heavy forests surrounding the parking lot. Other than that there was nothing—no vehicle noise, no distant rumble of main roads, no sound of humanity. Angela wasn't used to such peace, but if anything it set her more on edge.

"Where is the Fold from here?" she asked Ahara. The wisp was a vague shape in the back seat, and as dusk faded to night, she was becoming more difficult to see. Soon they wouldn't be able to tell whether she was with them at all.

"The Kin-killer is heading east," she said. "A different road, a different route, but soon the roads will end for him too."

"Then everyone's on foot," Vince said. He sounded on edge, and his nervousness was contagious. None of them was dressed or equipped for hiking. They had no food or water, no fresh clothing, and although Angela wore boots, they were only meant for casual walking.

"Yeah, either on foot, or on hoof or wing," Meloy said. "We'll be slower than most Kin in this landscape."

"Let's hope your friend can help with that, if she's even here." Angela turned a slow circle, scanning the shadows and watching for movement. Everything indicated that they were alone, yet at any moment she expected the hairy cannibal Jeremiah to burst from the trees ready to beat them to a pulp. They would put up a fight, but how could humans fight such a beast? Never a fan of firearms, she wished more than ever that they had brought some guns.

Something caught her eye. The sun was down, but dusk still hung over the hillsides, feeding deep shadows beneath the trees and silvering the open space. Close to its far end, a shadow parted from the darkness beneath the branches. It stood motionless, so still that Angela doubted it had moved at all.

"There?" she whispered.

"Yeah," Vince said. He stood close to her right, and as the shadow started walking toward them he held her hand.

"Which one of you's Meloy?" The voice seemed small in such a vast landscape.

The gangster walked forward a few steps, glancing at Angela and Vince as he went. The shadow stopped and changed shape, and Angela realized she'd been carrying something slung over her shoulder. Now she pointed the shape at Meloy as he approached.

Someone had brought a gun, at least.

Meloy and the woman met. She could hear them speaking, but their voices were too low to catch the words. Lilou paced nervously back and forth. Of Ahara there was no sign.

After a couple of minutes Meloy turned and walked back toward them, the woman a few steps behind him. She still had the gun aimed at his back. He didn't seem to care. Angela guessed he'd had guns pointed at him before. As he approached she stopped a dozen steps from them and kept the rifle at waist level, pointing in their general direction. Meloy looked at Angela, smiled, nodded.

"Meet Jolene Jameson," he said. She seemed comfortable holding the weapon, casual, as if it were a permanent fixture. She was tall and thin, gray-haired, but it was difficult to discern her true age. Her skin was smooth and uncreased, but her eyes were old. She moved like someone with aches and pains, or old injuries that had healed badly. Her clothing was loose and brightly colored, an explosion of rainbow shades across her short-sleeved shirt, trousers a bright red. There were shapes knotted into her hair. Angela thought they might have been small ribbons.

"People call me JJ," she said. "Or, you know, just Jay is fine if you don't wanna waste your breath."

"Evening, Jay," Angela said.

"Yeah."

"Frederick tells us you might be able to help."

Jay looked back and forth between them, and then her gaze settled on Lilou, and the older woman's breath caught in her throat. The rifle barrel wavered, dropping lower until it was aimed at their feet.

"Holy shit," Jay said.

"Hello," Lilou said. She must have been used to this reaction, but she sounded uncertain. Perhaps people only ever saw through her mask when she allowed it. Jay saw past it without any effort.

"What're you?" Jay asked.

"A nymph," Lilou said. "A napaea, to be more precise."

"Right. Russian guy offered me a napaeae's left tit once. Least, that's what he said it was. I didn't believe him. He was prone to selling false shit. Dead now, found in a ditch in Minnesota. Best place for the motherfucker."

"We're kind of in a rush," Angela said. "There's a Kin-killer close by, and he's kidnapped my niece."

"She Kin?"

"No."

"We don't know for sure," Vince said. "But this is much more complex than that."

"Yeah, Meloy told me some of what's up. And you need my help."

"If you *can* help?" Angela said.

"Sure I can. Where's this Kin-killer taken the kid?"

"Up into the hills," Meloy said. "We're not sure where."

"So how are you following?"

"With my help," Ahara said. The wisp manifested close to Jay, and Angela was worried that the older woman would panic, swing the gun, squeeze the trigger. But she didn't even twitch.

"Wisp," Jay said. "Seen a couple of your kind before. Knew one a few years back, little place just north of Chicago. Name of Bale. You know Bale?"

"No," Ahara said. "Wisps keep to ourselves."

"So why're you helping these folk?"

"Help them, I help myself," Ahara said.

"Right," Jay said. She nodded again at Meloy. "So, Frederick, you still collecting?"

"No," Meloy said. "Well, maybe. In a way. I'm helping the Kin that are alive, but stopped gathering bits of those dead. I like to think I'm collecting friendships."

Jay stared for a while, then broke into a loud, harsh laugh.

"Friendships!" She bent down and rested the rifle barrel on the ground, using it to lean on while she guffawed even more, strong, helpless exhalations. "You Brits!"

After a while she stood upright again, wiping tears from her eyes and shouldering the rifle.

"We need to leave," Angela said. "Do you know these hills? Can you guide us?"

"In the dark? No, no way. Get lost out there and you'll wander around for a week, then die raving and drinking your own piss. No, I can't help you on my own, but there are those who'll help me help you."

"Who?" Vince asked.

Jay uttered a long, low whistle. More shadows moved around them, and shapes came out from the dark spaces between trees. Emerging from hiding.

Angela heard the unmistakable clop of hooves. Beside her, Vince gasped. Memories of the brutal satyr Ballus flashed across her mind. This was no satyr, however. The centaur stepped closer until it was almost at Jay's right shoulder. Angela could smell it, a familiar horse smell with a more subtle, mysterious underlying scent, a warmth that reminded her of cooking and sex. The wonder of what she saw smothered the disbelief and the rush of questions she knew she should be asking, like *How is this possible, where does it live, how has no one ever seen it?* Maybe later there would be time for answers.

The centaur stomped one of its front hooves, the movement more bullish than equine.

A shorter, more humanoid figure stood further back, squat but strong. She could see that it was naked apart from several wraps of cloth, weak moonlight glimmering from muscles and damp skin. Its face was wrong. The dimensions were untrue, confusing to her brain, used as it was to seeing a certain aspect. Only when it blinked did she realize the creature had one large eye above the bridge of its nose.

The sight took her back to Vince's rented London apartment, paid for by the gangster Fat Frederick Meloy so that he had a base from which to mount his relic hunting missions. That was when her world had been knocked askew. There she had unwrapped the parcel in the apartment's bath to find the mummified head of an infant cyclops, after which the creature began haunting her with visions in which it opened its eye.

This cyclops seemed to be staring right at her. She feared it could sense what she was remembering, smell the scent of a dead infant on her hands.

Something passed by overhead. Startled, scared, Angela ducked down, as did Vince, Meloy, and even Lilou. A shadow drifted past and swerved around, floating over the centaur's head and approaching the tree line on their left. Branches and leaves rustled as the creature took to its roost. Wood cracked as claws gripped. The Kin was large, at least human sized, but she couldn't yet make out what it was.

"Any questions?" Jay asked.

"One or two," Angela said.

"But not for now," Lilou said. "Meloy says you're willing to help, and I trust him."

"You do?" Jay asked, raising her eyebrows. "Well, okay then. That's good. I see he's worked his magic." She chuckled as if sharing a private joke.

"How much has he told you?" Vince asked. "You've heard of Ascent?"

Jay grew serious. "The worst idea in the history of bad fucking ideas. It'll be the end of the Kin, doesn't matter how powerful this so-called fairy is."

"Not 'so-called,'" Lilou said. "She's real, and that's an interesting take on things. The way I see it, Ascent would be bad news for humans more than Kin."

"Yeah, well, whatever. You're in the USA now. My friends here…" She waved a hand. "They've survived well enough out in the wild. Your mad fucking angel does his thing, then everyone with a gun and delusions of fame will be up here. It'll be open hunting season. You ever seen a dead Kin, girl?"

She was speaking to Angela.

"Plenty."

Jay grunted, looked her up and down. "They're not things meant to be dead."

Angela nodded her agreement, and in that moment she felt a connection form with this strange woman.

"So of course we'll help," Jay continued. "Me and these three friends of mine. Let's talk while we're walking, huh? This place may be remote, but this time of day you'll get kids coming up here to take drugs and fuck." With that she headed right toward the line of trees and the mountains and endless wilderness silhouetted beyond.

27

I never believed Aunt Angela was a murderer, Sammi thought. Despite the news stories, the dreadful reports from London, the international search for Angela and Vince, and her dramatic escape from a police station in Boston, Sammi's father had never believed it either.

Right then, she had to believe that Angela was there to help, and that made her more determined than ever to help herself.

She pushed the man's arm away from her, smooth and quick. Digging her nails into his skin, she gouged and twisted, careful to stay away from the curved blade still clasped in his hand. It was a stupid move, but for whatever reason, she was certain that he didn't want to kill her. Not yet. He needed her as some sort of bait.

Gregor shouted something incomprehensible. He jerked the truck's wheel left, then right. Sammi moved in her seat but tensed, grabbing hold of his arm even tighter. She felt blood dripping from where her nails bit in.

"Not again, you stupid little bitch!"

She shoved, leaning forward and banging his arm against the dashboard, trying to dislodge the knife, grab it, stick it in him and jump from the moving truck before it crashed or rolled. He was stronger than she thought.

Still driving, Gregor let her push his arm forward, then slammed it back into her face. An explosion of white-hot agony erupted in her nose. Her eyes watered, and pain filtered out across her cheeks, blazing tendrils setting fire to nerves and blinding her. She tried to cry out, but he struck her again. She fell back into her seat and waved her arms in front of her, trying to ward off the killing blow she feared from the knife.

She hit his arm, his hand, then something cool and sharp. Her hand went numb, then a flare of pain bloomed across the meaty pad of her thumb and she felt warm blood, cooling as it flowed.

"Calm down!" Gregor shouted.

Sammi couldn't calm down. The things she had seen, the things she'd touched, all conspired to steal away her calmness, her sense of things being normal, and shred them to pieces in the falling darkness.

She could still smell Mallian. He wasn't human, however much her mind tried to attribute human traits to him, and humanlike appearances. He was huge, and the scent of him was something animalistic, like the whiff of a forgotten tomb or the aroma of magic.

She could never forget the woman, head ripped from her shoulders by Mallian's right hand while he still grasped Sammi in his left. The splash of blood she'd felt speckling her cheek and throat, the slumping body, the head tossed to Gregor, and then…

And then the other people being killed.

Most of it she'd only heard, but that had been bad enough. Then she'd seen the hairy, stocky man, fists and forearms coated with gore, climbing from the ditch with part of the dead woman in his hand, part of her in his mouth as he chewed and grinned.

"I only need you alive," Gregor said. "That doesn't mean whole. Got it? Got it, girl?"

"Don't call me girl," she said.

"You *are* a girl!"

"My name's Sammi. My mother and father called me Sammi."

"So?"

"My aunt calls me Sammi, too. She'll come for me. She knows what this is, more than you think." Somehow Sammi was sure of that. It was all to do with why Angela and Vince had been falsely accused in the news. Hidden stories, hidden histories… somehow, Sammi felt at home with them.

The pain still burned in her face and blurred her vision, but feeling blood dribbling from her nose seemed to drain some of the pain, as well.

"She knows nothing," Gregor said. "She won't have time to learn."

"She's smart. She'll learn. Then she'll take that knife and stick it up your ass."

Gregor took in a sharp breath and tensed, and Sammi had to use every ounce of strength and composure to not squeeze her eyes shut.

So fighting won't work, Sammi thought. *It'll have to be something else. I won't end up like that old woman with her head ripped off. I won't die and be eaten. Wherever he's taking me, whoever the fairy is and whatever the Fold is, I'm going to win.*

* * *

Soon after, Gregor pulled the truck off the road and drove into the woods, the vehicle bouncing on uneven ground and scraping past trunks. It soon stopped and he killed the engine.

"We walk from here," he said.

Sammi had been banking on that.

He climbed out and pulled her behind him. This time she didn't resist.

Standing beside the truck, the only sound she heard was the hot engine ticking as it started to cool. *"It's snoring,"* her mother used to say when a younger Sammi asked about the noises coming from under a car's hood. *"Going to sleep after a long drive."*

Sammi was ready to run, but she had to choose her time carefully. Just out of the truck Gregor would be cautious and alert, expecting her to do something stupid. She had to wait until he wasn't so prepared. He kept one eye on her as he shrugged on a jacket and shouldered his backpack. He didn't ask if she was warm enough. He didn't care.

"Where are we going?" she asked.

"Nearly there," he said.

"Nearly where? Where are we going?"

"Somewhere amazing. Somewhere I can finish my journey." He paused, looking at her as if ready to open up, divulge. He shook his head with a snort and grabbed her arm, pulling it out straight. "Hold your hand up... like this."

"Why?"

Instead of replying, he took a ball of thick twine from his jacket pocket and wrapped it a dozen times around her wrist. He tied it tight.

"Ow, that *hurts!*"

"Pull on it and it'll hurt more."

He passed the twine ball twice around his waist, knotted it off, and flicked the tense string between them. He'd left six feet of string, no more. If she tugged hard enough maybe she'd snap it, or maybe not. Either way it would hold her back long enough for him to use his knife.

"I only need you alive. That doesn't mean whole."

"Let's move it," he said. "It's getting dark. We'll move as far as we can, then wait until dawn."

The landscape here was heavily wooded, rolling, remote. The roads were rough, and she'd seen lots of signs for camping grounds and picnic areas. A couple of times when the road crossed a ridge or came to the top of a hill, she'd looked ahead and around. A sea of green extended into the distance ahead of them. Sammi loved the woods, but here and now she felt isolated and alone.

"You're looking for the Fold," she said. She'd remembered part of the conversation she'd heard back on the road. "Maybe I can help you find it."

"You don't even know what it is."

"Sure I do. I've been to one before."

He frowned. "Keep your trap shut, kid."

She'd rattled him. That was what she wanted. Heading into the forest away from the snoring truck, she made sure her mind was alert and prepared. With Gregor still carrying his blade and not averse to using it, she'd only get one chance.

28

Angela wondered at the history between Meloy and Jay. They obviously knew each other, but she got the impression that they hadn't actually met before today. If Meloy was larger-than-life, Jay was on a whole new level.

Leading the way into the dense, dark forest, away from the parking lot and any signs of civilization, the woman seemed entirely in her element. She'd slung the rifle onto her left shoulder. That reassured Angela less than it should have. Just because Jay didn't appear to sense immediate danger didn't mean it wasn't out there.

She'd never met Mallian.

An urgency scorched at Angela's heart, a burning need to hurry, not go slow. Rush ahead rather than be cautious. The time for caution was over. Hours, minutes, seconds were ticking, counting down. She'd made contact with Sammi, and with that contact broken again Angela felt even more bereft than before. Responsibility hung heavy, and she felt to blame for what had befallen the girl and Jim, her poor dead father.

It had to be Sammi's connection with Angela. Why else would she be targeted by Grace? The fairy must have remembered Angela's role in her release. Then when Sammi came close to the creature's final eternal home, her "Fold," it had piqued her interest.

But why?

There was no figuring out such a creature. Even Lilou said that the fairy was beyond understanding, as different from the rest of the Kin as the Kin were from humankind.

"Hills're coming," Jay said.

"Huh?" The words startled Angela from her thoughts. The dark forest was heavy around and above them, its shadows wrapping them in its embrace, warm and somehow cloying. Soft branches brushed her hair, shoulders, arms, like tentative fingers testing and tasting. Fine webs broke across her face and forehead.

"Up ahead," Jay said. "Easy bit's over. Gets harder from here. Save your breath." It was a strange thing to say, because Angela hadn't been talking. Now, though, with the woman walking beside her, a hundred questions vied for space.

"Your friends..." Angela said, and that seemed to be question enough.

"Ah, yeah, them, my friends," Jay said. Her voice still managed to be gruff even though it was barely above a whisper. She scanned ahead, left and right, up and down, pausing every now and then and holding up her hand. The others watched for her signal. Vince and Meloy walked behind Angela, Lilou further back and to their right. Ahara was nowhere to be seen, but Angela knew she was there, taking her own route through the trees and the darkness.

"Well, I've known them for some time. Some time." She paused and held Angela's arm. Her hands were rough, fingers calloused, and Angela wondered just how old she was. "You like the Kin?"

"No." She surprised herself with the answer. She'd never really considered it a yes or no question, because the concept was complex. She was fascinated by the Kin—enrapt, scared, troubled, and sometimes terrified. Sometimes she pitied them, too. But *like* them? She thought not.

Jay chuckled, a rasp in her throat. "Me neither. But I do love them."

"How long?" Angela asked.

"Seventeen years, three months, give or take," Jay said. "Three days after my Dizzie died. Cancer got 'im. One month fine, few weeks later gone, like that." She snapped her fingers. "I took to walking. Even before he was in the ground I'd leave our house and drive up here, into these woods. We don't live very far away. I used the tourist parking lots to begin with, wandered the trails, never quite alone enough, always with people having goddamn picnics or taking fucking pictures, as if this was all for them, and when they leave and go home nothing happens here. I knew it wasn't here for me. Whether I walk here or not, the mountains don't give a shit. You know that saying about a tree falling in a forest?"

"I know it."

"It's like that with us humans walking here. The mountains, the forests, they don't even notice us. So we ain't really here at all. Once we're gone, give it a hundred years and there'll be nothin' of us left. Roads and buildings and reservoirs and parking lots and rubber tires and mobile phones and McDonald's wrappers and used condoms tossed out of car windows, all gone and forgotten. That's why I liked walking up here. Thinking about Dizzie and how that gruff bastard

263

was at least half of me and my life, probably more. With him gone, I'm incomplete.

"So not being noticed began to suit me," she continued. "Went deeper, across the gas pipelines that snake through these places. Then deeper still, found some older trails leading higher into the mountains and ancient parts, then eventually no trails at all. You can get lost out here. People do, every year, and they're never seen again. I reckon some of 'em are a bit like me." She lowered her voice even more, as if the words were only for Angela. "I reckon some of 'em make the decision to not get noticed, forever."

"But you got noticed," Angela said.

"Yeah, but not by the forests, and not by the mountains."

"Which one?"

"Her name's Tah." She glanced behind them, left, right. "She's out there somewhere. They all are. They're all good at being quiet, being hidden. That's why they're still here."

"Which one's Tah?"

"Old one-eye." Jay chuckled. "She can be a real fucking bitch."

They passed through a low, level stand of trees and the ground below them began to rise, the slope punctuated by rocky outcroppings and heavily wooded clumps, too dense to penetrate. Jay led them through and around these overgrown areas. She paused now and then to examine the surroundings, and once or twice Angela saw her poised, staring into the darkness with her head tilted, as if listening to a voice only she could hear, or watching a shadow. Then she moved on.

The slope grew steeper, so that here and there they had to grasp onto trailing plants and low tree boughs to help themselves up.

Vince walked close to Angela's other side, always there, brushing her arm with his to reassure them both. He remained silent, listening. Being a listener wasn't something he'd ever been good at, but since learning about the Kin she'd noticed that he sometimes fell into these quieter moments. She thought she knew why he was quiet now. Being told the story of one of the Kin, in a roundabout way, was a rare privilege.

"It was late one evening," Jay said. "I'd taken to spending days in the hills, wild camping and trapping rabbits for food. I became pretty good at foraging and surviving. Most people come out here don't know a rabbit from a skunk, but I was doing okay. Dizzie taught me all that. I was collecting by then, too." She trailed off, perhaps going back to her own first sight of a relic, something so obviously not animal or human, yet real, tactile. Angela didn't ask what it had been.

"There are places up here," Jay muttered. "Not so many this low down, but higher in the hills, deeper in the wilderness. Places where you can find things if you know where to look. Know what I mean?"

"Vince is the relic hunter," Angela said. "I was just drawn into it."

"Right. Vince. So he'll know what I mean."

Vince didn't reply, but Angela caught a nod from the corner of her eye. Moon and starlight showed her a little, filtered down through the forest canopy in a silvery glow, and her eyes had adjusted.

"There's a ravine eighteen, maybe twenty miles from

here with a couple of caves in its wall. Entrances are really fuckin' narrow, and they slope down. First time I crawled in I didn't know how narrow they'd become, and how steep the slope might be. You know when someone says delicious fear? Yeah. Delicious fear. I might've got stuck there, thirty feet in with my head wedged between rocks, starved to death.

"Didn't though. Found a cavern, and from there a deeper network. It's huge, and I still haven't gone as far as I can. One day I will. Need food, lights, batteries— might be down there for weeks. And who the fuck knows where I'll pop up? Or if I'll even pop up at all." She chuckled, and something rustled off to their left.

Angela gasped and crouched. *We're totally in her hands*, she thought, and the realization sent a chill through her. *Delicious fear.*

"Cottontail," Jay said.

"You're sure?"

Jay only glanced at her, then carried on walking and telling her story.

"Tah found me in the third cavern, digging around in the remains of her ancestors. I was being delicate with the bones. They're precious. Even dead Kin are precious, I knew that even back then. I was honoring them, and she's told me since that it's the only reason she didn't kill me.

"I heard her first. The scrape of rough skin on rock, a movement, a breath. I shone my flashlight around but saw nothing, only shadows moving as the light switched around. Then I saw her. Peering at me from over a rock, one eye blinking in the light. Just one eye."

"Better than both of yours," a voice said. It was

surprisingly high and light, and Angela caught her breath as Tah manifested from the shadows to their left. She moved silently and with confidence, and there was a grace about her movement that Angela rarely saw in a human. Perhaps it was a survival skill handed down through generations, a desperate evolution all to do with survival.

"Only because I'm old and keep losing my glasses," Jay said.

"I'm two hundred and seventeen," Tah said.

"And still just a girl." Jay's voice was lighter than Angela had yet heard it. Tah came in close, she and Jay merged into one shape, a kiss and then she was gone.

They walked in silence for a few minutes. Angela was filled with more questions, but she knew they could never be asked, because to answer them all was impossible. Each fact about the Kin inspired more questions. It was wonderful and infuriating, and she had learned that sometimes ignorance was best.

The slope increased even more, and soon they were scrambling toward a vague ridge line high above. Tah went with them, a shadow off to the left, and from the right Angela heard heavy sounds of undergrowth crackling and small branches snapping. The centaur was with them, too. Above them, silvery moonlight caught the shape of something flying high up.

She was panting by the time they reached the top and rested, sipping from one of the two bottles of water Jay had brought along. Angela sat close to Jay.

"Tah saved my life," Jay said. The story was eager to come up, and the older woman took no prompting. "I thought she was going to kill me there under the mountain, but instead she let me go. Gave me something to fuckin' live for, after that old bastard Dizzie went and died on me." Her eyes glittered, adding to the starlight.

"Maybe she liked the company," Angela ventured.

"Yeah," Jay said. "She's young for a cyclops, orphaned eighty years ago. I was company, and we became friends, and then more than friends. She saved my life and gave me a whole new one. And all with one fuckin' eye." Jay stood and looked around, staring out across the heavily wooded slope they had just ascended. Somewhere far down and away was the parking lot they had left several hours before. "We'll wait here a while," she said.

"Wait?" Angela said. "No. No waiting, we have to go on."

"It gets more dangerous from here, girl," Jay said. "The terrain's rough, and there are things in the hills—"

"Some of them are with us already."

Jay frowned, then smiled. "True. True."

"Where are they?" Angela asked. "I want to meet them. If they're helping us, I want to meet them."

"Maybe you don't," Lilou said. She and Meloy sat against a large rock. Vince stood beside them.

"Nymph lady's right," Jay said. "Tah you've seen close up, and the mothman has no name."

"I thought that's what it was!" Meloy said, excitement getting the better of him. He jumped up and looked around.

"He won't be seen if you want to see him," Jay said. "Most of the time you won't want to. He's here to help, but only because he understands the threat."

"What about the centaur?" Angela asked. "Where does he live? How does something like him get around without ever being seen?"

"If I told you his secrets, they wouldn't be secrets anymore."

"He trusts you with them?"

"No, girl." Jay sighed and shook her head, and it might have been the first time she'd been wholly herself in front of them. "Baylor trusts no one and nothing. That's how he's still alive."

Angela looked around for Baylor the centaur, but he was nowhere to be seen. Of course. That was how these Kin survived. Defying expectations, denying themselves to humanity, protecting themselves behind veils of mystery and myth. The cyclops might still inhabit her network of caves deep beneath the mountains, but even in revealing that, Jay hadn't betrayed her in any way. These mountains and forests continued for hundreds of miles, and trying to locate a certain crack in a ravine wall would be like trying to find a particular leaf.

29

Lilou listened to Jay and Angela, taking the opportunity to walk slightly apart from the rest of the group. Meloy remained close to her, but she ignored him. Shut him out. It didn't make her feel good, but it was required.

Even she wasn't used to such long exposure to human company, and this, combined with being so distant from home, left her unsettled. She hadn't been alone since she got on the plane. A gentle queasiness played at her gut, and dizzy spells plagued her on the steepest part of their climb. She took in deep, slow breaths, conscious that Meloy was throwing worried glances her way. Clinging onto plants, she scrambled up the slope on her hands and knees.

Her thoughts had become so confused and uncertain that she craved time on her own. An hour to sit and contemplate. A day to hide away and recharge, let darkness soothe away the fears that plagued her. Back in London in their safe place she'd had such retreats, rooms shut away from the outside where she could spend time pretending she was far from the human world. In truth she'd been at the heart of it, and some of the Kin had perfected the trick of hiding in plain sight.

That was something that these American Kin

seemed less able to achieve, but it was hardly a surprise. The three that accompanied them—centaur, cyclops, mothman—would hardly look at home in a shopping mall or walking along a city street.

In the darkness, with only a silvery sheen of starlight to provide illumination, it was Ahara they turned to when they reached the ridge. Sitting back against a rock with Meloy by her side, Lilou watched the wisp. Ahara brought back bad memories, and Lilou couldn't find it in herself to trust her. Surely her aims were selfish. Surely she sought Grace for reasons they could not discern.

Though the same could be said for Lilou.

"Moving," Ahara said. She stood looking north, across valleys and toward the ragged shadows of higher mountains in the distance. Her head projected forward as if she was sniffing, and she moved it slowly left and right, eyes wide, mouth slightly open. "The Fold is not one place. It drifts. Even where it touched our world, it shifts."

"Then how can we find it?" Angela asked.

"We'll know more when we're closer," Lilou said, watching for any reaction from Ahara. There was only a nod.

"The nymph is right," the wisp said, and she pointed. "It's that way, north, a little east. The closer we draw, the clearer the entrances will become."

"So we've got to move," Angela said. "No time to rest."

"No time at all," Ahara agreed, and she was the first to head down from the ridge and into the next dark, deep valley.

Lilou remembered her wisp. Her Ecclehert. He had taken her heart and then broken it, and the hate she had exuded for wisps ever since was a display, like the mask she pulled into place whilst in human company. The hurt was still so great that she betrayed it as anger and rage. There was something in Ahara that reminded her of him, and that only made it worse.

Their love had been deep, intense, passionate, fed by the fury of those times. Lilou had let herself go and opened herself up, dropping her defenses and reveling in a newfound vulnerability. It was he who had entranced her, rather than the other way around, a freeing sensation that she had never grown used to. She had not been given time.

Since that betrayal, Lilou had not trusted a wisp. A thousand years bearing a grudge, so long that it no longer weighed so heavy. It had become more a habit than a driving force. Yet on those few occasions when she had encountered a wisp, the past had reared up again.

Now there was a far greater betrayal to consider, and she wondered whether Mallian would ever trust a nymph again.

"He'll probably kill you," a voice whispered in her ear.

"Fuck off, wisp."

How Ahara had come so close she did not know, but little about wisps could surprise her now. Not their secretive, silent movements, nor the idea that this one seemed to know what Lilou was thinking. Ecclehert had been much the same.

"How his bitch nymph has turned."

Ahara spoke the truth, and that made it painful. Lilou looked up and behind her, at Meloy working his way down the rocky slope. He paused and smiled, not appearing to notice a shape hovering and muttering into her ear. Maybe the voice was all her own. She looked ahead and down the winding, rough path, and Jay walked with Angela by her side.

They followed the hazy disturbance that must have been Ahara.

"What is it?" Meloy asked when he drew alongside. Vince passed them by with a curious glance.

"Nothing," she said. "Just thinking."

"About what?"

"Friends."

"Don't let Mallian and his gang worry you," Meloy said, his voice low and angry. "We're your friends now." It was such a naive, childlike statement that she couldn't help the soft laugh that escaped her.

"Yes, Frederick, and I value that."

Real or imagined, Ahara did not whisper to her again, yet Lilou felt the weight of her own betrayal hanging around her heart like a dead weight. Remembering Ecclehert and the effect he'd had on her made her angry all over again—being lovestruck was such a human emotion, so weakening and revealing, something that would open her to danger in the tough world of the Kin. Yet perhaps it was love that set her and Mallian apart.

Even back in Ecclehert's time she had known Mallian. He'd wandered more then, using the dense forests for cover and rarely revealing himself to humans. With a more rugged terrain and far fewer humans inhabiting it, the Kin had enjoyed much greater freedom in those times.

More regular meetings in the centuries that followed had cemented their great friendship, and sometimes in Lilou's eyes their relationship might have been deeper. But only in her regard. Her nymph's wiles did not affect the angel. The Nephilim stood proud and aloof, despite his fallen nature.

She felt a hint of shame for not supporting him. It was a chink in their friendship, perhaps a fatal flaw that would slice through all the ties of the centuries, and rip them apart. Yet she could not deny her beliefs. The faster Ascent approached—coaxed by Mallian, brought closer by his ever more rash actions—the more she railed against it. In the past, his desires had seemed almost an abstract notion, a potential uprising that would never happen. Now, as it approached, she could only imagine it being catastrophic.

They walked into the night, descending the treacherous mountain path into a dark valley where very little starlight penetrated the canopy, and moonlight was shielded by the bulk of the land they had crossed. Angela and Jay remained at the head of the group, with Vince now close to his lover. Lilou and Meloy followed behind.

She was often aware of the other Kin around them— the rustle and snap of Baylor the centaur working through the woodland, the darting shadow of the cyclops, Tah, and occasionally the drifting shape of the mothman swooping effortlessly above.

They paused again by a stream, with Angela and Vince standing close and whispering to each other. The mothman landed with a swirl of wings and a waft of stale, old air. The aroma was one of secrets.

"Something's coming," he said.

"Where?" Jay asked. "What?"

"From upstream. Something big."

The night was ripped apart by a deep roar.

30

"You'd better step aside," Jay said, but Angela was already reaching for Vince, the two of them tripping in the dark to splash down into the edge of the stream. The cold stole her breath as it soaked into her clothing. She rolled onto her side, propped up on one elbow, and watched the figure closing on them. It splashed along the stream, throwing up sprays of water that caught the weak starlight.

Meloy and Lilou were close behind her, and behind them Angela saw the mothman streak skyward again with barely a flap of his vast, fine wings, launching himself out of harm's way.

A gunshot sounded, harsh and shocking in the darkness. Jay stood on a rock, rifle braced on her shoulder, leaning into the shot as she fired a second time.

In the muzzle flash, Angela saw the hairy cannibal man Jeremiah leaping for Jay with clawed fists.

He never reached her.

A shape struck Jeremiah square in the torso. Much smaller than he was, still it moved faster, and the impact sent him back into the stream, slipping on wet rocks and losing his footing. As he fell onto his back he roared and brought both hands around to pummel his attacker. Water closed around him as his fists struck only his chest.

Tah stood breathing hard on the stream's opposite bank. She crouched down, ready to pounce again.

"Jay!" Angela shouted, and the woman took a step forward and fired down at the prone form.

The bullet struck home.

It only pissed him off more.

Jeremiah sprang to his feet and landed running. He went directly for Jay, and this time when Tah barreled into him he was ready, flinging his fist out and connecting squarely with her face. She slumped into a deeper reach of the stream and started floating, limp and loose.

"Vince!" Angela said, but he was already moving into deeper water. For a second she thought the cyclops was going to drift past, but he snagged her clothing and pulled. They both were dragged further into the stream before he used her momentum to swing her in toward the bank. Lilou helped drag her from the water, and then Angela joined in. Together they hauled the cyclops away from the water, turning her on her side so that she could breathe. Being so close to her, touching her, was strange, and seeing her one large eyelid continually flicker brought the strangeness of the moment crashing home.

Another roar came from behind them, and when she turned Angela saw a shape being borne aloft. At first she thought it was Jeremiah being lifted by the mothman, but he was too large, too violent. This was Jay being hauled up out of harm's way.

The mothman was struggling. His wings flapped hard.

Jeremiah plucked a rock the size of Angela's head from the stream and hurled it high. It was a strangely beautiful sight, trailing droplets of water that caught the starlight. It nicked one of the creature's wings and he dropped to the left, swooping down in a tight curve toward the tree line close to the rocky streambed.

As the mothman struck the ground and Jay tumbled from his grasp, Baylor burst from the trees close by and reared up, kicking out with his front hooves. Angela could swear she heard them swishing at the air.

Jeremiah charged.

A shape rose up from where it had been hiding, swinging the heavy branch. It connected with Jeremiah's face. Only then, seeing Jeremiah alongside the big man Meloy, did she realize just how strong and apelike the Kin was.

"Meloy!" she shouted.

Too late. He was a man who would never back down. He'd proven that at Mary Rock's house. He hefted the branch and swung it again, this time striking the Kin across the chest. The branch snapped.

Jeremiah did not waste time. He swung a heavy fist down onto Meloy's head and crushed him into the ground, then rushed on toward Baylor, Jay, and the mothman.

"Boss!" Vince shouted.

Angela's heart sank. "You go," she said. "But careful. I'll stay with Tah."

Vince crouched, hesitating.

"Go!" she said. It was pointless staying together. If Jeremiah came for them, being together or alone would mean nothing.

Vince dashed along the stream's bank and crawled over rocks toward where they had seen Meloy fall.

Beneath her hand, Tah groaned.

"Easy," Angela said.

"Run," Tah said.

"No."

"We have to… run. He won't be… alone."

Angela had already thought of that. She scanned the dark forest, the jingling stream, the flood plain, looking for shadows that should not move. Running would do no good. They had to make their stand.

When Vince reached his former boss he was already expecting the worst. What he saw only confirmed it. Blood gleamed in the starlight. Meloy was huddled down between several large rocks, as if rolled up and jammed there by something trying to hide a prize. He thought of animals concealing food for later consumption, remembered Jeremiah chewing on the dead woman's arm, Ballus and his unnatural appetites.

He wondered if humans had caught their insanity and evil from the Kin, or the other way around.

From his right came a roar, a hiss, and the sound of something hard hitting something harder. Jeremiah and Baylor struggled together, the hairy man battering with his meaty fists, the centaur rearing and kicking, hooves striking up sparks each time he struck rock. Jeremiah was circling, and Baylor kept between the enemy and his fallen friends. Jay was already on her feet, and Vince saw the mothman stagger upright and fade back amongst the trees. If his wing was damaged he was done for, and no more use in this fight.

"Fuck," Meloy said, and Vince had never been so pleased to hear the gruff man's voice.

"Boss." He crouched beside him, but any relief was short-lived. There was lots of blood. It glimmered in the poor light, and Vince could smell its rich warm tang on the air. "Where'd he get you?"

"Everywhere." Meloy's voice was harsher than before, as if coming from somewhere broken.

"Can't believe you stood up to that thing."

"Like hitting a tree with a twig."

"Just keep still," Vince said, and he leaned in closer, trying to make out Meloy's injuries. It was too dark. He pulled out his phone, but Meloy's hand clasped around his wrist. Even his fingers were bleeding.

"Not yet!" he rasped. "Might not just be him."

"Right," Vince said. If he used his phone's torchlight, any other creatures closing in on them would have a bright target to home in on.

"Not good," Meloy said. His voice, still harsh, sounded weaker. "Feel like shit."

"Keep still, boss," Vince said.

From the tree line came more roars and the sounds of combat, fists and hooves clashing, meaty thuds... breaking bones. Baylor and Jeremiah were locked together, rolling and writhing in the midst of a fight to the death. Vince could smell them, a rich, cloying stench like the rankest body odor, piss, decay.

Meloy said something, and Vince had to lean in close to hear him.

"They're amazing," Meloy said. "All of them. To know them..." He drifted off.

"Yeah, boss. All amazing."

"I'm still collecting. Now it's memories."

"Hang in there," Vince said. "Look at me! Keep talking!" He squatted down and reached for the man's hand. He held and squeezed, and Meloy squeezed back.

"A most amazing honor," Meloy said, and then he fell silent. Vince felt his body tense, and then go limp. He shook Meloy's hand, squeezed again, but this time there was no response.

From behind him a gunshot rang out.

With Jeremiah and Baylor engaged in their bloody, brutal fight, it was easy enough to edge across the stream and circle around toward the first of the trees. Angela had to feel the way with her feet, keeping her full attention on the conflict. She glanced around, expecting more shadows to rise up and attack at any moment.

The mothman seemed to have disappeared back into the forest, perhaps nursing his wounds. Jay had gone with him. When Angela reached the spot where they had landed, she peered into the trees but could see nothing. Perhaps they gazed back out at her, but if so they did nothing to signal her.

Jeremiah and the centaur fought less than thirty feet away, and she felt the impact of each assault through the ground and transmitted on the air. Grunts and roars, thuds and snaps, she didn't think either of them could sustain such violence for much longer.

Scrambling around, she searched for an unnatural straight line in the darkness. She found it faster than she could have hoped, leaning against a rock close to where she'd seen the mothman and Jay fall. She grabbed the rifle. It was heavier than she'd expected. Her heart hammered, a thumping echoed in her ears, and time seemed to slow as the weight of events pressed down upon her. Sammi's danger, the violence, Vince close by with an injured or dead Meloy, the slaughter of people on the road. Mallian.

Ascent.

She wished for a life free of the Kin, and every moment that passed, every event, made that seem less and less likely.

Angela had fired guns before, when she was a kid and her cousin had taken her shooting. It had been a long time ago, and never a rifle. She hefted the weapon, hoping the safety was off, and braced it against her shoulder.

Sighting on the struggling shadows, she wondered whether she should just fire into their mass until the weapon was empty.

She breathed deep and slow, finger teasing the trigger and concentrating only on what was in front of her. The shapes roiling in the darkness. The pale flashes of bare skin, the twists of fur and hair. Starlight glimmering from sweat and blood.

Baylor reared up and away, and Jeremiah pulled his fist back for a strike.

Angela squeezed the trigger. The shot was so loud, the kick into her shoulder so hard that she stumbled back a couple of steps, ears ringing and all sound lowered into the distance. She gathered herself and brought the rifle up again.

Just as a screaming, raving Jeremiah filled her vision and leapt at her with hands raised.

She shot him in the face.

The beast's scream rose into a sharp, high whine and he tripped, sprawling so close that she felt one of his hands brush against her jeans. She stepped back and aimed the rifle down at him, pulling the trigger one more time.

Click.

Empty.

Stay down, she thought, *stay down, be dead.*

He wasn't dead. He raised himself on all fours, his face a mask of wet, dark hate in the starlight. His tongue slipped out and slurped at his own blood.

Then Baylor was there, stomping down with his two front hooves again and again, rising and falling. Tah was there, too, lifting a massive rock above her head and bringing it down on the fallen Kin. The sounds were horrible. Angela turned away, not wishing to see Jeremiah's beaten, broken fate. Whoever and whatever he had been, it was a terrible way to die.

She dropped the rifle and circled around toward Vince and Meloy. As she reached them she saw the look of hopelessness on her lover's face.

"I think he's dead," Vince said.

31

"Mallian left him behind to stop us," Lilou said. "He'll have left the others, too."

"I notice the hairy fucker didn't go for you," Jay said.

"Mallian and I go back a long way," Lilou said.

"So you're for him or against him?" Jay asked. She'd reloaded her rifle and held it in one hand, not yet slung on her shoulder. Ready to be used again.

"In this, against him," Lilou said. "That should be obvious."

"Fuck knows," Jay said. "I've never pretended to understand any of you."

They were gathered around Meloy. In the east, the forested horizon was growing brighter. Vince was using his phone torch now, and the damage the big man had sustained was apparent.

"Finish him off and move on," Tah said.

Angela stood between the injured man and the cyclops, as if ready to fight.

"We don't finish anyone," Lilou said.

"I'm not heartless," Tah said, blinking her one large eye. It was wet, wide, expressive. "It's just for the best, that's all. Look at him. He's broken. We leave him behind alive, he'll die a slow death."

Meloy appeared to be unconscious, but Lilou wondered whether he was listening.

"We're not killing him," Lilou said. Yet at the same time she understood what Tah was saying. "How is he?" she asked Vince.

"I'm no doctor, but it's not good. Compound fractures in his legs, slashed scalp, maybe cracked skull. And inside, who knows? That thing hit him pretty hard."

"I hit back," Baylor said.

Lilou looked around at them, taking stock. Jay and Tah stood close together, the cyclops nursing a bruised face and shoulder. Baylor was a little way off, washing his hooves and blood-spattered legs in the stream. Of the mothman there was no sign.

Her human friends were together, Angela and Vince close to the battered, broken Frederick Meloy.

"Where's the wisp?" Lilou asked.

"Always here," a voice said from behind her.

"Thanks for your help."

Ahara shrugged. "Not my fight."

"It's everyone's fight!" Lilou spat. "Mallian fears us, otherwise he wouldn't have left Jeremiah to slow us down."

"We carry him," Baylor said. The centaur's voice was a surprise—soft, high, almost delicate. It belied his appearance. "He can go on my back. We need to move, and if we're not putting him out of his misery, he has to come with us."

"So let's move out," Jay said. "Dawn's here. We can move faster."

"So can Gregor," Angela said.

"What about the mothman?" Lilou asked. "He could

scout ahead for us, search for Gregor and the girl. They'll be on foot, too."

"Where is he?" Angela asked.

"In the trees," Jay said. "I'm afraid that rock might have damaged his wing. What's a mothman who can't fly?"

"So will he do it?" Angela asked.

"Why ask me?" Jay said. "I'm not his master."

"Then I'll ask him myself," Angela said. "Lilou?" She nodded, and together they went after the mothman.

He was huddled close to the base of a tree, just inside the forest. He looked somehow reduced, and Lilou feared she had seen the expression he wore, many times before. Lost, subdued, resigned. He held one pair of wings wrapped around his torso like the flaps of a dark, iridescent robe. The other pair drooped away from his body, and the damage to them both was obvious. The rock had done more than nick a wing, it had passed through both of them, shattering fine bones and ripping the thin leathery skin that stretched between limbs. It was a miracle that he had glided in to land safely, with Jay in his grasp.

He watched them approach, big eyes dimming as a filmy lid blinked.

"I'm so sorry," Lilou said.

"Sorry doesn't help me."

"We'll help you," Angela said. "What do you need? What can we do? We need your help, too. Do you think you'll be able to fly and—"

"Angela," Lilou said, touching the woman's arm.

Angela looked at her, blinked, and seemed to understand the gravity of the situation.

"It doesn't matter," the mothman said. His voice was gruff, old, weak. Lilou wondered how old he was, and what he had seen and done. More than any of them would ever know, probably. Such was the story with most Kin.

"Of course it matters," Lilou said. "We all matter, more so now than ever before."

The mothman held up one of his damaged wings, wincing as some of the fine broken bones grated together. His face was pale, and his big eyes were wet with tears.

"You'll be going to the Quiet Place." Lilou jumped as Jay spoke from behind.

"It's long past my time," the mothman replied.

"What's the Quiet Place?" Angela asked.

"Somewhere secret," Jay said.

"Where they go to...?" Lilou could not use the word in front of the wounded Kin. It didn't seem fair.

"Where they go when they can't live in the world anymore. You don't have Quiet Places back in your country?"

"I don't think our country is big enough," Angela said.

"Safe places, yes," Lilou said. "But they're hiding places in the midst of the human world. Hiding in plain sight."

Jay only nodded, then stepped between the human and the nymph to approach the mothman. She glanced back over her shoulder. The situation had stolen her gruffness, and Lilou saw that something private was about to take place.

"Come on," Lilou said softly, and Angela seemed to

understand, too. They walked away together. Lilou glanced back only once, to see Jay and the mothman standing close, whispering into each other's ears.

It was a feeling she should have become used to, but was pleased that she never had. The mothman might or might not have been dying, but his removal from the world seemed certain. With the injuries he had sustained, his time here was at an end. A flying creature with no wings could not survive in the wild. Whatever their Quiet Place was, wherever it hid itself away, it was about to receive another poor soul.

She guessed it was somewhere high in the mountains, perhaps in a hidden valley or ravine, or deep within a cave network whose entrance was protected by weak glamors. It was the sort of place a collector like Meloy would give a limb to find. It was somewhere the likes of him must never see.

Yet Jay seemed to know where it was.

Perhaps they do go there to die, Lilou thought, and she imagined taking her own walk into the wild mountains, following a trail only Kin could find, to a Quiet Place where all the noise faded away, all the troubles of surviving in a world that no longer acknowledged their existence drifted into memory and myth. She had often considered her own passing, and knew of a Kin back in Britain who was cursed with knowing the time and place of his own death. He never told anyone, and no one ever asked.

Lilou was old in human years, but as Kin she was still young. Mallian sometimes made her feel like a child with his reminiscences of the Time. The fairy Grace was older still, old as the mountains, old as the cracks in the land, the rivers, and the seas. Yet more and more of late, the possibility of Lilou's own demise presented itself to her, because the age of the Kin was long gone, and their Time was dead.

Mallian's desire to create a new Time for the Kin was misplaced and ill-informed. They were creatures of myth and legend now, known to humans almost entirely in books and stories, their exploits only guessed at, and rarely with any truth. Regaining the Time was like trying to restart a heart that had stopped beating, and bringing life back to a dead, corrupted corpse. Only tragedy could result.

Even though her own time might be coming close, she was becoming more and more certain that her direction was the only one for the Kin. She knew where they should be. They *had* to know their place.

That place was not at Mallian's side.

"So sad," Angela said, startling Lilou from her thoughts.

"Kin often die in the human world," she said, as if in response.

"So what now?"

"Now we split up," Lilou said. "Make it harder for Mallian to stop us."

Angela didn't object, though Lilou had thought she would. She had to know that it made sense.

"And what about Meloy?"

"We move Meloy without killing him."

32

As dawn broke across the wild hillside, Sammi knew she was running out of time. Gregor forced her ever onward, and the rising sun didn't bring the usual sense of peace and anticipation. Back on the Cape she would have been preparing for another day of swimming or kayaking with her father, meeting up with friends, wondering what the future might bring.

Here, her future was short and dark. But though exhausted and afraid, still she was determined to fight. She would not let this monstrous man win.

"The Fold's that way," she said pointing.

"Shut up, kid."

"Suit yourself."

They continued climbing. He made her choose the route, remaining behind her. That way she couldn't surprise him again. She felt his eyes on her back. The heavy string that stretched between them meant she sometimes had to pause while he caught up, and she used every moment to catch her breath. She was hungry and very thirsty, but requests for food and drink had been met with silence. He didn't care about her. He cared about what was at the end of this journey, at the Fold, whatever hell that was.

"I told you, I've seen a Fold before, I know where it's likely to be, and on top of this mountain isn't the place."

Gregor tugged on the string, bringing them to a stop, then looked past her up the long slope they were climbing. Sammi looked, too. She couldn't see very far because trees, undergrowth, and rocky outcroppings blocked her view. The only certainty was that the slope was steep.

"You haven't seen one before," he said. "No one has."

"How do you know? You don't even know what it is."

"Just shut up and keep moving!"

Sammi started climbing again, but she didn't shut up. She was getting to him, and she needed to keep him annoyed, unsettled. That way his guard might slip. He wouldn't kill her as long as he thought he needed her.

"It was on the Cape last year," she said, "just after my mother died. Dad and I were on a sailing boat. He doesn't sail, but his friend Glenn does and he took us out. We were going out to see if we could spot porpoises, and the Fold was about half a mile along the shore from where we moored for a beach picnic. It was just sort of… there. We all looked, amazed. None of us knew what it was at the time, of course. Just like a… thing."

She grabbed a tree and hauled herself up and forward, and Gregor followed. He no longer told her to shut up. She hoped it was a sign that he was uncertain about her story, and not that he was preparing to use the knife.

"But later, someone arrived to tell us what it was. He wasn't as big as your friend Mallian, but he was just as weird. Very strong, taller than anyone I'd ever seen. He walked along the beach and had a couple of burgers and a fish from our barbecue. And he came from the Fold." Sammi thought that was inspired. She even heard Gregor catching his breath. "He told us it was lovely there, and if we wanted a look—"

"Shut the fuck up!" He slapped her across the back of the head, a solid impact that made her ears ring. She grimaced but didn't react. "Keep walking." She obeyed.

The rise turned even steeper, and she had to lean into the slope to continue. At the top they emerged onto a flatter area of hillside. To the right was a sheer drop, a bowl in the slope that might have been the result of old mining activity or some ancient cataclysm. Across the other side of this wide, deep ravine, on an area of hillside almost stripped of trees and scattered with boulders and scree, something was... wrong.

Sammi rubbed at her eyes, thinking that sweat might have dripped into them, or exertion had misted her vision. The thing she saw couldn't be described. It had no real form or substance. It was an uncertain area, a blurry smudge on the firm landscape of this dawn mountainside. She couldn't tell how far away it might be, but she guessed not more than a mile.

"Keep moving," Gregor said. "We'll go up to that ridge, cut across the top of the ravine, then back down to it."

Sammi obeyed, scrambling upward and glancing frequently across the wide open space at the strange thing. Was there a faint glow coming from it? Or were its surroundings simply darker? She couldn't tell. All she knew was that it was amazing and terrifying, like nothing she had ever seen or even imagined. Nothing of this world...

"Fold," Gregor breathed.

"'Course it is," she said. "I've told you, I've seen one before."

"No one would have offered you a look into a Fold!" Gregor shouted. He stopped walking. "You're making this up to—"

Reaching for a tree to pull herself upward, she wound the string twice around a broken branch, held onto the stump, braced her other hand against the ground, and kicked back hard with both feet. She felt the impact, heard Gregor's surprised "*Oof!*" As he fell to the ground she felt and heard the string snap.

The release of pressure on her wrist was instant.

She didn't have time to enjoy it.

Scrambling up the slope, she risked a single glance behind her.

Gregor had fallen onto his back and slid down the slope, coming to a halt against a large tree root. There was a splash of blood across his lower face, and she hoped she'd mashed his lips and knocked out some teeth.

He was already trying to roll over and regain his feet, but his movements were slow, confused. The shock and pain might give her another couple of seconds.

This was when Sammi hoped her youth and fitness would give her an advantage.

Grabbing onto trees, shoving hard with her feet, trying to keep her breathing slow and easy, she propelled herself up the steep slope toward whatever might await them up above. There was no going back now. If he captured her, he'd make sure this wouldn't happen again. He'd already said that he only needed her alive, not whole. Maybe he'd cut off her foot, gouge out her eyes. She wouldn't put anything past him.

"Come back here!" he roared, as if that would make her obey.

Using her hands and feet to drive herself on, she closed her left hand around a loose rock the size of her fist. She hefted it and turned, leaning back against the hill and not out where she could fall into space.

Gregor was already coming after her, face down as he concentrated on climbing. She threw the rock at him. All those hours playing baseball in their back garden returned to her, along with her dad's advice about picturing exactly where she wanted the ball to go. The rock struck Gregor's left shoulder.

Damn.

He grunted and paused, looked up. His face was splashed with blood, lips split from her kick.

Sammi started climbing again.

"I'm going to hurt you!" he bellowed.

She didn't respond. Every breath he used to shout was one less available to climb.

"And when you've got me into the Fold, I'll kill you!"

Whatever the Fold is, I'm not going there with you, she thought.

Something snapped.

Sammi shouldn't have let it stop her, but it did, and as she tilted her head to listen another snap came from the distance, echoing from the hills.

Gunshot! she thought. She glanced back at Gregor, and he was listening, too. He grinned up at her.

"That'll be the woman who came for you, having her head blown off."

Aunt Angela!

Sammi started moving again. Maybe he was wrong. Maybe it was hunters. These forests were huge and wild and seemed endless, and there would be other people out here enjoying the wilderness, rather than dreading it. But this early in the day, and this close, she couldn't help thinking the gunshots had something to do with them.

After a couple more minutes of climbing, breath burning in her chest and sweat stinging her eyes, the ground leveled. She came to a narrow path that ran along the steep hill's side, glanced left and right, chose right, and started running. This was when she had to take full advantage of her head start. If she could get out of Gregor's sight, then she might give him the slip. Double back down the hillside, perhaps. Or slip up the slope and gain ground. Maybe she could even find somewhere to hide.

Despite the lack of food and water, adrenaline gave her renewed energy. She leapt over a fallen tree that spanned the rough trail. The forests were alive with birdsong now that the sun was up, and the heat was building. It was going to be another scorching day. She only hoped it wouldn't be her last.

The blood from a fairy's second heart, Gregor thought. That was his focus, the focus of his entire life, and he was so close that he would let nothing steal it from him. The girl was his passport into whatever the Fold was, but the fairy was his true target.

He'd heard of fairies, but never seen one. Some stories said they were hard to kill. Others said they were immortal. He didn't let any of these thoughts trouble him, because he had come too far to be halted by a story. He was making his own.

The blood from a fairy's second heart.

Combined with the relics he carried in his backpack, it would form the end of the Script and the beginning of something else. The ingredients for the rest of his life. His transmutation into Kin, something that would embrace those small horns and tattooed eyeballs he'd suffered as a younger, more naive man. Perhaps he'd have a choice over what he would become, or maybe the ritual would choose for him.

Either way Mallian, the creature he had once known as Jace Tan, would guide him on his way.

He had no doubt that Mallian would be following, along with those other Kin who accompanied him. The gunshots didn't trouble Gregor. Whoever went up against the Kin would be stomped into the ground, flesh and bones turned to mush.

The end of his journey was so close, the anticipation so high, and he couldn't entertain the idea of failure. He had to catch the girl. Nothing else mattered.

Ignoring the pain in his arms and legs, the burning in his chest, the blood on his lips, Gregor pushed on until he reached a level path. He glanced right and saw Sammi disappearing over a fallen tree.

She had maybe twenty seconds head start.

Once he caught her, he'd make sure she could never run again.

33

Everything feels so close.

He experiences no doubt. He hasn't for a long, long time. No doubt at all that this must be the way of things. Now that he's taking action, rather than planning, his certainty is greater than ever. Soon he will be back in the Time where he belongs. A new Time, a precious Time. A Time of reality risen from myths, and new stories that will be told for ages to come.

It's good to be out in the open again, moving without fear of being seen. It's too early to reveal themselves fully, yet Ascent is on the rise. Once he has the fairy on his side, there will be no reason to hide anymore.

He has practiced the rite many times over the centuries, since obtaining the Script long, long ago. Each practice, however, has been in his head. It's too risky a spell to try before the time is right, too dangerous to reveal, even to those who profess to follow him.

Besides, until now, he hasn't possessed the necessary ingredients for it to work. The gullible human has almost finished gathering those ingredients for him. Perhaps he could have sent one of the Kin, but he liked the idea of using a human to bring closer humanity's subjugation. Besides, Kin needing to travel so far would have taken much longer.

Half a human lifetime has been no time to wait.

It was difficult to be so close and let the ingredients go again, but that final gamble will gain him what he wants. The relic hunter will obtain access to the Fold, because of the child he holds prisoner. And Mallian will be close behind.

His only doubt—and the greatest disappointment—lies with Lilou. He is furious at her, yet sadness overrides the rage. They have spent so long together that being apart leaves an emptiness within him, a void which he struggles to fill. If she was with him now he would probably strike her down for her betrayal. But it would be with love, and tenderness.

He has no wish to see her suffer.

She senses someone approaching one of the entrances to her Fold.

This might be the last of them. Nineteen deniers have been brought to the Fold by nineteen wraiths, and soon she will be ready to perform the final spell, closing off this new world forever. Twenty Kin will be sufficient company for her. She could find more out there, send more bolts, draw more to her new home, but she has no wish to wait any longer.

She hasn't felt this fresh and alive in a long, long time. Almost like a child facing the big wide world, wide-eyed and optimistic at the future. The arrivals have made themselves at home. Most have embraced their heritage, and denied their denial. None of them are ashamed, because they have survived, and being deniers has meant that they can now move on to this new place and Time.

She wanders the valley. This is a big, wide space, and the longer she spends here the larger it seems to be. Perhaps the Fold is growing in some unexpected side effect of the glamor that formed it. Perhaps not. Either way, she revels in this new world she has created.

Yes, there is definitely someone drawing close.

Perhaps she will go to meet this final new arrival.

34

Meloy screamed as they heaved him up onto Baylor's back. It was a horrible sound. Vince had always seen Meloy as strong, hard, invincible. His reputation in the London underground was solid, and more than once Vince had avoided trouble or confrontation because someone discovered who he worked for. Fat Frederick's reputation preceded him, and to see him suffering didn't fit into a worldview that made any sense.

Vince glanced at Angela and saw the same expression on her face. Her experience with Fat Frederick Meloy was far different from his, but he knew that despite it all, she respected the man. That he could suffer such pain brought reality crashing home.

"We split up," Lilou said. "Gregor's got something, is doing something, that benefits Mallian, so he's our priority. We have to stop him reaching Grace. If he does that, he achieves something that Mallian wants. And by definition, that's something we *don't* want."

"My priority—" Angela began.

"I know who your priority is, Angela," Lilou said, cutting her off. "Capturing Gregor saves Sammi. So we split into two groups and pursue them both. That gives us twice the chance of stopping him."

"We're running blind," Vince said. "We've no idea where Mallian and his supporters are, or even how many he has with him. There's no saying we saw them all back at the road."

"What do you suggest?" Lilou asked.

"Splitting up might weaken us."

"And staying together presents a single target. If we get ambushed again, we're all held up for longer while we deal with it. That is, if we aren't all killed."

"She's right," Angela said.

Vince raised his eyebrows in surprise.

"It makes sense," Angela continued. "If Mallian's sent them out to stop us, they're running blind, too. Otherwise they'd have come down on us by now. So if they're waiting out there in the forest, we've got more chance if we're in two groups."

"So how do we split?" Jay asked. "'Cause, you know, your crippled friend here won't be much help."

Meloy groaned. Vince wasn't sure if it was a conscious response, or just another moan of pain.

"Baylor's the strongest of us," Vince said, hating the doubts he was feeling. Maybe they *should* leave Meloy behind, at least until this was over, one way or another.

"I can move just as quickly carrying him," Baylor said. "If there's trouble, I'll dump him until it's passed."

Angela nodded.

Vince agreed.

"Angela, Tah, Ahara, come with me," Lilou said. "Vince, you go with Baylor and Jay."

Vince didn't want to be split from Angela, but it made some sort of morbid sense. If one of them died, at least the other might still survive to take care of

Sammi. The chances of both of them being killed were increased if they traveled together.

He doubted that was Lilou's thinking, though. All of her focus was on capturing Gregor and stopping Mallian from gaining whatever advantage he'd come all this way to achieve. Taking control of the fairy would give him terrifying power, and Gregor was part of that.

"We need to stay in touch," Vince said.

"No reception," Angela said, holding up her mobile.

Vince checked his own. The battery was dead.

"We can help," Tah said. She looked at Baylor and nodded. Baylor smiled, nodded back.

"What is that?" Vince asked.

"Something Kin," Jay said. "Don't worry about it, you won't understand, but the two of them have been close for a long time."

A dozen questions jostled in Vince's head, but he asked none of them. He'd got the impression that Jay and Tah had some sort of relationship, but he couldn't pretend to understand anything so complex within the Kin. He was only just beginning to understand people.

Angela came and embraced him. Though afraid, he felt strong and determined. They hugged tight, squeezing as if to mold themselves together, one person not two.

So much had changed, and while their love still burned fierce and strong, everything around it—their support network, the comfort of routine and civilization—had been burned away by the heat of pursuit and the simmering mysteries of the Kin. But they still had each other, and his world still felt strong.

"Love you," he whispered into her ear.

"Yeah," she said. She kissed him beneath his left ear. "Don't leave me again."

Don't die, she was saying. *Don't get yourself killed and leave me in this strange new world.*

"Do my best," he said.

"Come on," Lilou said, but not harshly.

The two groups parted company. Lilou, Angela, Tah, and Ahara headed uphill. Vince, Baylor, Jay, and the unconscious Meloy headed east, intending to turn upward around the next ridge.

"Fucked-up day," Jay said.

"Right," Vince said. He feared it was going to get even more fucked up.

"What else can we expect?" Vince asked a few minutes later. Angela and the others were out of sight, as if the wild landscape had swallowed them up.

"Huh?" Jay seemed distracted.

"Mallian had a pixie with him, called Thorn. Vicious bastard. I've seen him in action before, back in London. But there was something else, a woman who kept sort of flickering back and forth, sometimes a woman, sometimes something like… an otter? A fox?"

"Huh." Jay carried on walking, resting her rifle in the crook of her left arm and looking ahead.

"What does that mean?" Vince asked.

"Means you better hope we don't meet her. Sounds like a kooshdakhaa. Never seen one myself, heard about them though. Baylor?"

"Not pleasant," the centaur said.

Vince followed Jay in silence, suddenly realizing how

isolated he was, at the mercy of this woman who Meloy had brought in to help them. She was someone he'd never met, didn't know, and now Meloy was on the verge of death. Vince could be in as much danger from her and Baylor as from Mallian and his crew.

As Jay had said, *Fucked-up day*.

The morning sun was warming the air and lifting a haze of mist from the forests, making the atmosphere heavy with moisture. With each minute that went by it grew more and more humid, and he became soaked with perspiration. Jay soon altered their route and took them straight up the hillside toward the mountain's hidden peak. That didn't help.

"The others are well," Baylor said. Jay grunted. Vince didn't ask any questions, but took comfort from the centaur's pronouncement.

Angela had never seen Ahara so solid, so *there*. She led the way, heading into the mouth of a steep gorge and seeming never to tire. Lilou followed silently. Whether or not she trusted the wisp, she seemed content to follow her higher into these mountains.

Angela was close behind Lilou, and behind her came Tah. The cyclops fascinated Angela. A mummified cyclops head had been her first ever sight of a Kin relic, back in Vince's secret flat in London when life was simpler and she'd merely suspected Vince of having an affair. Tah was dressed in loose jeans and a checked shirt, and she'd produced a baseball cap from somewhere. From behind she might have looked like any normal woman. Bigger in the shoulders perhaps, stockier than most, with a strength that would immediately set her apart.

But the single, big eye was animalistic, more like a bird's than a human's, lidded with a fine skin layer that flipped down and back regularly to clean her vision and lubricate the large eyeball's surface.

"The others have started uphill," Tah said.

The silent communication between Kin was a mystery, but Angela didn't want to know. All she wanted was for Sammi to be safe. Then, *only* then, she might consider her future with the Kin. Whatever she decided, she was sure they would now always be in her life. It was too dangerous for them to let her go.

If Mallian got what he wanted, everyone would know about them, soon enough. The implications of this—his intentions, the methods he might use, their effects—had never really been discussed, but she feared that she knew what it meant.

Humanity wasn't ready for the Kin. Creatures like these would threaten the foundation of every belief system, and throw every human being off balance, whether or not they were people of faith. Like anything they feared or didn't understand, people would greet the Kin with suspicion and violence. With Grace on his side, Mallian would return that violence in kind.

Magic against guns. Myth against military might. The slaughter on both sides didn't bear thinking about.

"Close," Ahara said from up ahead. The gorge had widened into a deep valley, a sheer cliff to their left leading up to a curving ridge line, a wider bowl-shaped formation to their right, clogged with trees and tumbled boulders. Ahead, the slope rose even more steeply toward an escarpment high above. It was a wild, rough landscape, beautiful and brutal.

"Where?" Lilou asked.

Ahara grew still, tilting her head as if listening, looking left and right.

"Closer."

"Closer where?" Angela asked. "What are we looking for?"

"And… here," Ahara said.

Undergrowth rustled. Birds took flight from trees around and above them, singing out in alarm.

"Is this it?" Angela asked, wondering what the Fold would be, how it would manifest, and whether they'd even realize they were there.

But this wasn't the Fold.

She smelled Mallian before she saw him emerging from the shadows beneath the trees. That such a large creature could conceal himself until he was so close to them shouldn't have surprised her. *Nothing* about him should surprise her.

He appeared to be alone, and that didn't surprise her either. The Kin allied with him would be out there in the wild, tasked with stopping Vince and the others.

"Lilou," Mallian said, as if no one else existed.

Ahara had faded back, becoming hazy now that her betrayal was complete.

"This is so wrong," Lilou said. "I can't let you—"

"'Let'?" Mallian said, and he chuckled. Angela wasn't sure she had ever heard him laugh before.

An explosion of movement erupted behind her, then past her, as Tah went for the Nephilim. Angela opened her mouth to shout a warning, but felt herself winded with shock at **what** was happening, and what she was about to see.

She wished she could close her eyes. She wanted so much to turn away, to not witness something that would stay with her forever. But her mind was already scarred by violence, and the same shock that stole her voice froze her to the spot.

Tah seemed to flow across the twenty feet between the small group and Mallian, dodging a couple of small saplings, her passing barely touching the undergrowth. A couple of leaves shimmered, and a cloud of flies parted and then closed again behind her. It was almost too fast for Angela to take in.

She reached Mallian and leapt.

Mallian flitted to one side and brought his fisted right hand around and down onto Tah's back. He struck her between the shoulder blades and drove her into the ground. All her grace, speed, and suppleness was shattered by the impact, replaced with a heavy grunt and a crunch as she struck.

"Mallian—" Lilou began, but the big Nephilim seemed suddenly aflame with movement and rage. Before Tah had a chance to move or catch her breath he grabbed her up in both hands, one clasping the back of her neck, the other clenched around a big thigh. He lifted her high and brought her down with all his might.

Bones broke. Blood splashed. He did it again, and again, then threw her limp body into the air. He caught her lower leg while she was still above him, and used his body weight to swing her around and down, slamming her head into a heavy tree. The sound of splintering was more than wood.

Angela managed to close her eyes at last, but she still heard. Tah was probably dead already, but over the space of the next few seconds Mallian made sure.

"Mallian, *no*," Lilou said, and in her words Angela heard a hopelessness she too felt.

"Where are the others?" he demanded. His voice was deep and angry, but he didn't sound the least bit out of breath.

"Dead," Ahara said.

Angela's eyes snapped open. Lilou lowered her head to look at the ground, and as realization of the double deception bit in, Angela felt tears blur her vision.

"All of them?" Mallian asked. He was gazing at Angela now, knowing where to look for the greatest reaction.

She stared back at him, defiant behind the tears. Her jaw trembled. She made herself glance down at the bloody, broken remains of Tah, steaming in the morning sunlight where parts of her that should never be seen were splashed and slopped out to view. The horror of the sight fed into her shock and grief.

"It doesn't matter," the Nephilim said.

"It all matters," Angela said. "Vince mattered to me more than anything. It's called love. You don't understand it, and that's why you'll lose."

"Lose?" Mallian said, tilting his head. "I never looked at this as a competition."

"You've gone so wrong," Angela said. "It's so sad. Even with the fairy, you'll never gain whatever you see in your dreams. You know that, don't you?"

"I know I have to try," he said. He wiped his hands across his body, leaving smears of blood and gore. "You're all coming with me."

"I thought you'd just kill us," Angela said. "That's what you're good at."

"Ahara, no, because she led you to me. Lilou, no, because I love her and she's my oldest living friend, however misguided she's become. But you, Angela? A human who has no love of the Kin?"

Angela stared at the Nephilim. Her heart hammered, and every instinct strove to tear her gaze away. But she denied those instincts. Few humans had ever seen anything like this majestic, horrific creature and lived.

"Come on then, you bastard," she said. "I'll gouge your fucking eyes out."

Mallian blinked, then smiled.

"You come with me," he said.

"Why?"

"To bear witness," he replied. "It's a great day." He looked down at the ruined Kin at his feet. "A *great* day! Surely you can feel that, Lilou?"

Lilou said nothing.

"You will," he said. "You all will." He pointed up the slope toward the escarpment. "We're close. She's close. Walk."

They all started to move. With Mallian bringing up the rear they headed uphill. Angela could already see something strange up on the escarpment. Part of the forest seemed less solid than the rest, more uncertain. Like heat haze, only more fluid, slower.

Part of the world was not their world anymore.

35

Sammi went downhill. It was an instant decision, one informed by the strange area she'd spied up on the ridge line ahead. It was hidden behind trees now, but the few glimpses she'd caught were troubling. They played on her mind.

It's somewhere else, she kept thinking, and running away from it made her feel better.

She tripped over a hidden root and went sprawling, sliding through undergrowth and feeling brambles and thorns prickle across her neck and shoulder. She pulled herself upright, wincing against the pain but not letting it slow her. A few scratches and cuts wouldn't matter. She'd been struck by lightning twice, and survived.

Gregor would do so much worse if he caught her.

Scrambling over a fallen tree, she scanned ahead to pick the best route. There were no paths or trails here, and she had to make her way between trees, following the contours of the land to avoid slipping into a ditch or a hollow. The idea of being trapped somewhere deep while Gregor appeared above her was terrifying.

She had to believe that he was still pursuing her, although she could no longer hear him. She might have lost him on the flatter ground, sprinting ahead and disappearing while he still struggled up the steep slope. She couldn't rely on that. Moving as quietly and rapidly as she could, Sammi felt his breath on her back with every step.

After running for what might have been fifteen minutes, still cautious, still quiet, Sammi heard a strange sound from up ahead. She skidded to a halt, kicking up fallen leaves and twigs as she bumped down a slope and came to rest against the trunk of a big tree.

The sound came again. A long, slow moan, like something in pain.

Edging around the tree, peering downhill at an open area of forest below, she saw Vince and some of the creatures he'd been with before.

Her heart stuttered. *Aunt Angela!* she thought, but there was no sign of her. Only Vince, and a strange man-horse with another man splayed across its back, and a woman carrying a gun. They were tending to the man on the man's... horse's... thing's back, and he was the source of the long, low moaning.

Sammi felt freedom and help closing in. She barely knew Vince, had only met him a couple of times, but he had been with her aunt, and now she knew that he was here to help.

She certainly couldn't sit here for too long, trying to debate what to do.

"Vince!" she whispered, and they all turned to look at her.

Vince, with wide-eyed disbelief and a smile breaking across his face.

The horse-man with a look nothing like a real man's.

The woman with the gun pointing at her face.

"Sammi!" Vince said. "Are you—"

His gaze shifted behind her at the same time as she heard the sound. She knew it was Gregor, so instead of pausing to turn and look she launched herself from the side of the tree and curled into a ball, hitting the slope hard and rolling several times before coming to a halt. Scrambling on hands and knees, scratched and cut in a hundred places, she scrabbled toward Vince.

He was there for her, grabbing her under the arm and pulling her upright. Beside him, the older woman was standing in a shooting stance.

Sammi twisted to look behind her.

Gregor was at the bottom of the slope. Sweating, panting, curved knife grasped in his right hand, he was also grinning a mad, toothy grin. There was blood on his face from where a branch or thorn had slashed him across the bridge of his nose. Blood smeared his teeth red.

"Give her to me," he said, and the woman tensed.

"You want me to kill him?" she asked.

"Yes," Vince said.

"No!" Sammi shouted. "Not because of me."

The woman breathed hard, grumbling in her throat.

"It's not only for you, Sammi," Vince said. "Shoot him."

Sammi actually heard the metallic strain of the trigger tightening when another sound broke the air. A heavy, unbelievably loud crack. Not for an instant did she believe it was a gunshot, because she'd heard that sound before.

Not again, Sammi thought, and the fading marks across her shoulder, chest, and arm tingled with static. *Oh no, not again.*

* * *

As Grace makes her way toward one of the remaining open routes into and out of her Fold, she stretches out her senses and probes beyond. It is unpleasant—sensing out into the human world is distasteful, like putting herself into the mind of a madman. With these bridges still connecting the Fold to the world, however, she can do it with relative ease.

Where she has recently felt one Kin approaching, now there are more. Confusion takes hold for an instant, then she gathers herself. Quickly she moves down the sweeping valley side toward the floor, leaping several tumbling streams, cooling herself in the mist from a waterfall, reaching the river and following its course downstream. Soon this river will come from and flow to nowhere, and she has begun thinking about how she will stock it with fish and keep the waters fresh. Her magic will make it happen.

The powers inside her, dormant for so long, are relishing this new explosive use. This is a wonderful sensation.

As she follows the river she hears something calling out in the distance. It is a vibrant, exultant sound, and it gives her a frisson of delight. One of the deniers she has brought here has found itself again, reassumed its real form, shed whatever pretense allowed it to exist openly within the world of humans. With every day that passes, her Fold is becoming a true place of the Kin.

She feels no need to walk to the open portal at the end of the valley. Instead, after assessing the orientation of the Fold and the location she needs to reach, she reaches out with her magic to make a rent in the Fold's skin. Her magic comes as easily as breathing, thinking, being, and with a sharp crack the temporary tear opens up.

She peers through into the human world and sees the final Kin she seeks.

She doesn't even have to move. She reaches out, grabs the denier, and pulls her through.

Then with a blink she closes the rip and drops the girl to the ground.

"No," Vince breathed.

"No!" Gregor shouted.

Jay fired, but he had leapt toward the place where Sammi had been standing. The bullet slammed into the hillside.

Gregor tripped and landed on his face, clawing at the ground, hauling himself closer to the place where the impossible had happened.

I saw, Vince thought. He reached out and pushed the rifle down before Jay could shoot again. "We might need him." He didn't know how, or why, he thought that, but he was acting without thinking, some strange instinct moving him while his thoughts…

… his thoughts wallowed in shock.

I saw the fairy, I saw into the Fold, another world, her world, and now Sammi is in there, too.

Grace had reached through and grabbed Sammi's hand. Time moved differently—out here manic, panicked, the witnesses watching in stunned disbelief. In that strange other place, slow and considered, almost calm. Sammi had stood and walked through, guided by the fairy who had glanced past her at the others.

Her eyes had met Vince's. Less than a heartbeat, less than a blink, but in his memory that gaze felt like forever, as if he had been born staring into her eyes, and still did now. They held him pinned to the world.

"I saw…" he said, but he couldn't say what he had seen. It made so little sense that words couldn't describe. In his memory it was already a dream, so solid and sure moments ago, now faded and hazy. He tried to remember, to hold onto what they'd just witnessed. He closed his eyes.

"What happened?" Jay asked.

"I saw," another voice said, and Vince turned to Baylor. The centaur was motionless, eyes wide and staring past Vince. But it was Meloy who had spoken. Splayed across the beast's back, his head was raised. He locked eyes with Vince. "She took Sammi?"

"The fairy took Sammi," Vince confirmed, and stating the truth out loud made it awful. He turned to Jay. "How do we get her back? How do we go through there and bring Sammi back?"

Gregor was raging, dashing back and forth where they'd seen the split open and close. He clawed at trees, kicked at the ground, swung his hands at the air.

"How the fuck should I know?" Jay asked. She raised the rifle again and aimed it at Gregor, but her urge to kill him seemed to have abated. "I don't really know anything," she said, voice quieter.

Vince rushed across to Gregor. The man was in a panic, unaware of his approach. Vince grabbed him, punched him in the face, hard, and he stumbled and fell back.

"Where were you taking her?" Vince shouted.

Gregor blinked up at him. He wasn't there.

Vince circled around from the fallen man's feet and kicked him in the ribs. Breath hushed from him and he rolled onto his side. Vince kicked him between the shoulders, knelt, and started tugging the backpack from his back.

That brought Gregor around to reality. He fought, swinging around to punch Vince in the leg. The fallen man paused, looking in surprise at his hand, as if something should be there.

"Bastard!" Vince hissed, kneeing him in the back and pushing him face down. "Jay! Get that rifle in his face!" She was already there, pressing the gun's barrel down against Gregor's cheek. She leaned on the weapon and Gregor groaned as his cheek was forced inward against his teeth.

"It'll blast your lower jaw off," Jay said, "but you'll still be alive. Give me the smallest excuse, you murderous shit."

Vince dragged the backpack from the man's back.

"Mine!" Gregor said, a hopeless wail through pain.

"Mine now," Vince said. "Let's see what's so precious to you." He ripped open the top flap and upended it on the ground.

A dozen wrapped objects tumbled out, maybe more. They varied in size and weight, but all were packaged in fine gray cloth. Vince knew what he might find. Gregor's reputation, the reason he was here, told him everything he needed to know. It made unwrapping even one of them even harder.

"That's *mine!*" Gregor hissed, his words twisted by the rifle pressing into his face.

"None of these are yours," Vince said. He plucked the cloth away from the object and opened it up to the sunlight, then gasped. It was something that should have never seen light, because it belonged inside a body, not outside.

Jay saw it and pressed her lips together, leaning more weight on the rifle. Gregor groaned and squirmed against the pain.

Vince couldn't tell exactly what the object was or what it came from, but one thing was obvious. It had come from a living creature. Gregor had killed to acquire it, as he had for every other wrapped item in his bag.

"Where were you going with Sammi?" Vince asked. "Where were you going with *this*?"

Jay eased back so that the Kin-killer could talk.

"Across the ridge, up on the escarpment," he said. "Look. Just look."

Vince left the backpack and its objects, left Jay pressing the rifle against the killer's face, and climbed a steep outcropping to try and see past the trees. He looked up the slope to a ridge that curved around to the right, forming a lip around a steep-sided ravine.

And he saw.

Whatever it was, it didn't belong in the world. This had to be the Fold. It had to be where Sammi had been taken.

He jumped down from the rock just as a gunshot rang out from below.

36

As soon as Angela heard the gunshot she knew what it meant.

Ahara glanced back, knowing that her deception had been revealed. She grinned at Angela and Lilou and flitted away to nothing, a point of light quickly swallowed away in the sunlight.

"Never can trust a wisp," Mallian growled.

"That way," Thorn the pixie said. He pointed to their left, toward a sheer climb and the forest slopes above.

"The Fold," Angela said. Ahead of them, higher up at the head of the ravine, the strange area of woodland blurred and pulsed, drawing her in. If Gregor still had Sammi, that was where he'd be taking her.

"What I want is there," Mallian said, nodding in the direction from which the gunshot had come. "We climb."

"What if we don't?" Lilou asked.

Mallian shrugged. "You do, you don't, it doesn't matter to me anymore. But you either come with me, or I'll leave you here dead."

"You won't be able to kill me," the nymph said. It was almost a challenge.

"I think I could," Mallian said, and Angela believed him. "If I really had to. Her, though? Easily."

Angela felt ice in her spine when Mallian looked at her and said that. She was nothing in his eyes, just another human, no matter that she'd helped rescue the fairy in London. Humans were beneath him. It was Kin prejudice, and she couldn't imagine him ever changing. The Nephilim displayed a very human stubbornness.

They headed for the cliff, and as they approached Angela saw the diminutive figure of Thorn dashing back and forth across the shale slopes at the cliff's base. By the time they reached him he was already climbing a narrow trail he'd found on the cliff face, a natural fault that was scattered with dried animal crap and shreds of fur snagged on the sharp rocky surface.

Angela and Lilou started up, and she glanced behind to see if the Nephilim was following. *Maybe once he might have flown*, she thought, and not for the first time she wondered at his story, his history. The immediate truth of him was there before her, a tactile thing she could smell, touch, fear. The implications of his existence, the wider story implied, terrified her.

Mallian found the cliff path easy going. Though he was almost twice her height and four times as heavy, he walked the path with an easy grace, clasping onto the cliff with his big hands, bare feet treading in her footsteps. Despite everything he wanted to achieve, and the awful things she had seen him do, he was magnificent.

Thorn reached the cliff top first, dashing back and forth as he waited for them to complete the climb.

Angela felt a heaviness in her guts. Her hands were sweating. She'd never liked heights, and sometimes Vince sent her YouTube links of idiots scaling tall buildings and standing on the tops of cranes or aerial masts, defying gravity and death for a selfie that would make them famous if they fell. She never liked looking, but always had to. It was a similar thrill she felt riding the biggest roller coasters.

By comparison, her climb up the steep slope was terrifying. She faced the rock wall and walked sideways, looking down at her feet and trying not to see past them to the drop into the woods below. They'd only just passed the highest of the trees, but it was still a long enough fall to make jelly of her when she hit the ground.

"I'd catch you," Mallian said, and the sudden rumble of his voice almost sent her tumbling.

"I didn't think you cared," she said.

"Oh, I don't. If you die here, it'll be on my terms."

"Thanks. Nice. Good to know. Prick."

"You humans are weird."

Taken by a fit of giggles she carried on climbing, and soon Lilou grabbed her hand and pulled her up from the rough path and onto the cliff top. Laughter might have turned to desperate tears, but Angela bit her lip. Crying wouldn't help Sammi.

"Through there," Mallian said, stepping past them and pointing into the trees.

"I don't hear anything," Thorn said.

"Nor do I. But I smell blood."

"He moved, he went for me, I had to," the woman said, and although Gregor knew that she was lying he could say nothing, do nothing. The shock and pain was all-consuming. Everything felt wrong. Sickness threatened, but he knew that if he threw up, his body might finish the bullet's job.

He was on his feet, walking in a tight circle and trying not to touch his face. On the ground where he'd been lying a spatter of blood glimmered in sunlight that filtered through the tree canopy. Too much blood. There were other things there too. He didn't want to see but couldn't help looking, and he saw teeth, and shards of bone, and gristly shreds of flesh that were already attracting flies.

I'm not dead yet and they're eating me already, he thought, and he fought back a hysterical shout.

He couldn't see the damage that had been done to his face, but the expressions of those around him provided the perfect mirror.

Despite her protestations, the woman looked pleased. The man, Vince, stared at him in shock. The centaur had averted his gaze, and the man resting on his back, head against the centaur's thick neck, had a strange smile on his face, despite his own deformative and still-bleeding injuries.

"Ugh…" Gregor said, and agony pulsed through his face, head, and neck. Everything above his chest felt wrong. When he moved his head swayed back and forth, a weight swinging at its base and driving spears of blazing pain through his scalp and skull. He didn't think the woman had blown off his lower jaw, but it felt close.

"The gunfire will bring them," Vince said.

"Good," the woman said. She turned her back on the man she had shot and aimed the rifle into the forest.

"Just…" Vince said to him, but it was clear he didn't know what else to say, what advice to offer.

"Uhhh," Gregor said. He reached up at last and touched the ruin of his face. His fingers found parts of it before they should have. Shreds were hanging too low. They were wet and meaty, warm.

"Something!" Baylor said, and as the horse-man stomped his hooves, Gregor sensed a shape coming at them through the trees. The clarity of his vision shocked him but he grasped onto it, because for a second or two it diverted him from the pain.

A shape, a shadow, a smear of pale light danced from tree to tree as it came closer, shaking leaves and branches, startling birds that had only just landed again following the gunshot.

Jay raised her gun but something knocked it from her grasp, sending her flying through the air as if punched by a train. She hit the ground and rolled, winded, hugging her knees up toward her chest.

The attacker became motionless, a woman or an otter, an otter or a woman. Between blinks she changed from one to the other, before manifesting into a tall, naked woman, sleek and shining, her auburn hair hanging down across her shoulders.

She picked up the dropped gun and bent the barrel into a question mark over her raised leg.

"Mallian is here," she said. Her voice sounded strained, as if she was more used to growling or howling.

And then Mallian was there, along with the small man who had accompanied him down on the road. Angela and Lilou were there also.

They all looked at Gregor with a mixture of disgust and shock.

And now he'll save me, Gregor thought. *My Mallian,*

my angel, I've done everything he's asked, and he can steal the blood from the fairy's second heart and save me. Make me more than I ever was before.

Mallian walked to Gregor and stood before him, huge and proud and devastating in his sheer presence.

"Poor Gregor," he said. "Where is it?"

Gregor tried to speak but pain throbbed through him, lava in his veins, acid in his muscles. He stumbled and fell, and Mallian's arm was there to hold him up.

He killed the witch for me to dig out her inner eye. He'll kill the fairy and squeeze her second heart. For me. Always for me, because he sees how special I can be.

"Where?" Mallian asked, and his big hand squeezed. Too hard. It hurt.

"Uhh!" Gregor grunted, and blood hazed the air before his face.

"It's here," Vince said. He held up the backpack, straps retied.

"Ahh," Mallian said. He lunged forward and snatched the bag away. Then he looked down at Gregor, and Gregor looked up into the face of his angel.

He didn't see what he had been hoping to see.

There was cruelty in Mallian's eyes.

"And now your story is done," the Nephilim said.

Gregor shook his head, feeling his shattered lower jaw swinging on shreds of gristle.

"You've done well."

But my change! Gregor thought. *I was always destined to be Kin. It was all for me, for the change, for the spell you promised to cast. I was going to be the bridge between species.* He wished he could say these things, but the bullet had stolen his voice.

Mallian reached up with his free hand and closed it around Gregor's head.

Careful, it hurts, it hurts!

And then he realized that Mallian did not care, and never had. He had only ever cared about himself.

Gregor felt the initial exertion of immense pressure, heard the first crunch of bone, and then he felt and heard no more.

37

He drops the body and turns away, shakes his hand, spattering brains and gore across the ground. He splays his fingers and examines the bloody, jellyfish gloop strung between them.

Human waste, he thinks. *Nothing like the Kin he dreamed of becoming.* He feels no pity for Gregor, and he never has. Some small gratitude, perhaps. Even respect that the sad, deluded human managed to achieve so much.

"Watch them," he says. Thorn giggles and skitters around the small group. The kooshdakhaa hangs back, a naked woman in the shadows, a beast in the sun. He has seen her killing before, and knows that she regards humans as even less than he. She has lived in the wild for so long that they intrude into her world, not the other way around. He knows that he can trust her.

Perhaps he should kill them all now. But he is afraid that such violence will urge Lilou to act, to protect those human friends she has made.

He has no wish to harm Lilou.

When his plan achieves fruition, she might appreciate the sense of Ascent. With the fairy in his thrall, the power he wields will be endless. Then she will understand.

"Mallian," Lilou says, "this isn't the way."

"Is there any other?" he asks.

Lilou goes to reply, but she has nothing to say. She understands that she cannot change his mind.

That makes her dangerous.

"Don't let them follow me," he says. "We're almost done. Everything changes today."

"Everything!" Thorn says.

The kooshdakhaa says nothing, but she, it, smiles.

Mallian turns and lopes away, the rucksack safe in one hand. He hears raised voices behind him as Lilou and the humans appeal to him one last time. Even if he heard the words they would mean nothing. Everything he has lived for over the past few decades has been edging toward this moment. The human Gregor has gathered everything he needs for the spell, and soon the fairy will be under his control.

It doesn't take him long to climb the hill and reach the escarpment. The entrance to the Fold is there, a shifting haze on reality. A wafting breeze washes over him from that strange phenomenon, and for a moment it startles him. He gasps and breathes in again. The scent inspires such memories.

Then with one great step he passes out of the human world, and into another.

With a crushing sense of failure, Angela watched Mallian leave. She had failed Sammi, and all the people who would suffer if Ascent came to pass. She had achieved nothing by coming here, dragging Vince with her, apart from getting people killed. It was becoming the story of her life.

As the Nephilim disappeared uphill into the forest, Thorn circled them warily, and the woman-beast hung back in the trees ready to strike. Though sometimes she was a naked woman, she was one of the least human-looking Kin Angela had ever seen. It was as much about her aura as her appearance. She exuded strangeness.

Vince sat down and leaned back against a tree. Angela was shocked at his apparent submission, but then she saw the look in his eyes, and knew. He was feigning it to try and gain an advantage. He didn't have to say anything. It reminded her of how well they knew each other. Not only did they sometimes finish each other's sentences, they shared the same thoughts.

We look as though we've given in and they'll lower their guard.

She walked to Baylor, who still carried the injured Meloy on his back.

"How you feeling?" she asked.

"Like Godzilla stood on me," Meloy said, but he was sitting up. He was astride Baylor, leaning against the centaur's thick neck and holding onto his flowing mane. Meloy had bled onto the Kin's pelt. The blood was drying now.

"We'll get help," Angela said. "A hospital. Or something." It sounded ridiculous and she knew it. They were miles from anywhere, and unless they airlifted him out he'd likely never survive a journey through the forest.

Meloy smiled. Baylor shifted, and it turned into a grimace.

"Watching you!" Thorn said. "We're watching, both of us."

Angela glanced back at Vince. He was leaning against the tree, eyes closed. Lilou was sitting beside him now, and she caught Angela's eye. She was in on their charade. She knew this couldn't be the end of it. But how to fight back when Thorn and the woman were there?

"I'll help," Meloy whispered. "I've got a surprise or two in me yet." He spoke as if something was broken within him, but the passion in his voice was palpable. Everything he'd been was changed, everything he had become was determined to help the Kin. Even injured like this he was a formidable man.

"What about Jay?" Baylor asked.

"I don't think she's good," Angela said. Jay was sitting up a little way from them, hugging herself around the stomach. She didn't seem able to move, nor was she paying them any attention. She stared at her feet as if willing them to carry her away from here.

"What do we do?" Angela asked.

"We wait," Baylor said.

"What?"

"Not long. Don't worry. I suspect a minute, maybe less."

"I don't—"

"The more we talk about it," the man-horse said, "the more likely they'll hear. Go and sit with your husband. Be ready."

"They're not married," Meloy said, and Angela held back a laugh. It was such a mundane comment, something that held no relevance at all. Turning away, she hoped it wasn't the last thing she would ever hear Meloy say.

Slumping to the ground between Vince and Lilou she leaned against the tree, closed her eyes until they were only open a slit. Thorn was still circling them, a small shadow darting through the trees. The inhuman woman remained where she'd been when Mallian left, perfectly still, watching, waiting.

Angela had seen how violent and brutal Thorn could be, but it was the woman who scared her most.

"What?" Vince whispered.

"Don't know," she said. "Baylor said wait."

"I think I know," Lilou said, and she sounded strange. Angry and sad at the same time.

Only the wisp can make her sound like that!

The darting, leaping shape of Thorn suddenly tripped and struck the ground with a heavy grunt. He shrieked a warning. Ahara manifested atop him, pummeling her arms down into the pixie's face, and as Thorn cried out again, Angela saw movement deeper in the forest.

"She's coming!" she said, and she, Lilou, and Vince stood. They had no weapons, and weren't prepared to confront the kooshdakhaa. As she came for them she flickered between woman and beast, pale and dark, lithe and muscular, and Angela crouched to pick up a short, heavy stick.

With a single leap, Baylor launched himself into the woman's path. He punched out with his front hooves but she was ready for him, dropping onto her back and sliding beneath him, slicing ragged nails across his chest and stomach as she went.

The centaur cried out in pain and shock.

The woman grinned as she stood. Not ten feet from

the humans, she looked determined to kill.

Angela saw the movement, recognized what was about to happen, and she almost cried out. Lilou grabbed her arm and squeezed to keep her silent.

The kooshdakhaa glanced down at the movement. It grabbed her attention, and that gave Meloy another vital second.

The injured man leapt from the centaur's back and landed on the Kin. If he'd been expecting her to crumple and fall beneath his weight he was disappointed, but he did not pause. As she stumbled two steps forward, he wrapped his muscled arms around her neck and face, his legs crossed around her thighs.

"Go!" Meloy shouted.

"Meloy," Lilou said. He looked at her, and smiled. She took a step forward. This time it was Angela's turn to hold her back.

"He's giving us time!" she said.

The kooshdakhaa flitted between human and animal, struggling to loosen Meloy's grip. His face was a grimace, eyes squeezed shut, and Angela couldn't imagine the pain he was in. She was a naked woman, skin slick with sweat, his arms slipping and legs almost losing their grip. She was an otter-like creature, fur thick with dirt and dried blood. She screamed obscenities at the air, then gnashed at Meloy's arms with sharp animal canines, piercing and slashing to the bone, ripping, crunching.

Meloy gritted his teeth but did not scream. He held on tight. He couldn't fight this thing, but he could restrain it.

"Go!" Jay called. She was still seated and nursing her

own pain, but she saw the chance they were being given.

Angela knew there wouldn't be another one.

She glanced across at Thorn and Ahara, engaged as they were in their own fight. Then, without another word, she, Vince, and Lilou started uphill, following the route Mallian had so recently taken toward the entrance to the Fold. Angela still gripped the stick she'd picked up, and she slammed it against a couple of trees to test its strength. It was solid, but didn't give her an ounce of comfort or hope.

However they faced Mallian, they would need something more than a broken tree to help them.

They climbed in silence, pushing themselves hard to take every second they could from Meloy's selfless act. The silence was a heavy pressure that none of them wanted to break, a pressure that built as Angela awaited the sound she dreaded.

When the scream came, Angela felt it crawl inside and scrape claws across her soul. Lilou let out a sob.

They kept moving, faster if anything, all of them understanding that Meloy's sacrifice gave them this one chance to achieve their aims. For Lilou, to stop Mallian. For Angela, to rescue Sammi.

"She'll be coming," Lilou said. Neither of them replied. There was no time, they had no breath. Every word spoken took strength, and they needed each gasp to reach the Fold before the changeling reached them.

When they broke out of the forest onto the escarpment it came as a surprise. Even while Angela rested on hands and knees, panting and sweating and trying to catch her breath, Lilou was up and urging them on.

"No time to stare," the nymph said. "Follow me." She started running toward the thing that should not be there.

Vince and Angela shared a glance and followed.

Everything is telling me to run the other way, Angela thought. *Maybe that's how the Kin have survived for so long. Everything about them makes us want to look and run the other way.*

All but a few of us.

Part of the landscape was somewhere else. The rocky escarpment, home to some isolated trees, steep shale slopes, and spreads of moss-covered stone, was blurred and uncertain a hundred feet from where they had climbed from the steep forest. Still they ran, not hesitating, not risking a moment of their advantage.

At the last second, as Angela passed through the shimmering mass, she wondered whether only Kin could enter the Fold.

Maybe she and Vince would be turned inside out.

Eyes squeezed shut, she ran on.

38

She has not felt shock like this in such a long time.

The fairy shivers in the warm, comfortable atmosphere of the world she has created. The shivering is from surprise and a deep-rooted clenching of her soul, a feeling she has not believed possible for many centuries, perhaps more. Uncertainty stalks her like the ghost of the fairy she used to be.

This was all about being on my own, she thinks, and the figure before her mimics her quivering fear.

The girl stares at her, eyes wide, breathing fast and shallow. Behind the girl she sees the wide, beautiful landscape that she is so eager to close off from the rest of reality and call, finally, home. She has peopled it with her own kind, or at least fellow Kin, creatures who she will come to know better over time. This girl should have been the last of them.

I never knew. I never even suspected.

It's that deficiency in her knowledge that shocks her as much as what she sees before her.

Somewhere in this girl is fairy.

"Who are you?" the fairy asks, and the girl frowns and takes a few steps back. *It should be her asking me that question*, she thinks. *It should be me with the authority here.* Without even speaking, the human-looking girl is taking charge.

She takes another step back.

The fairy whispers something in her own ancient language. It's a sound she rarely makes anymore because only she is there to hear and understand, and she will not talk to herself. It's barely a language at all, more a muttering of insinuations and an exhalation of hopes.

The girl's eyes grow wide. Is that a flicker of understanding?

"No," the girl breathes. And then she opens her mouth and says something else, something in the fairy language.

She drops to her knees.

The girl has fairy in her, and now she is talking to me in a language she cannot know. This is more than denial. This is ignorance. How the human-ish child could have existed for so long without knowing is beyond her grasp.

Five generations ago, eight, twelve... this child's ancestor lay with a fairy.

"Travesty," the fairy says. She is angry that such a word must taint the air of her Fold. "Corruption," she whispers, the word heavy and dirty on her breath. She mutters an incantation in her fairy language. The ground shakes. Grasses wave back and forth in rippling patterns of fear.

The girl turns and runs.

But as the fairy stands to follow, to tear the girl down and rip out the part of her that should not be, a great invisible hand slams down onto her, driving her into the soil of her own Fold and knocking the breath from her lungs.

At first she thinks it is the girl, and she berates herself for not recognizing such power. But lying on her side she can still see the girl sprinting like a frightened child down into the valley in her flight of fear.

This is not the girl. This is something else.

He has not felt a thrill like this in such a long time.

Inside the Fold is like the Time, and for the first couple of minutes Mallian forgets everything he is here for. He walks and looks, breathes and remembers, and for the first time in a long, long while he sheds a tear for everything that has passed.

Then he grows more determined than ever before about everything that is to come.

He senses that he is being watched. He cannot see the watcher, but he can smell it, and he knows that it is Kin. He is happy to let it watch. Perhaps in times to come the watcher will tell stories about what he or she saw, and sing songs. Mallian rarely lets pride obstruct his actions, but he allows himself this.

Emptying the rucksack, he unwraps the items which Gregor spent his adult life collecting from across the world. Most of these relics are memories from the past, old, withered things from creatures that once thrived, or at least survived. Mallian feels sadness that they had to die for him, but bears no guilt. He cannot allow that. With all the things he has done, guilt will drive him mad.

The glamor is one he has harbored to himself for many decades. One of the few left to him—a shred of magic, a dreg of something once so much more powerful—he has nurtured and practiced its performance and charms every year for all that time. Always alone, always in private, never revealing the talent, he has constantly been preparing for this moment.

He looks around for the fairy. She will soon know that he's here, and he has to ensure that he's ready for her when that moment arrives.

The spell is in two parts—subdue and contain. When Grace is subdued he will be safe from her great power, for a time. And once she is contained, he will own her.

He spreads the relics on the ground before him. They will be used in two parts, to coincide with the two portions of the glamor. He concentrates on the first, arranging seven of them in a half-circle around him. Kneeling within the arc, he touches each relic and experiences a brief, powerful memory of its owner's life. It's a humbling experience. He accepts each memory with a mutter of thanks, and a promise that their lives will be remembered—even those whose lives ended in hiding, ashamed and terrified.

Even those, he honors. Every Kin, no matter how beaten down and petrified of what this world has become, is worth a hundred humans. A thousand. More.

Soon, such numbers will begin to pay their dues.

Mallian mutters the glamor. He has its Script once again, but he does not need to consult it, because he remembers every word, turn of phrase, and incantation perfectly. Concentrating all his focus on the seven relics, he remembers where this magic originated. His senses thrum with memories of the Time, and some memories are fed by this new place. It would be a good place to make a home, but he quickly shoves that idea aside.

The fairy has built this Fold as a retreat. Hiding is what Mallian has been doing for far too long, and the ethos of Ascent is the exact opposite.

He repeats the glamor again... again... and with each repetition he is closer to completing the first part of the spell.

He takes a deep breath and sees what is watching him. One of the Kin, a denier, given freedom by the fairy. But this valley is not real freedom.

Mallian shoves, and the spell is made. He feels it surging outward, and somewhere in the Fold the fairy falls to the ground, subdued. He grins.

I'm so close, he thinks, and the Kin has vanished. Perhaps his delight has scared her away.

He sweeps aside the seven relics. They have served their purpose, and already he can smell the scent of decay as time catches them and they begin to putrefy. He begins to spread the second seven items, ready for the spell that will contain the fairy and place her in his thrall.

Such power to command. Such potential—

There are only six.

He pauses, breath held, then looks again. Still six.

Mallian knows the Script word for word, letter for letter, and there are seven items required for each spell. Gregor gathered all of them. A witch's third ear and eye was the last, and Jilaria Bran gave herself up for that great honor.

He counts the parts. Six.

He closes his eyes and thinks of Vince holding the rucksack up to him. That deceitful human.

Mallian roars.

* * *

She rises up. Shoved face-first into the dirt of her world, she knew exactly what was happening. It is an ancient glamor, one not used on a fairy for millennia. It might be the one thing she still fears, greater than an eternity alone, so she pushes back against it, struggling to regain herself before the second part of the glamor is cast and she is forever in thrall to whoever is doing the casting.

It's him, she thinks as the Nephilim comes to mind. Of all the Kin she has encountered in recent memory, he may be the only one with access to the spells, and the wherewithal to gather the parts required. *He rescued me only to contain me.*

She grimaces as she stands, casting her own conflicting glamors to fight against the weight that is crushing her down. Pushing back, pushing hard, she realizes that the second glamor is not yet cast. If he knows what he is doing, he must know that his time is now short.

Something must have gone wrong.

Still moving against the stifling weight of subjugation, she starts down the hillside toward the entrance to the Fold, following the fleeing girl. She can see traces of her on the air like echoes of her passing. Signs of her trace of fairy blood hang everywhere—a shimmer to the air, a sheen against certain flowers. It is something incredible. Perhaps if she can recapture the girl, she will not have to rip out the fairy part of her, buried in human flesh, blood, and bone. Perhaps over time, the girl might become what she always craved for her eternity in the Fold.

True companionship.

Moving faster, shrugging off more and more of the glamor with her own powers, she eyes her future with the brightest eyes yet.

39

Sammi had never run this fast before. Leaping from rock to rock, pounding across grassy slopes, dodging holes in the ground, jumping over a ravine and just making the other side without slipping and falling, her focus was on the valley floor and its end, where she saw the shimmering opening that she'd first experienced from the other side.

The other side was home. She didn't know what this side was, only that it was a long way from home. The Fold looked like a valley she might know, but although there were trees and grasses, a river and signs of geological time having formed this place, she knew it was somewhere else. The fairy had made this place.

The fairy had seen something in her.

Sammi wouldn't allow herself to think about that, for now. Her only aim now was to escape, run back into her world where Angela and Vince were searching for her. Gregor might still be there, but at least he was a danger she could understand.

Something about this place felt so wrong. It was a feeling in her bones, a whisper coming from deep inside in a voice she didn't quite know, but felt like she should.

Her mother wasn't here. That had been a lie all

along, and she guessed she'd known it for a while. She couldn't beat on herself for hoping, though. She hated Gregor all the more.

Jumping over a stream she landed in marshy ground, falling forward and losing a sneaker in the muck. It didn't matter. She crawled, then stood and started running again, despite the discomfort. She was on the valley floor now, and ahead of her she could see the air shimmering with the exit from the Fold. Perhaps this was her only way out. She hoped it was safe.

But it wasn't, and Sammi knew that even before she heard the cries and saw the beast kneeling close to the Fold, raging about something that had been done to him. It was Mallian, his fury unleashed, power unrestrained. There were small objects scattered around him, and close to his feet lay Gregor's backpack.

Sammi skidded to a halt and hid behind a huge fallen tree. She looked around, through a gap where the tree lay against a tumble of rocks. Mallian stood between her and the way back home. Perhaps she could run past him and be through the portal before he caught her. Or perhaps in his rage he would snatch her up and tear her in half out of pure spite.

She had never been so far from home. The distance seemed to be a hollow within her, readying to explode, as if the infinity between here and there had its own terrible gravity. Then something inside calmed and soothed her, and told her that if she only kept her wits, then things might still end up all right. The Fold was a universe and just a step away from home. All she had to do was take that step.

Edging around the fallen tree, she eyed the best route past Mallian.

As she tensed and readied herself to run, heart hammering, sweat glimmering on her face, she saw movement in the blurred portal.

Three figures came through.

Angela, Vince, and the woman who had been with them.

Mallian stopped shouting and stood motionless as he watched them pass through.

"You!" he said, pointing at Vince. "You stole from me."

Angela looked past the towering Nephilim and locked eyes with Sammi. Sammi smiled. Angela frowned.

And then Sammi sensed something approaching behind her.

Glancing back she saw Grace floating down the valley side and leaping across the stream, moving so quickly that her feet barely seemed to touch the ground.

Mallian turned, too, and saw the fairy at the same time. His face dropped. His shoulders slumped.

"Sammi!" Angela shouted.

Sammi broke cover and ran.

This is when everything changes, Angela thought, and she rushed ahead without giving herself time to pause. Instinct took over. She focused on Sammi, running to meet the girl who was sprinting toward her. Nothing else mattered.

Between her and Sammi stood Mallian, and she had never seen him looking so fearsome, so furious. Past the fallen tree, Grace rushed toward them all.

Mallian glanced at her, growling. He looked past her at Lilou and Vince, his expression melting into one of pure hate.

Then he twisted and faced the fairy, hands turning into claws. He roared, and his anger filled the sky.

Sammi was past him now, skirting around so that she remained out of reach, and Angela stopped and held her arms wide, welcoming in her lost niece and hugging her tight.

"We have to run," Angela said.

"All the way home," the girl said.

They turned and headed back toward the doorway. Lilou and Vince were there, watching, and as she caught Vince's eye he gave her a strange smile.

"Run and don't look back," he said as they passed, but of course that meant Angela had to look back. Even as Lilou grabbed her beneath the arm and urged her faster toward the portal. Even as something about it began to change—the shimmers settled, the size of it dwindled, and the sense of it being a fluid, hollow place began to fall away.

She looked back and knew that Vince wasn't coming with her. Her fiancé, her lover, was walking toward Mallian as the Nephilim took three huge strides toward them. He was coming for Sammi, for Lilou, and for her, perhaps to exact revenge while he still could, or maybe he thought he might still salvage something from his doomed efforts.

Maybe he thought they had been stupid enough to bring the relic Vince had taken.

"Faster!" Lilou said.

"But Vince—"

"Jump!" The nymph pulled her and Sammi as she leapt at the doorway, and as they entered Angela had her final glimpse of him.

The Nephilim was twice his size and ten times as furious, but Vince was already swinging a fist, punching out to hold Mallian back. As Angela fell through and back into her own real, harsh world, she saw the Nephilim's arms swinging down to crush the man she loved.

"No!" she screamed, but passing through had stolen her voice, and all that emerged was a dull croak.

Angela struck the ground and scrambled back to her feet in one movement.

"Take her," she said, pushing Sammi toward Lilou. She turned, ready to rush back through into the Fold and confront whatever awaited her there.

But there was nowhere to go. The mountain escarpment was bare, wild, harsh, and home to nothing out of place.

"No!" she cried, and this time the scream came out. But no matter how many times she tried to deny it, the truth was that the Fold was closed.

Grace had made her new world whole.

Angela held hands with Sammi, and with Lilou and Jay walking on ahead they began to make their way down out of the mountains. It was dusk again. Jay was limping and in pain, but too proud to accept a ride. Baylor was still there to support her as much as she would allow. The old woman sobbed silently.

Angela had never felt such a sense of deep loss. It was bad enough seeing the body of Fat Frederick Meloy, a big man reduced in death. His murderer had vanished by the time they came back through, the kooshdakhaa melting back into the vast woodlands when she realized Mallian was not returning. Whether she actually cared about his cause, Angela did not know, and Lilou and Jay wouldn't hazard a guess. She was now just another Kin in hiding.

They spied Thorn now and then as they headed down the mountainside. Something about him had changed. He seemed uncertain, even afraid, and though still cautious, they no longer felt threatened by him. Long before they reached the first of the hiking paths that would take them back to the vehicles, the pixie disappeared.

"He doesn't like me," Sammi said. Something about the way she spoke troubled Angela. The girl had a depth of knowledge in her voice that she was afraid to examine.

"That's no normal girl," Jay said when she was out of earshot.

Lilou said nothing, even when Angela asked.

Losing Vince left an unknowable void. If she had seen him die, could touch his body, she might not have felt so hollowed out as she did now. One second he had been there with her, the next he was a universe away. That cutting of ties had been a physical thing, inspiring a flush of pain through her core and a sickness of the soul from which she wasn't sure she'd ever recover.

Where is he? she wanted to ask, but there was no good answer.

Is he alive? Once, she might have been able to tell. She wasn't one to believe in mystical links and the tight bondings of love, but the sickening sensation when the

Fold closed would be with her forever. At that moment she and Vince had been split in half, one core cut in two, one love ripped forever. It was a horrible, empty feeling.

Maybe Sammi might help her fill some of it. Maybe not. That was something for the future.

"Where to now?" Lilou asked when they stopped for a rest, and Angela was surprised by the question. The nymph had lost something, too, Angela realized. Whatever the relationship between her and Mallian, that had also been torn asunder, even before the Fold closed. Perhaps she was feeling that same sense of deep, unfathomable loss.

"I have no idea," Angela said. She looked at Sammi, who was sitting on a rock and staring down across the valley. There was a road in the distance, vehicles moving along it like single points of light. It was a comfort seeing signs of civilization, but it also brought back the familiar worries. "I'm still wanted by the law, and that'll never change."

"I can help," Jay said. "Know a few places that'll be safe. Cabins outside of small towns, easy to get stuff delivered, private communities. No one asks questions."

"I don't think I'll ever feel safe among people again."

"Welcome to my world," Lilou said. "So, what about…?" She nodded at Sammi.

"I'll look after her," Angela said. At the same time, she had the odd feeling that part of their relationship might go both ways.

There was something about the girl.

40

Time moved unevenly in this strange new world.

Sometimes it felt like hours since the Fold had closed and he had felt that brutal, irreversible dislocation that separated him from Angela. Other times it felt like days, even weeks. The sickness was the same, the sense of loss uniformly awful. Time did nothing to dispel that.

Vince had taken shelter in a small cave close to the river. Here he had water, and food in the form of berries growing on nearby bushes. He didn't recognize the berries. Hunger had driven him to try them, and he wasn't dead yet.

The sun rose and fell, but the length of each day felt arbitrary. His watch had stopped working. He'd tried his phone, but then remembered that the battery was dead. He suspected there would be no signal even if it wasn't. It made him feel even more isolated.

There were small animals here, and he'd seen several deer higher up the slopes. Sometimes he heard creatures calling wild, ebullient cries that sounded almost human. He saw them in the distance, and once or twice he thought they'd come closer. He couldn't pretend that he was here covertly. He was not that foolish.

Leaving his cave to walk to Mallian once again, something felt different about this journey. He knew it wouldn't take long—he'd been five times before, and the geography of this part of the Fold was already starting to feel familiar—but there was an air of danger about the place now. It was as if the land held its breath, waiting for something to happen.

Mallian was still there. His hands and feet remained pinned to the ground by whatever magic Grace had used to secure them. The Nephilim rolled his head so that he could watch Vince approach. Was it imagination, or did he appear weaker than he had last time? Diminished, denuded? Perhaps, even for Kin, hunger and thirst eventually did their worst.

Vince sat ten feet away and they remained silent for a while, as they had on his previous visits. Sometimes they didn't talk at all. He wasn't sure why he came here. It might have been because Mallian offered some shred of familiarity in this place. A vague link to Angela.

Today, the Nephilim seemed more eager to talk.

"You said the girl wasn't Kin."

"Angela said that."

"Hmph. Humans. They know nothing."

Vince had wondered about Sammi, but the fact that she and Angela had escaped gave him peace. Worrying about the girl's origins could achieve nothing, not while he was trapped here. But now, this.

"So what is she?"

"What is she?" Mallian said, repeating his words several more times. "She's what many humans are. Touched by Kin."

"Meaning what?"

Mallian rolled his head left, right, cricking his neck. He grumbled, a growl or a sigh.

"Release me and I'll tell you."

"I can't. Even if I could, I wouldn't."

"I see none in you," Mallian said. "Interesting."

"You see no what?"

"No Kin blood."

Vince frowned, and then raised his head as realization set in.

"You think so many generations of human and Kin can keep apart?" Mallian asked. "Countless numbers of you are blessed, and you don't even know it."

"The deniers?" Vince asked.

"The mongrel humans. The half-breeds. Our pure, honored blood diluted by your human… filth." He spat the last word.

"So what is Sammi?" Vince asked.

"Help me and I'll tell you."

"I can't."

"You won't."

Vince frowned and stood to leave. This new information swirled in his head, and although so shocking, it was also painfully, patently obvious. *Of course* Kin and humans would have come together, perhaps even fallen in love. Not so much now—at least not as far as he knew, although there might have been something between Meloy and Lilou—but centuries ago, creating bloodlines that simmered down through the years.

"She won't let you live," Mallian said. "You're not company for her. None of us are."

Vince paused. "What do you mean?"

"You'll see," Mallian said. He chuckled, a dry, throaty rasp. "I should have known."

"Known what?"

The Nephilim turned his head and stared up at the sky. By day, the sun was a constant comfort. By night, strange constellations passed over this new place.

"Known *what*?" Vince asked again, but he was wasting his breath. Mallian sighed and closed his eyes.

Vince left and walked back along the river toward his cave. There was no point trying to hide, and as yet none of the Kin in this place had bothered him. He mused on what Mallian had said about Grace, and wondered whether he and the Kin were in the same situation.

Close to the cave, something caught his eye up on the hillside. It was a creature loping on two legs, nude yet with feathered limbs and a sharp, avian head. It didn't seem able to fly, but it could certainly run, as if hunting something. Deer or rabbit, perhaps. Then as Vince watched, he realized that the creature was hunted, not the hunter.

Grace darted across the hillside and brought the Kin down. Vince heard a faint squeal of pain and alarm. He moved beneath the shadow of a willow tree growing by the river, parting drooping branches to watch.

You're not company for her, Mallian had said. *None of us are.*

The creature's struggles were useless, and when Grace bit down into its arm, its squeal became a screech of pain.

Vince gasped. Shock bit in.

Grace shook her head and ripped away a chunk of flesh, the vivid red wound visible even from this distance. Then she turned and stalked away, leaving the injured Kin to escape in the other direction, holding its wounded arm across its chest. Vince wasn't sure, but it sounded like it was weeping.

He rushed back to his cave, making sure to keep to the shadows and the cover of trees and rocks. He felt vulnerable now, rather than simply abandoned and alone. He felt eyes upon him.

As his cave's coolness welcomed him in, he remembered something he'd heard back in London. Something Mary Rock had said to Angela. It was a phrase that made everything that had happened and continued to happen here much clearer.

A fairy has to eat.

ACKNOWLEDGEMENTS

Thanks as ever to the whole splendid gang at Titan. And a very special thanks to my agents Howard Morhaim, Michael Prevett, Caspian Dennis, Danny Baror, and Ed Hughes. I wouldn't be doing this without them.

ABOUT THE AUTHOR

TIM LEBBON is a *New York Times*-bestselling writer from South Wales. He's had over forty novels published to date, as well as hundreds of novellas and short stories. His latest novel is *Blood of the Four* (with Christopher Golden), and other recent releases include *Relics*, *The Family Man*, *The Silence*, and *The Rage War* trilogy.

He has won four British Fantasy Awards, a Bram Stoker Award, and a Scribe Award, and has been a finalist for World Fantasy, International Horror Guild, and Shirley Jackson awards. Future novels include *The Edge*—third in the *Relics* trilogy—and others.

A movie of his novel *The Silence*, starring Stanley Tucci and Kiernan Shipka, is set for release in 2019, and the movie of his story *Pay the Ghost*, starring Nicolas Cage, was released in 2015. Several other projects are in development for television and the big screen.

Find out more about Tim at his website
www.timlebbon.net